THE WHITBY WITCHES

ROBIN JARVIS

ILLUSTRATED BY JEFF PETERSEN

BOOK ONE OF THE WHITBY WITCHES TRILOGY

chronicle books · san francisco

First published in the United States in 2006 by Chronicle Books LLC.

Book design by Mary Beth Fiorentino.
Production assistance by DC Typography, San Francisco.
Typeset in Stempel Schneidler.
Manufactured in China.

Library of Congress Cataloging-in-Publication Data
Jarvis, Robin, 1963-
The Whitby witches / by Robin Jarvis.
p. cm.
Summary: Ben and Jennet, an orphaned brother and sister, are taken in by an old woman
in the quaint fishing village of Whitby, where they soon learn of the town's ancient
lore and become involved in an epic struggle between good and evil.
ISBN-13: 978-0-8118-5413-9
ISBN-10: 0-8118-5413-2
[1. Orphans—Fiction. 2. Witches—Fiction. 3. Supernatural—Fiction.
4. Whitby (England)—Fiction. 5. England—Fiction.] I. Title.
PZ7.J2965Whi 2006
[Fic]—dc22
2005026778

Distributed in Canada by Raincoast Books
9050 Shaughnessy Street, Vancouver, British Columbia V6P 6E5

10 9 8 7 6 5 4 3 2 1

Chronicle Books LLC
85 Second Street, San Francisco, California 94105

www.chroniclekids.com

CONTENTS

THE INHABITANTS OF WHITBY

BEN

An eight-year-old boy who comes to Whitby with his sister. Ben unnerves the people around him because he sees things they do not.

JENNET

She is Ben's older sister and has looked after him since the death of their parents. Jennet will not stand for any of his nonsense, however, and refuses to talk about the strange things he sees.

ALICE BOSTON

An eccentric old lady who adopts the children. Most of the people in the town think she is an interfering busybody, but there is more to her than they realize.

PRUDENCE JOYSTER

Like most of Alice Boston's friends, Mrs. Joyster lives alone. Her late husband was in the army and his strict, military manner rubbed off on her.

MATILDA DROON

Known to her friends as "Tilly," Miss Droon is renowned for her love of cats and keeps umpteen of the creatures. Consequently, her house reeks, and there are cat hairs all over her clothes.

DORA BANBURY-SCOTT

Not only is she the richest woman in Whitby, but she is also one of the fattest. Mrs. Banbury-Scott refuses to grow old gracefully and has the most revolting peach-colored hair that money can buy.

EDITH WETHERS

She works in the post office and is a terrible ditherer. She suffers from all sorts of allergies and would be lost without a tissue tucked up her sleeve.

ROWENA COOPER

A mysterious stranger who arrives in the town, she is keen to usurp Alice Boston's position as leader of the ladies' circle.

SISTER BRIDGET

A novice from the convent who wanders on the cliff top at night, she harbors a sad secret and weeps to herself.

NELDA SHRIMP

The youngest of the strange fisher folk who live in caves deep below the cliffs, she is concerned for her father who has disappeared.

HESPER GULL

Nelda's aunt and Silas's wife, she is a comical figure who collects seaweed and shells but is driven by her search for the mythical moonkelp.

TARR SHRIMP

Hesper's father and Nelda's grandfather, his greatest pleasure is sitting before a fire smoking his pipe with nobody fussing around him.

SILAS GULL

The black sheep of the fisher folk tribe, he is missing along with Nelda's father, but it is not long before he reappears.

*L*ook, look! Down on the sands of Tate Hill Pier; see there, my friend. Three small, strange figures—do you not see them? Listen to them calling to the cliff. Ah, the sound is lost on the wind. But, there, you must see them—they are searching for something. One of them stops and turns to us—its jet-black eyes glare up at me.

It is not quite dawn, and the light is poor, perhaps that is why you cannot see. You tell me to come indoors, you say the damp morning has chilled me and take my arm. I glance back; the figures have gone. Can I have seen the fisher folk? The old whalers of Whitby town?

The boats will soon return with their catches. I must speak to no one. I shall let the fisher folk be and try to forget them. Perhaps when I sit by the fire, as my toes uncurl and my head begins to nod, that face shall haunt my dreams.

No, they are but childhood fancies, and I am too old. The kettle whistles on the stove, and I draw on the pipe that trembles in my shaking hand. Yes, it is a cold morning, and I am chilled.

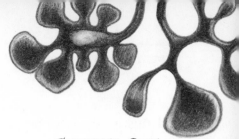

CHAPTER ONE

DIFFICULT CASES

Mrs. Rodice perched herself on the edge of her spartan desk and sucked her watery afternoon tea through sullen lips. She was relieved. Two of her more trying charges had left today; she had put them on the train personally. A delicious shudder ran down her spine as she sank her small, irregular teeth into a dunked biscuit. This was her favorite part of the day—a special, secretive hour when she could close the door and relax with her Royal Doulton and the occasional romantic novel.

Margaret Rodice ran a home for children whose parents were dead, indifferent, or "inside." It was a difficult, demanding role: trying to manage a maximum of 16 young people while at the whim of the local authority grant policy. If only Mr. Rodice had not departed from the world so shortly after their wedding. She wondered how different her life would have been; perhaps there would have been children of her own—even a grandchild by now.

Mrs. Rodice rattled the cup on its saucer in agitation and placed them both on her desk. She really must stop dwelling on the past. Donald was a vague shadow from her youth, and she rarely thought of him now—up until recently, that is. But now that creepy little boy had gone, and she hoped things would get back to normal. Oh, for the run-of-the-mill occurrences: the runaways, the girls who stole, even (God forbid) lice would be welcome after the turmoil of the last three months.

She rose to peer out of the narrow window and watched the rain streak down over Leeds. After some minutes of contemplating, Mrs. Rodice returned to her desk, but refrained from draining her cup. The tea leaves at the bottom would only remind her of the recent troubles.

"Of course I was right to send that letter," she reassured herself. "Even if the old bat *does* know someone on the board, she had to be aware of what she was letting herself in for." Mrs. Rodice shook her head at the folly of the old woman in question.

"At her age! I ask you," she addressed the table lamp. "Well, it won't last—it never does with *them*." A thin smile twitched her mouth. "Still," she muttered, shuffling her papers, "whatever happens, they're not coming back here."

She bent her graying head over the spread of forms and took up her pen purposefully, then with a tut of consternation looked up at the ceiling and groaned. "I hope Yvonne won't wet again tonight."

Ben stared out of the window and watched the green landscape race by. He pressed his face against the glass, and the motion of the train vibrated through his nose.

"Don't do that," sighed the girl beside him, as she pulled him back to his seat.

The boy squirmed and plucked crumbs of sausage roll from his sweater. "Bored, Jen," he grumbled.

Jennet fished a comic book out of a large, blue canvas bag beside her and shoved it under her brother's nose.

"I've read it," he said, without bothering to look.

The girl let the comic sprawl on the table and turned away. Ben's eyes flickered over the colorful pages. He pursed his mouth with his usual show of contempt and returned his attention to the window. A curtain of silence and resentment fell between the children.

The train slowed and pulled into Middlesbrough. Ben twisted on his seat, his eyes following the people who got off. He was eight years old, a serious-looking boy with mousy brown hair and eyes that were set unusually deep below his frowning brows. His sister, Jennet, had the same oval face and unremarkable, blobby nose, but her long, wavy hair was darker, and her eyes were less troubled.

The conductor strode by, slamming the doors of the train cars, and Ben kicked the seat impatiently with his heels. Jennet said nothing but looked at him disapprovingly. Ben considered himself scolded, and the kicks subsided.

"We nearly there?" he asked suddenly.

"I don't think it's far now," she answered.

Ben abandoned the delights of the window and faced his sister. With one of his disconcerting stares, he asked her soberly, "Jen, what do you think it will be like this time? Will we be there long?"

The girl shrugged. "Miss Boston's old. That's all I could get out of the Rodice."

At the mention of that name, Ben screwed up his face. "I hated her," he said passionately. "I'm glad we're not there now. She used to frighten me."

"Not as much as you frightened her," remarked his sister dryly. "Listen: remember what I said." A warning note crept into her voice. "You're not to talk of *that* with this one, right?"

Ben nodded and hastened to change the subject. "Will we really live near the sea, Jen?"

"Yes, I think I heard Rodice say Whitby was on the coast—it's the end of the line, anyway."

"And did Peter Pan live there too?"

Jennet picked up his discarded comic book and flicked through it herself. "Peter Pan?" she asked, puzzled.

"Yes. Mr. Glennister who put them flags down last week told me Captain Hook came from there."

"He must have been pulling your leg, then," said Jennet flatly.

"Oh." Ben was deflated and slouched back.

"Didn't like those flags anyway," he mumbled. "There's no grass left now."

"Rodice said it would be cheaper in the long run," said Jennet distractedly. Then she raised her head and, imitating Mrs. Rodice's humorless nasal tones, added, "Grass needs regular mowing in the summer, and in the winter the passages are covered in mud."

Ben chuckled; he approved of anything that made fun of the dreaded Rodice. He rubbed his eyes, then asked, "Don't you know anything else about this place?"

But Jennet was trying to concentrate on the comic book and ignored him. A year—perhaps eight months—before she would have been nervous and excited at the prospect of moving to somewhere new. She might even have looked the place up in the library to learn something about it beforehand. But that was four different foster homes ago.

"I think I'll like the sea," continued Ben. "Have I been to the seaside before, Jen?"

"When you were five."

"Were *they* there too?"

She coughed and stared at the comic book intently. "Yes," she replied curtly.

Ben frowned and put on his most serious face. "What I mean is . . ." he struggled to choose the right words, "were they *really* there?"

Jennet threw the comic book down and snapped sharply, "You've seen that photo of us, haven't you?"

Ben's eyes grew large and pleading. "Not for a long time, Jen—you won't show me the photos any more. Couldn't I see just one of them now?"

"No, they're at the bottom of the bag. Besides, *you* don't need to see photos of Mom and Dad, do you?" It was an accusation, spat out bitterly. She folded her arms crossly and stared down the car at a toddler sleeping in his mother's arms. Ben began to kick the seat again and rested his head sulkily on the window.

Jennet was tense. In the past, they had always met the foster families before going to stay with them, but this time everything was different and rushed. Mrs. Rodice was probably only too glad to get them off her hands and no doubt had hurried the procedures along. Still, it was very odd. The first Jennet had heard of this Miss Boston was two weeks ago, but presumably negotiations had been going on long before that. Jennet was curious. Why would an old woman go out of her way to foster two children she had never even seen, and why would the authorities let her? If only the Rodice had said more. But then Jennet had not bothered to probe into the matter very deeply. She and Ben had never had much to say about where they were shunted off to, and now that they were categorized as "difficult cases" they had none at all.

Jennet was now beginning to regret her lack of interest. Miss Boston seemed such a mysterious figure. All she knew about her was that she was old. Would Miss Boston be there in person to meet them at Whitby station, she wondered, and just how old was she?

Jennet allowed a smirk to spread over her face; perhaps some wizened hag in a wheelchair would be waiting for them. A new thought struck her. Maybe the old lady had money? That would explain the haste with which their fostering had gone through the system. The wheelchair vanished abruptly from beneath the imaginary figure and was replaced by an ancient Rolls Royce, with a chauffeur in gray livery holding open the door. Inside was the same old woman, now swathed in furs, her wrinkled hands dripping with diamonds.

If money was involved Jennet wondered whether she would be sent to a posh school. That's what rich people did with children. It was an unwelcome thought, and she mulled it over miserably. She and Ben had not been separated since the accident. Jennet could not imagine life without her brother, however much trouble he caused.

The stations the train stopped at were becoming smaller, their names spelled out in whitewashed stones on well-mown slopes. Some even had hanging baskets dangling from the eaves. It was like taking a journey back to the age of steam, and Jennet half-listened for the "chuff chuff" she had heard in old films.

The scenery was beautiful. Wild expanses of rolling moorland dotted with sheep shot by, then a dense pine forest, some farm buildings with a gypsy caravan parked outside, and then more wide acres of heather, cut through by a little brook.

The railway track became a single line. Just how far away was Whitby? It seemed as if they were going beyond the reaches of the civilized world. Jennet wondered how regularly the trains went there and wished she had thought to look at a timetable when they had changed at Darlington.

"Look," said Ben excitedly, "there's a river, and there's a boat. See?"

A ribbon of water ran parallel to the track. For some moments, it was obscured by dense trees, then it was revealed once more, wider than before. Buildings clustered on the far bank, and the river swelled into a marina, with yachts. Jennet caught a glimpse of a high cliff, then the vision was snatched from view and the train, wheezing with exhaustion, finally drew into Whitby station.

"I saw the sea," declared Ben, jumping up and down on the seat. "And there were lots of fishing boats. Listen to the seagulls, Jen."

She grunted an acknowledgment and stuffed the wreckage of the journey into her large blue bag. She left the empty can of lemonade and two brown apple cores on the table and told Ben to put his coat on.

"But it isn't cold," he protested obstinately.

"Put it on," she insisted.

Ben mumbled a sentence, but the only word Jennet could catch was "bossy." When he had fastened the top button of his coat, she guided him in front of her and swung the heavy bag over her shoulder.

There were only a few other passengers on the train; they filed past the children with neat little suitcases and bags, smiling as they gave their tickets to the man at the barrier. Ben stared at the sky. The rain had left behind a bright August day with big white clouds rolling inland. The seagulls circled high above and cried raucously.

"I can't see anyone," said Jennet, looking up the platform. "Come on, maybe she's waiting for us outside in her car."

They trudged up to the barrier and Jennet began to rummage in her pockets for the tickets. The ticket collector cast a weary glance their way and held his hand out impatiently. Ben stared up at him and pretended to pick his nose. The man set his jaw and glared down icily. Jennet, meanwhile, was still rifling through her pockets.

"Come on now, miss," said the man.

Jennet was flustered; she could not think what had happened to the tickets.

"Has it arrived, George?" came a brisk female voice.

The ticket collector turned and nodded to the newcomer. "Aye, an' three minutes early, Miss Boston."

Jennet looked up sharply. There, with her hands clasped firmly behind her back, stood a stout, white-haired woman. She wore a jacket of sage-green tweed with a matching skirt, and on her head sat a shapeless velvet hat. The cobweb lines around her gray, birdlike eyes suggested the old lady's age to be about 70, but her stance was like someone much younger.

"Ah, three minutes, is that so?" Miss Boston spoke challengingly and raised her eyebrows at the ticket collector. "Well, well, what a day for wonders, to be sure."

Then the old woman saw the children, and her face lit up. The eyes blinked and disappeared and the rolls of skin beneath the chin shook like jelly. "Oh, these must be mine," she cried, clapping her hands together like an eager child.

"Yours, Miss Boston?" asked the ticket collector, baffled.

"Yes, yes, George. Now let them through that wretched thing."

"But they an't give me their tickets."

"Oh stuff!" she exclaimed in exasperation. "Let them through at once, they're with me." And she stamped her foot and gave the man a look that no one would have dared to disobey.

"This is most irreg'lar," he said as the children squeezed past him, "most irreg'lar."

Miss Boston clucked gleefully as she ran her keen eyes over Jennet and Ben. "Let me have a good look at you," she demanded. "So, you're Jennet."

"Yes," the girl replied, returning the interested stare.

"Pretty name—far better than Janet or Jeanette. Now I believe you are twelve, is that correct?"

"Yes."

"Mmm. You look older—act it too. Not surprising, really," Miss Boston nodded as though satisfied with the girl and turned her attention to the boy.

"And this is Benjamin, I presume." It was a statement rather than a question.

The child stared back and said nothing.

"He's shy with strangers," put in Jennet.

"Of course he is," the woman returned. "All sensitive children are timid."

"Ben's not sensitive, just shy," corrected Jennet firmly.

"Ah, yes—you must forgive me." Miss Boston's face looked like someone guiltily sucking a boiled sweet. "Well," she went on, "I trust I shan't be considered a stranger for very much longer—by either of you." Her smile was warm and genuine. "Now, come," she cried, waving them out of the station, "let us retire to my home and have a bit to eat before you unpack."

As they left the station, Jennet saw for the first time the town of Whitby. The girl stood stock-still and absorbed the sight breathlessly. The station was close to the wharfside and the harbor was filled with fishing boats, from large fat vessels with wide hulls and tall radio masts down to the simplest coble, painted red and white. Close by, there was a long red boat that ran fishing trips for the tourists.

On the far side of the harbor was a jumble of buildings with roofs of terra-cotta tiles, nestling snugly alongside each other like a line of nervous swimmers waiting for someone to take the first leap into the water. They were built on a steep cliffside and the hotchpotch of sandstone and whitewash somehow seemed to be a natural feature of the landscape. They felt right, as though they had been there from earliest times, and without them the land would be naked and ugly.

Jennet's eyes scanned up beyond the houses, to where the high plain of the cliff reached out to the sea. She gasped and stared. For there, surmounting everything, was a ragged crown of gray stone—the abbey.

The building was in ruins, but that did not diminish its power. The abbey had dominated Whitby for centuries, and waves of invisible force flowed down from it. The ruin was a guardian, watching and waiting, caring for the little town that huddled beneath the cliff. It was a worshipful thing.

Miss Boston nodded. "Yes," she sighed dreamily, "the abbey. It is indeed lovely. There has been a church on that site for at least fourteen hundred years. One gets a marvelous sense of permanence, living under such an enduring symbol of faith. If one believes in the *genius loci*—the spirit of place—then surely therein dwells something divine. The Vikings came, Henry did his best to destroy the abbey with the Dissolution of the Monasteries, and in the Great War, German ships bombarded it. Yet still it stands—stubborn and wonderful. They say a true inhabitant of Whitby is lost if he cannot see the abbey." She paused and looked at the ground. "Well," she went on again breezily, "there I go, off on tangents again. You two may have eaten, but I have not. Come; tea awaits."

Jennet dragged her eyes from the cliff and glanced about the road. "Where's your car?" she asked curiously.

Miss Boston puffed herself up indignantly. "A car?" she cried, her chins wobbling. "I don't need a car. Whitby is not big enough to warrant the use of an automobile, child. However, I do have transport, now that you mention it." She strode around to where an old black bicycle was leaning against the station wall.

Jennet bit her lip to stop herself cracking up with laughter at the thought of the old woman riding around on that. Had she and Ben come to stay with the local eccentric?

Miss Boston announced that she would not ride but walk, for the sake of the children. "Now, this way," she declared, setting off. The bicycle clattered and whirred beside her.

Ben had been silent since they had met, but by now he had decided that the old woman was harmless and much friendlier than the Rodice. There were none of those phony smiles and patronizing looks that were a feature of the Rodice's way with children. He was also relieved that this adult had not tried to pat him on the head or ruffle his hair, like some others had done.

Now his excited eyes saw the fishing boats with their gleaming paint, orange nets, and lobster pots. A twinge of pleasure tugged at his insides when he thought of actually sailing in one of them. It was not impossible. If the old woman liked him and Jennet and if he kept quiet about certain things, they might stay here just long enough.

Ben was already beginning to find Whitby a thrilling place, full of possibilities. Suddenly, he remembered again what Mr. Glennister had told him. As he walked behind his sister along New Quay Road a determined expression crossed his face and, forgetting his bashfulness, he pulled at the old woman's sleeve.

"Where's Peter Pan?" he demanded.

Miss Boston stopped and blinked. "Whatever does the dear boy mean?" she asked Jennet in surprise.

"He was told Captain Hook lived here," explained the girl in an apologetic tone.

Miss Boston hooted loudly and frightened some gulls on the wharfside. "Bless me, Benjamin," she chuckled, "it's Cook, not Hook. Captain Cook lived here."

"Oh," murmured Ben. He felt babyish and all the shyness returned in a great flood. He waited for the old woman to call him stupid, but instead she said something quite unexpected.

"Peter Pan, eh?" Miss Boston mused to herself. "Do you know, young man, you have crystallized something I have felt without realizing. For some time, I have sensed that there is—oh how shall I say?—something special about this place of ours. It almost seems to have been neglected by time. Oh yes, we have motor cars passing through and amusement arcades on the West Cliff, which scream of the twentieth century, plus of course the summer visitors snapping their cameras, yet . . . there is an aspect of the town that belongs to the past. Never-Never Land is a good comparison . . . yes, most interesting. How perceptive you are."

She wheeled her bicycle on once more. Ben looked up at Jennet, who gave him a frosty stare.

"Just don't be too perceptive," she whispered harshly.

"Captain James Cook was a very famous mariner," Miss Boston called to them over her shoulder. "He lived for some time in Grape Lane on the East Cliff—we shall pass by there on the way to my cottage. He discovered Australia, you know. Still, we must not hold that against the man."

They came to a bridge spanning the river. It was only wide enough to take one line of traffic at a time and was jammed with pedestrians, swarming everywhere.

"Our busiest time of year," Miss Boston explained as she plowed her way through. "We've just got over our regatta, and the Folk Week starts in two days."

"Folk Week?" queried Jennet.

"Yes, with lots of dancing—people come from miles away. The town is always packed with bearded men who paint their faces and walk about in clogs—such fun."

When they were halfway across the bridge, Ben glanced back. The road they had left was just beginning to get interesting. He heard the crackle of electronic guns and the amplified voice of the bingo caller. A row of glittering arcades stretched out toward the sea beneath another cliff.

"That is the West Cliff," said Miss Boston as she negotiated her way through a crowd of giggling girls. "Traditionally the East Cliff was for the fishermen and the West for the tourists. Of course it's got a little mixed up over the years; most of the fishermen can't afford to live here any more, so they have to travel in."

They reached the far side of the river. "Down there is Grape Lane," indicated Miss Boston, waving her hand.

The buildings of the East Cliff were more densely bunched together than Jennet had at first thought. They had been built in the days before planning permission was heard of and their higgledy-piggledy clusters formed a vast number of dark alleys, lanes, and yards. The Whitby of the East Cliff was gazing at the world from an earlier time all its own.

Miss Boston led them up a narrow cobbled road called Church Street. It was the main thoroughfare of the East Cliff, yet still cars had difficulty making their way down it. Old buildings hunched over on either side in a forbidding manner, and tiny lanes led off through sudden openings to unseen doorways.

"Afternoon, Alice." A thin, elderly woman greeted Miss Boston courteously. She had the palest blue eyes that Jennet had ever seen, and her silvery hair was scraped tightly over her head, to be bound in a fist-sized bun at the back. She wore a gray cardigan over a lemon yellow blouse, fastened at the neck by a cameo brooch, and clasped a brown handbag primly in front of her.

"Oh, Prudence," returned Miss Boston hastily. "Did you manage to come across that book?"

The other shook her head and sniffed. "Sorry, Alice—must have thrown it out with Howard's things after all. Never kept much of his stuff you know." Her voice was clipped and precise. Then she regarded the children and waited for an explanation.

"My guests, Prudence: Jennet and Benjamin."

"Yes, well. They're younger than I thought. I hope you know what you're doing." She then continued the conversation, ignoring the children completely. "Actually, Alice, I have just come from your cottage. That Gregson woman told me you were not at home." She shook herself and adjusted the cameo. "So I was about to take myself off to call on Tilly. Haven't seen her for over a week—more kittens, I imagine. It's all getting too ridiculous. Well, must cut along. Good-bye." And with that, she walked briskly away.

"Don't forget Sunday," Miss Boston called after her.

Without slowing her brisk stride, the woman raised her hand dismissively and called back, "Naturally." Then she was lost in the crowds.

Miss Boston turned back to the children and sucked her breath in sharply. "That was Mrs. Joyster," she informed them. "Rather a cold woman, I'm afraid—husband was army, and it rubbed off on her. Sometimes I feel as though I'm being drilled when she talks to me. Mind you," she added, "she can be very pleasant at times."

The bicycle began to clatter once more. "I recall how I used to hate it when adults pretended I wasn't there; dear me, that was a long time ago now. Do you prefer blackberry or raspberry jam? I confess I have a passion for both—especially on hot scones. My cottage is not far now."

Jennet and Ben were beginning to find Miss Boston's abrupt changes of thought bewildering. It did, however, occur to them that they would have no difficulty polishing off a plate of jammy scones.

An odd, square building on the left caught their attention. It was set a little apart for one thing. Pillars supported the upper story and right at the top, in the middle of the roof, was a clock tower and a weather vane shaped like a fish.

"This is Market Place," said Miss Boston, waving a proud hand. "If you'd like to, you could go on this." She pointed to a black sign with white letters advertising a Ghost Tour.

Ben's eyes widened, and he swallowed nervously. The sign drew him like a powerful magnet. Jennet pulled him roughly away as if from a fire.

"No!" she told the old woman. "We don't like that sort of thing at all."

If Miss Boston was surprised by the severity of Jennet's outburst, then she did not show it. "Really, dear?" she said mildly. "Then I'm afraid you have come to the wrong place entirely. You know I sometimes think Whitby has more ghosts than living residents." She waggled her chins at the sign and muttered, "Just as well, really—I've been banned from going on the tours anyway. Well, the young man who runs them seemed to resent my chipping in. Got quite irate once when I corrected him. He gave me my money back on the condition that I never bothered him again. Astounding state of affairs."

They had come to another of those sudden openings, and Miss Boston wheeled her bicycle through it. After about 15 feet, the alley opened out into a spacious yard. She walked up to a flight of steps, rested her bicycle against a rail, opened a green door and said, "Well, come in then."

Jennet was downstairs, talking to Miss Boston. Ben lay on an embroidered quilt and stared at the primroses on the wallpaper. It was a small room but just big enough for him, and for a change, he had it all to himself. There was a bed, a small wardrobe, and a chest of drawers next to it with a lamp on top. He licked the jam from his chin and rolled over to gaze at the sloping ceiling.

It was a funny house. There were lots of weird prints on the walls and old sepia photographs of Victorian Whitby. There were also a good many corn dollies hanging up all over the place. A table in the hall was reserved for things Miss Boston had found while out walking: pine cones, bright orange rosehips, a bunch of heather, sheep's wool found in a hedge (complete with twigs and fragments of leaf), the broken shell of a blackbird's egg, several interesting pebbles, a gnarled piece of driftwood, and a white gull's feather.

This was not what he or Jennet had expected, and it certainly disproved the idea that Miss Boston was rich—unless she kept a secret stash of money under the mattress. It was not the sort of house you would expect an old lady to live in, whether she was rich or not. There were no china statues or rows of dainty cups, no bits of fussy lace, no piles of women's magazines heaped in the corner, no obvious signs of knitting, no fat lazy cat sprawled on the sofa clawing away the cushions and—best of all to Ben—the place did not smell of lavender. He thought he would like it here. Miss Boston was not an average old lady; there was something vital and a little bit eccentric about her.

An idea came to him as he lolled on the bed. Gingerly, he crept out of his room and went into Jennet's. He could still hear the faint hum of voices downstairs, so he knew he was safe.

Ben fumbled with the zipper on the blue canvas bag and delved through piles of neatly folded clothes and small treasures. There, right at the bottom, his groping fingers touched what felt like a book. Gently, he slid the photograph album out of the bag and stroked it lovingly with his hands. With great care and reverence, he opened it and turned the pages. This was a hallowed thing to him and Jennet, and lately she had been withholding it from him.

There were his mother and father on their wedding day, smiling up out of the album, about to cut the cake. Another page, and there they were on honeymoon in Wales. Ben's father was a tall man with thick, dark hair and a broad grin. His mother, a petite blonde, had blinked at the wrong moment, and here she was, frozen into an eternal doze. The opposite page showed Jennet when she was a baby, sitting on her father's lap.

Ben examined the photographs carefully. Here they were: images of his parents locked in happy events—birthdays and holidays sealed into the album forever. But the eyes staring out at him were unseeing. They were focused on the person taking the photograph and that had never been Ben. His mother and father were looking out at someone else, not him. He was confused. The memories of who they had been—everything they were—were now transferred to six inches by four inches of glossy paper.

He turned the last page. There was the photograph he sought above all. A younger version of himself sat astride a donkey on the sands of Rhyl, and beside him were his mother and father. Jennet must have taken the picture. Try as he might, Ben had no memory of the occasion. He imagined sitting on a donkey and hearing his father's voice, but no—there was nothing there. The photograph had been taken on the final day of their last holiday together. Six months later both his parents had been killed in a car accident.

Ben closed the album, frowned, and then chewed his lip. He understood that his parents were dead. He and Jennet had gone to the funeral and had watched the coffins being lowered into that deep hole. He remembered that because he had worn those shoes that pinched and Jennet had cried a lot and had to be put to bed. Yes, his parents were dead; everyone told him that. So why was it that every now and then, in a mirror or at the end of his bed before he went to sleep, he could see his mother and father smiling at him?

CHAPTER TWO

EURYDICE

"I knew your dear mama's aunt," said Miss Boston, above the buffeting wind.

Jennet sat on the tombstone and hugged her knees. "Great Aunt Connie?"

Miss Boston held on to her hat and nodded. "She was one of my pupils," she said. "A good student but never made any use of her education—shameful waste."

"And you say she wrote to you about Ben and me?"

"Yes, over the years we have kept a correspondence going. She was very fond of your mama, you know, and when she heard about the accident, well . . ."

They had climbed the 199 steps to the top of the East Cliff in order to see the abbey, only to find it was too late and the man in the office had gone home. Still, there was plenty to see. At the top of the steps was St. Mary's Church, a solid building surrounded by ancient graves whose stones were nearly worn smooth. They had settled themselves on a large, mossy tomb while Ben ran off to play among the stones and lean into the strong wind.

There was a magnificent view of the town below. On the West Cliff, directly opposite, bedroom lights were flickering on and the glitter of the arcades was becoming more notice-able in the gathering dusk. Dark night clouds were moving in from the sea, and the sun was pale and low, catching a last, weak glint from the tiled roofs before it set.

Miss Boston, wrapped in a tweed cloak, stared at the hori-zon and said, "Of course, if Constance had not been in that home she would have taken you and Benjamin in herself."

Jennet spoke into the darkening sky, tilting her head back and sweeping the hair out of her eyes. "She couldn't have coped with Ben and me, she's too old."

Miss Boston snorted. "Too old? My dear girl, Constance is a mere sapling compared to me."

"But Aunt Connie's seventy and uses a walker."

Miss Boston puckered her face up and asked, "How old do you think I am, child?"

Jennet looked at the figure blanketed in sage green tweed. Only the face was visible, and it was difficult to put an age to it. Miss Boston's skin was lined, yet one grin could banish the wrinkles. Only the tufts of white woolly hair poking out beneath the hat gave any real clue to her age.

"Seventy-five?" Jennet ventured uncertainly.

Miss Boston closed her eyes and raised her head. "I am ninety-two," she solemnly informed her. "Don't be alarmed, dear—some of us do survive for that length of time."

"But you're not frail or anything," Jennet declared in surprise.

"As to that," Miss Boston lifted a finger to her nose in a gesture of secrecy, "I have little methods all my own. Old age is terribly unfair. Usually either the mind or the body succumbs. Hospitals and nursing homes are filled with shambling near cadavers who still possess all their marbles: intelligent people who can't go to the bathroom by themselves or even get out of bed, in some cases. Then there is the other variety: the sprightly gibberers, I call them, senile but with perfectly healthy bodies. What a cruel joke old age is, to be sure."

A flock of gulls soared out over the sea, spreading their wings and hanging on the air. Miss Boston followed their course with interest. "They're not supposed to be able to fly over the abbey, you know," she told Jennet. "Legend says that if they try, they are overcome and fall to the ground. There they must pay homage to St. Hilda, the founder of the abbey, until she releases them."

"That's silly," said Jennet.

Miss Boston agreed. "I suppose so, but it is a lovely notion, don't you think? St. Hilda was a remarkable woman, after all."

They sat in silence for some time, listening to the wind rushing through the grass and hearing Ben's squawks as he chased the gulls.

"Why now?" asked Jennet, breaking the calm. "Why didn't you send for us before? Why wait over two years?"

The old woman put her hand on Jennet's and explained. "After the accident, Constance wrote to me and told me you had gone to stay with your father's brother."

"Uncle Peter, yes—and Aunt Pat, his snotty wife."

"You were with them for just three months, were you not?"

Jennet stared at the ground and mumbled, "Aunt Pat said she couldn't cope with . . . well, with us." She hesitated before adding, "Ben was having a bad time, and there were other things."

"I see," Miss Boston turned to watch Ben playing. "So they put you both into care."

"Yes, then we were put with another family who actually wanted to adopt Ben and me, until . . . well, it didn't work out that way."

"No," Miss Boston narrowed her eyes thoughtfully. "Nor did it work out with three other families after that. You asked why I had not sent for you before now. My dear child, I was hoping that you would find a good home with a family who would care for you." She sighed loudly. "Alas, it was not to be, so I decided to enter the fray and applied a little pressure here, called in some old favors there. Well, here you are; stuck with a terrible old woman like me. I'm sorry, but I could not stand by and let you stay in that home until you were sixteen."

Jennet shifted, uncomfortable on the tombstone. This woman had no idea why they had been unable to fit in. She looked around for Ben and suddenly saw that he was dangerously near the cliff edge. "Will he be all right there?" she asked in alarm.

"I think your brother has brains enough not to go leaping off cliffs," remarked Miss Boston. "Of course, he might get blown off. The wind is notoriously strong up here." She raised a hand and called the boy to them. "Do you know it gets so violent sometimes that it actually lifts the lead off the church roof? Last winter the vicar had to cancel the service because of the noise."

Ben began to make his roundabout way toward them. Miss Boston cleared her throat and said to Jennet, "I think I ought to tell you something before he rejoins us. It's only fair you should know. You've a sensible head on your shoulders—too sensible perhaps at times."

"What should I know?"

"I received a letter from Mrs. Rodice," Miss Boston made a sour expression. "Nasty, spiteful letter it was too. It concerned Benjamin. What an unpleasant creature she must be."

The color drained out of Jennet's face, and she dug her nails into the palms of her hands. "What did the letter say?" she asked shakily.

Miss Boston snorted her contempt. "She is obviously an ignorant woman—unbalanced too, I shouldn't wonder. She accused Benjamin of certain things that I refuse to believe. I threw the wretched piece of paper on the fire—wish I could do the same to her."

The girl glanced up and found Miss Boston looking at her steadily. Now was the time to tell her everything. If that was the end of their stay in Whitby, then so be it; at least she could put the old woman straight. Lord knows what the Rodice had put in that letter.

"Ben has dreams," she stammered. "Sometimes he has them in the daytime, and he gets muddled up. He used to think Mom and Dad came to see him after the accident. That—that's not all. He used to tell some of the other kids at the home funny stuff that frightened them. We had a new girl come who used to live with her grandmother before she died, and Ben told her that he could see an old woman sitting next to her when she was in the TV room, stroking her hair. Apparently that's what this grandmother used to do. Yvonne started to wet the bed after that, and the other kids used to look at Ben like he was some kind of freak."

"Go on," Miss Boston prompted her gently.

"Well, that's why we never settled down with the foster families. With Aunt Pat, the last straw came during one of her posh dinner parties. Ben came running downstairs saying he'd seen Mom. Aunt Pat went dead red; she hated the embarrassment of it, she didn't want anyone to think she had a retarded relative in the house. I heard her and Uncle Peter talking one night—their room was next to mine, and the walls were thin. She said she couldn't stand it any more, and Uncle Peter had to go along with her. It was horrible listening to them discussing us like that. I wanted to shout out that I could hear them but I never did.

"The other families were the same. One lot was really religious and thought Ben was possessed or something, and the others just looked at us funny."

Miss Boston frowned. "Yes, I can see that some people might not feel comfortable with that sort of thing—it unnerves them and upsets their established ideas of the universe."

"It got really bad, though, at the home," Jennet continued. "About three weeks ago Ben goes and tells the Rodice he's seen a man on the stairs. 'Course, there was nobody there, but Ben describes the man to her and says he told him his name was Donald. She got all angry and shook Ben, calling him a liar. He had bruises on his arms where she'd grabbed him. That frightened her, that did—they're not supposed to hit us, see. Well, after that she had as little to do with us as possible, and I actually saw her shudder when Ben pushed past her once."

Miss Boston put her arm around the girl and tried to comfort her. "Well, it won't bother me, I assure you, dear.

Benjamin can chatter to an army of ghosts, and I shan't mind—I'm nearly one myself, after all. Tell me, do *you* ever see anything like that?"

Jennet shook her head. "No. At first I thought Ben was making it all up to annoy Aunt Pat, but he wouldn't have kept it up this long, would he? I've told him to stop but he won't."

"Of course not dear—he cannot. It is the most natural thing in the world for him to see these things. I believe Benjamin is a very special child. He has 'the sight,' a marvelous gift that should be encouraged. He must not feel that it is something to be ashamed of or he will lose it. Yes, he is special—and so too are you, Jennet. Throughout all this, you have stood by him and protected him, even though you did not fully understand yourself. You are a very brave girl."

At this point, Ben sauntered up to them. "Come here, Benjamin," said Miss Boston. "Get under my cloak, and I shall tell you a tale. You too, Jennet."

The children huddled up to the old woman and sheltered from the bitter wind like chicks under their mother's wings.

"Do you see that?" she asked them, nodding to a tall, thin cross. "That is Caedmon's cross."

"Who's he, then?" Ben wanted to know.

"Ah," Miss Boston explained, "Caedmon was a cowherd, long before the Normans came. He used to tend the cattle on the plain back there when the abbey was just a monastery. He was painfully shy and awkward, poor fellow. In the winter when fires were lit and songs were sung around them, all the other servants of the monastery would do their party pieces, except Caedmon. He felt so unhappy because he could not sing that he would retire early and his friends would shake their heads and feel sorry for him.

"Then, one night, a vision came to him in a dream. It was an angel that bade Caedmon sing of the glories of God the Maker. Do you know, when he awoke he felt confident as never before and began composing his own verse. Caedmon is recognized as the first English poet." And Miss Boston ended her tale with a satisfied sigh.

"That's soppy," sneered Ben, greatly disappointed.

"You impudent rascal," cried Miss Boston with mock severity. "And what kind of stories do you like, may I ask?"

"Scary ones—with monsters," he whispered conspiratorially.

Miss Boston's face became grim as she shook her head and gasped, "You mean you don't know? Have you come here unprepared? Did you not pack your garlic?"

Ben squirmed happily on the tomb, shaking his head. "Why?" he giggled.

"Because, child," she moaned in a horrified voice, "the most dreadful monster ever created came ashore at Whitby— Dracula himself, King of Vampires!"

"He didn't!"

"Oh yes he did, young man—he changed himself into a great black dog and jumped from the doomed ship *Demeter* as she ran aground, just down there." Miss Boston paused for dramatic effect and they all stared down at the rough sea. "Now," she said in a bright, cheerful manner, "it's getting colder—let us return home. Don't pretend to be a vampire, Benjamin, you haven't got the cloak for it." And she flapped her own, although she resembled a large green chicken more than a bat. Benjamin, however, was still staring down at the rocks below. He seemed to be watching something.

The old woman squinted down and saw a blurred shape move quickly over the stones. "So," she whispered to herself, "he sees the fisher folk also." A slow smile spread over her face.

Jennet waited for them at the top of the steep flight of steps. "Did Dracula really live here?" she asked nervously.

Miss Boston chuckled. "Dracula is but a character of fiction. His creator, Bram Stoker, came here in 1890, a dozen or so years before I was born. Mind you, the black dog was a grisly creature of legend he borrowed from the locals—the Barguest. As big as a calf with fiery red eyes, it was supposed to stalk through the streets of Whitby at the dead of night. Anyone who heard it howling was doomed."

Jennet shivered. "That's horrible, Miss Boston."

The old lady sighed. "Really, Jennet, you must stop calling me Miss Boston; I gave up lecturing a long time ago. My name is Alice."

"I can't call you that. It doesn't sound right."

"Then how about Aunt Alice? Will that do?"

Jennet simply smiled in reply and slid her hand automatically into Aunt Alice's.

The seagulls woke Ben up; for a moment he wondered where he was and then remembered. Hastily, he pulled his clothes on and ran downstairs to the kitchen, where he found Jennet finishing off a boiled egg.

"Those seagulls are a bit loud, aren't they, Jen?" he said chirpily.

Jennet blinked at him wearily. "It's seven in the morning," she answered grumpily. "I'll never get used to this."

"Where is she?" asked Ben, heaving himself onto a stool.

Jennet emptied the eggshell into the garbage and rinsed her plate under the tap. "She went out ten minutes ago. Says she always goes for a walk before breakfast."

"Where's mine?" demanded Ben hungrily.

His sister poured some milk into a bowl of cereal and passed it to him. Ben picked up a spoon; it was an odd color, and he sniffed it suspiciously.

"It's nice here, isn't it, Ben?" said Jennet as she watched him munch his breakfast.

"Um," he agreed, with his mouth full.

"I hope we can stay here for a while; she's a nice old lady. I feel a bit funny calling her 'Aunt' though."

The latch on the front door rattled, and Aunt Alice stepped in looking windswept and rosy. She stayed in the hall to hang up her hat and coat.

"Don't like these spoons, Jen," hissed Ben, waving his in the air.

"Shush! They're probably made of silver and very old—behave."

Aunt Alice entered, undoing the top button of her blouse. "There," she puffed. "I like to climb the one hundred ninety-nine steps, whatever the weather. Blows the sleepy cobwebs away, it does." She bent down and opened the door of an old-fashioned refrigerator. "Now," she mumbled, "will it be kippers today or scrambled eggs? Kippers it is!"

Ben liked the smoky smell of the kipper, but the taste was too strong for him—he preferred fish fingers and said as much. Aunt Alice roared that he would get no fish fingers from her as long as he stayed in Whitby. He could eat fresh fish or none at all.

Twenty minutes later, she was dabbing the corners of her mouth with a hanky and praising the art of a Mr. Bill Fortune. "Well now, children," she addressed them as she pushed the plate away, "What do you intend to do today?"

They shrugged and looked at her blankly. "Explore?" suggested Jennet. "If you don't mind, that is."

"Why should I mind, child? I hope you enjoy yourselves. I shall want to know what you have discovered when you return."

"Oh," said Jennet disappointedly, "aren't you coming too?"

Aunt Alice raised her eyebrows. "Certainly not. I have far too much to do. You can look after yourselves—you won't get lost in a small town like this." She rose and scraped the kipper bones into the garbage, then washed her plate with Ben's breakfast things. "Now I think you ought to brush your teeth, don't you?"

Jennet was the first one down from the bathroom, and she took her coat from the peg in the hall. "When should we come back, Aunt Alice?"

"Oh, whenever you like, dear. I have to go out myself."

"But how shall we get in if you're not here?"

Aunt Alice came into the hall, dangling a key to the front door between her fingers. "A spare," she said.

Jennet thanked the old woman. It had been a long time since anybody had trusted her like this, and she appreciated it.

"Just come back when you get hungry," beamed Aunt Alice. "I should be here by lunchtime."

Ben struggled into his coat while Jennet wiped the toothpaste from his mouth, and then all three of them left the house. The weather looked promising. Aunt Alice waved good-bye to them and set off purposefully toward the West Cliff.

It was still early, and Jennet and Ben wandered through the narrow streets, gazing into shop windows that were filled with pieces of Whitby jet. It had been fashioned into all sorts of jewelry—rings, pendants, bracelets, and tiepins. Jennet looked longingly at a pair of jet earrings and stroked the glass dreamily. Ben tutted in disgust and walked away, muttering about the dullness of shops.

Then he spied a joke shop. He pressed his face against its windows and uttered little yelps of delight. It had everything, from facepaint to horrific rubbery masks. There were sugar cubes that turned to worms when placed in tea and ghastly sets of false teeth. He wondered what he could afford—maybe Aunt Alice would buy him something. He drooled over the possibilities until his sister came to look for him.

Eventually the children came to the harbor and watched some late fishing boats return. A fresh, salty tang was in the air, and they ran across the bridge to see the fish auction. It was being held in a large covered area on the West Cliff. Wooden crates filled with silvery fish were stacked into high piles, while an auctioneer in a white coat gabbled away, faster than they believed possible.

Jennet wrinkled her nose at the strong, fishy smell. Ben peered into one of the crates and tried, unsuccessfully, to out-stare the dead fish, until a gruff man in a black coat shooed them away.

They walked along the Pier Road, but as it was only half past eight they could not go into the lifeboat museum. Instead, they chased each other along the sandy beach. The morning wore on, shops opened, and the tourists strolled out of hotels and bed-and-breakfasts.

* * *

Jennet ran up to the green door and searched in her pockets for the key. Outside Aunt Alice's cottage was an old barrel that overflowed with geraniums, and above the door itself hung a curiously shaped stone with a hole worn into it.

"Mornin'," said a voice suddenly. Jennet dropped the key in surprise.

Leaning against one of the other doors in the yard was a thick-set, dark-haired, surly-looking woman. A cigarette was balancing on her bottom lip, and when she spoke it stayed in place as though it were glued on. Her face showed disdain as she looked Jennet up and down. She folded her bare, fleshy arms and said, "You one of them what's come to stay wi' her?"

Jennet nodded, mesmerized at the acrobatic skill of the cigarette.

"Given you a key as well, 'as she? Me an' my Norman know what she gets up to, her an' them friends of hers. Oh, she thinks she's so clever, bossing everyone about." The woman blew through the curling blue cigarette smoke. "Anyway, you make sure you keep your hands to yourself, you hear me? I know your sort, lass—don't you come thievin' round here. She might be daft, but I'm not."

Jennet was so taken aback by the woman's outburst that before she could think of anything to say the dreadful creature had gone back into her house and slammed the door. Jennet stuck her tongue out and turned the key in the lock.

Inside, there was no sign of Aunt Alice. Jennet took off her coat, wondering whether she was in the parlor, having a nap. She knocked, but there was no answer, so she turned the brass handle and peeped in.

The parlor was papered in rich burgundy and lined with shelves full of dusty volumes. A large round table dominated the center of the room, and in the corner a tall grandfather clock monotonously ticked the time away.

Jennet went into the kitchen and decided to make a cup of tea to await the old lady's return. Just as the kettle began to whistle, there came a furtive knock on the front door.

"You took your time, Ben," she began. "What happened to—"

But when the door opened, she saw that the new arrival was not her brother after all. Another old lady blinked in surprise at her.

"Oh dear," said the stranger. "I suppose you must be Janet."

"Jennet," the girl corrected.

"Of course. I'm Miss Droon—a friend of Alice's. Is she in?"

"No, but she should be back soon."

"Shall I come in, then, and wait? Thank you." And she barged through to the kitchen, where the kettle was whistling for all it was worth and steaming up the windows.

Miss Droon was an odd-looking woman. Her hair was dark gray and very wiry, like a pan scrub. She wore thick, black-rimmed spectacles and a chunky, blue sweater that was covered in short, white hairs. As she passed by, Jennet noticed a strong whiff of cats. This was rather appropriate because Miss Droon had whiskers; they stuck out above her top lip and bristled along her chin. It was quite a struggle to keep from staring.

Miss Droon made a pot of tea and helped herself to the Gypsy Creams. She planted her bottom on a stool and tapped the table distractedly; evidently there was something on her mind.

"I'm sure Aunt Alice won't be long," said Jennet, noticing the hairs that had fallen to the floor from Miss Droon's sweater.

"I hope you're right, girl," she returned, "for Eurydice's sake." She looked out of the window desperately.

"Eurydice?"

"Yes. She's wandered off again, and she could go into labor any minute." Miss Droon wrung her hands together anxiously.

Jennet had visions of some woman roaming around Whitby, ready to give birth. "Maybe she's gone to the hospital," she suggested hopefully.

Miss Droon looked at her as if she were mad and opened her mouth. But at that moment, the front door opened and in came Aunt Alice with Ben. They had met on Church Street, and Ben was giving her a detailed account of the morning's activities. "Then we saw a statue of that Captain Cook and two huge whale bones made into an arch, and I found a fossil thing on the beach—see?"

"That's an ammonite, Benjamin; there are lots of them around here."

Miss Boston removed her hat before the mirror in the hall. "Sounds like you two have been busy," she said. "You and Jennet must be ravenous. Oh," and she paused in the kitchen doorway, "hello, Tilly. What can I do for you? I've just been over to Pru's, looking for that wretched book she cannot find—said she'd seen you yesterday. Everything well?"

"It's Eurydice!" Miss Droon burst out.

"Again!" whistled Aunt Alice. "How many this time?"

"No, she's gone off, and they're due any minute."

"How tiresome," tutted Miss Boston, winking at Jennet. "And you would like me to find her for you, is that it?"

"Please, Alice—I've brought Binky along." Miss Droon pulled a well-chewed woollen mouse from her pocket. "I just can't bear to think of her coping alone."

"She probably wanted to get away from your ham-fisted interference, Tilly dear. Do help yourself to biscuits, by the way."

Miss Droon guiltily licked the crumbs from her moustache. "Oh, Alice," she pleaded, "there may be very little time."

Miss Boston sighed and filled a jug with cold water. "Very well. Come into the parlor, Tilly—and don't forget Binky. Oh, Jennet, could you and Benjamin stay here for a while and be very quiet?" The children nodded, greatly puzzled. "Excellent. Now, in you go, Matilda."

Ben looked at Jennet. "Who's that, then?" he wanted to know.

"A friend of Aunt Alice's, I think," she replied.

"What have they gone in there for?"

Jennet brushed hairs off the stool lately occupied by Miss Droon and shrugged. "I don't know. I think she's a bit loopy."

"What did Aunt Alice want with the water, Jen? There are no plants in the parlor."

"Maybe she's going to pour it over Miss Droon's head," she answered sarcastically. "How do you expect me to know?"

The sound of voices filtered through the parlor door, so the children kept quiet and listened.

"Do shut up, Tilly," boomed Aunt Alice. "I need to concentrate."

"What can they be doing?" breathed Jennet.

After a short while, the door was opened and Miss Droon bustled out. Aunt Alice called after her, pulling back the curtains, "It's either the old barn again or that empty house on Hawkster Lane—sorry, Abbey Lane. Yes, I'm certain she'll be there."

"I must go to her! Poor little Eurydice," cried Miss Droon, fumbling with the front door latch.

Aunt Alice emerged from the parlor and remarked wryly, "I'd hardly call her 'little' in her condition." But Miss Droon had fled from the house.

"Oh, confound the woman," said Miss Boston. "it's no good. I shall have to go with her. Do you children want to come? It isn't far, but perhaps you need your lunches right away?"

Ben began to say that he did, but Jennet elbowed him into silence and said of course they would go.

"Good," said Aunt Alice, putting her hat back on. Jennet watched her and Ben leave the house while she put her coat on again. Then, on a sudden impulse, she ran into the parlor.

A sweet, heavy scent laced the air; on the table was the jug of water and an empty black lacquered bowl. Jennet went up to it and ran her fingers around the rim. It was wet.

"So, Aunt Alice filled the bowl with water, drew the curtains, then poured the water back into the jug," she said slowly to herself. "But why? And what is that sickly smell?" Jennet was mystified; how could all these things, not forgetting Binky, lead to Aunt Alice's conclusion that Eurydice was in some empty house?

She left the parlor and ran outside, closing the front door behind her. Ben and Miss Boston were on Church Street before she caught up with them.

"The Blakelocks used to live in the house, but they moved out two years ago and went to live in Wakefield, I believe," Aunt Alice was telling Ben. "The house has been empty since then. I can't imagine anyone wanting to buy it now, too rundown and probably overrun with field mice. Perfect for Eurydice, though."

"Why's that?" asked Jennet.

"Oh, didn't she tell you? Eurydice's a cat."

Jennet laughed. "No wonder she gave me an odd look when I mentioned the hospital."

"Yes," continued Aunt Alice, "Tilly already has twelve of the perishing things, most of them Eurydice's offspring. Too popular with the local toms she is—Eurydice, not Tilly. But will she get her seen to? Not on your life. There's hardly a stick of furniture in her house that hasn't been used either as a claw sharpener or—well, a convenience. The place positively reeks."

The empty house they were heading for was just off the lane that ran behind the abbey, so up the 199 steps they had to go. Halfway up, they encountered a breathless Miss Droon. She was finding the climb rather too strenuous.

"Oh my," she wheezed, "I hope you're right, Alice—I don't want to have staggered up these ruddy steps for nothing."

Finally they reached the summit and walked through the graveyard to get on to Abbey Lane. The stately ruin of the abbey towered up on their right as they followed the small road that circled around it.

"There it is," said Miss Boston, pointing to a long, two-storied building. It was an ugly house with mean little windows, quite secluded. Jennet shuddered at the thought of living there; at night it would be pitch dark, for there were no streetlamps. It was a dismal, lonely place.

"Goodness me!" exclaimed Aunt Alice. "Look at that sign. Somebody's actually bought it."

The "For Sale" sign that had stood outside the house for two years now bore a garish red stripe proclaiming "SOLD," for all the world to see.

"They haven't moved in yet, though," Miss Droon observed. "Let's slip in and get Eurydice."

Miss Boston opened the garden gate, which creaked and groaned in protest. "Dear me," said the old lady, "what a state this is in."

Ben was the last through the gate and studied a grimy nameplate nailed on to the wood as he went through. "The Hawes," he read aloud.

The garden around the house was wild: grass and weeds had choked the flowerbeds and only the taller roses had survived. The house itself was shabby and dark, with several of the downstairs windows boarded up.

"Such neglect," commented Miss Boston sadly. "And look at the path, completely overgrown. We shall have to wade through—mind the nettles, children."

Miss Droon tottered behind, calling out, "Eurydice, Eurydice—come on daring, there's a love, now. Oh, no, maybe she's had them already. What shall I do?"

Jennet looked back at the overgrown path thoughtfully. "Aunt Alice," she began, "if no one's been here for ages—how come someone's bought the house? I mean they can't have been to see it, can they?"

"Good heavens, child," said Miss Boston, "you are sharp today. How curious; I wonder who can be moving in?"

"Might be council, Alice," suggested Miss Droon. "Perhaps they're going to knock it down and rebuild."

"I shall go around to Olive and Parks the real estate agent this afternoon and solve this mystery," Miss Boston decided. "I'll see if they're going to rebuild or not."

Ben's voice called to them from around the back. He had found the kitchen door, and the wood was rotten. There was a large hole at the bottom.

"Eurydice," cried Miss Droon, going down on her knees and calling through the gap. "Kitty, Kitty."

"It's no use calling," Aunt Alice told her, "she won't come. I certainly wouldn't. The poor thing doesn't want to have you fussing about and being a nuisance. You always annoy her when she's expecting, Tilly."

"But I can't leave her here," wailed the crouching Miss Droon.

"Shall I go in?" asked Ben. "I could easily squeeze through there if we made the hole a bit bigger."

"Certainly not," said Miss Boston sternly, "that's breaking and entering."

"Oh, let him go in, Alice. You never liked Renie Blakelock anyway."

"That's hardly the point, Matilda. The property no longer belongs to her."

Miss Droon clicked her tongue in annoyance. "But as it's going to be knocked down anyway, I can't see what's the harm."

"We don't know that for certain. That was just your idea."

Miss Droon countered with her master stroke. She looked squarely at Aunt Alice through those thick glasses and said, "What about that umbrella Renie borrowed and never returned to you—your mother's wasn't it?"

Miss Boston relented at once. "On the other hand," she said stiffly, "it is an emergency, and if Benjamin really doesn't mind . . ."

Ben pulled away more of the crumbling door and wriggled through. A dingy, yellow-brown light filtered through the filthy kitchen windows. The room was bare, and the noise of his movements echoed around as he searched for the troublesome cat. He looked in the low cupboards and out of curiosity inspected the drawers also, but they only contained a broken fish slice and quantities of brown paper bags. Eurydice was not in the sink either.

In the hall, the exposed floorboards moved as he walked on them; they had warped and no longer fit properly. He put his head around the door of the front room, but only a collection of empty tea chests stood morosely in the middle of the gloom.

The whole house smelled damp and musty. Ben shivered. What a horrid, dank place it was—he found it hard to believe that someone had actually lived there. The entire house reminded him of a large dungeon, and that made him think of other things, Whitby's most frightening visitor for one.

"Eurydice, Eurydice," he called out feebly as he stood at the bottom of the stairs. Then he heard a noise. "You would have to be up there, wouldn't you?" He gritted his teeth and hoped it was the cat who had made the noise and not some vampire opening the lid of its coffin. He tried to control his rising panic, but it was some minutes before he was able to put his foot on the first step.

The stairs still possessed their carpet—too worn to be worth removing, it was damp and spotted with black mold. Ben took hold of the banister and crept very slowly up the steps.

It was dark on the first floor, for there was no landing window, and all the bedroom doors were shut. There were

five doors; he opened the nearest. Only a bathroom. The next led into an empty pink bedroom. As he went, Ben left the doors open behind him to illuminate the landing; in the growing light, he noticed a square opening in the ceiling.

"Must be the attic," he whispered to himself. He did not like the look of that deep black hole. It made him uneasy as he passed beneath it. "I hope you're not up there, you daft kitty," he mumbled as he quickly opened the next door. Another bedroom, blue wallpaper this time. Then a toilet, and finally a room done out in lime stripes. This was full of cardboard boxes and old yellowing newspapers that the mice had chewed.

Ben tiptoed over to the boxes. There was a sudden movement, and he stepped back in alarm. A furry white head popped up.

"Eurydice!" sighed Ben, relieved. The cat meowed crossly, staring at him with one green eye and one blue. "Come on, Kitty," he said soothingly. Eurydice let him stroke her, and Ben slipped his hand down to her tummy. At least she hadn't had the kittens yet. Then he frowned; something was wrong. As he tickled the cat's stomach, she rolled over, and he discovered that she only had three legs. What a peculiar animal.

He picked up the box she was in, and Eurydice glared at him. "It's all right, Kitty," he said, carrying her out of the room. Only then did Ben begin to wonder: Who had shut that door in the first place?

On the landing, Eurydice grew agitated, and her ears pressed flat against her skull. She began to hiss and spit but not at Ben. The boy turned cold. As he passed under the dark loft opening, all the hairs on the back of his neck prickled and rose. He felt sure something was up there, watching him from the shadows—the same something that could close bedroom doors.

He made for the stairs quickly, but as he ran down them two at a time, he chanced to turn back and was horrified to see a small, dark figure drop silently to the landing and begin creeping after him.

Ben bolted for the kitchen and thrust the box through the gap, scrabbling frantically after it.

"Look at your clothes," sighed Aunt Alice, "all dusty and cobwebby."

"Eurydice, you naughty girl," scolded Miss Droon, "don't do that again. I shall lock you in my room from now on."

In the sunlight Ben's fear seemed irrational; he must have imagined the whole thing. Either that or the figure was one of his "visitors," although he had never felt frightened in their presence before. He decided not to mention it to anyone.

"What was it like in there?" Jennet asked him.

"Smelly and damp," he replied, shaking the dust out of his hair.

"Must have been cold, too," she added. "You're covered in goose pimples."

Miss Boston put her arm around him and said, "This young man has earned his dinner—come on. Tilly, do stop messing with that wretched cat and make sure you do keep an eye on it until the kittens are born."

"Eurydice has only got three legs," Ben told his sister.

"Really?" asked Jennet, staring at the two ears that bobbed up and down above the box.

"She lost one when she was a kitten herself," crooned Miss Droon dotingly. "A window sash broke, and the frame crushed her leg beyond repair. The vet had to amputate to save her, poor darling. Now I can't take her anywhere near the vet's—simply goes berserk. Don't you, Eurydice darling?"

"And that's why she's always expecting," said Miss Boston, "and of course why she's so popular with the toms."

"Because she has three legs?" asked Jennet. "I don't see the connection."

Aunt Alice laughed wickedly. "Well, she can't run as fast as the other lady cats."

The children roared, and Miss Droon looked away.

CHAPTER THREE

THE LADIES' CIRCLE

Ben turned the ammonite over in his fingers and stared intently at it. It was the same size as a fifty-pence piece and charcoal in color. Miss Boston had told him that it was incredibly old, older than the human race, in fact. Ben held it tightly. It felt safe to touch something so ancient—there was very little permanence in his turbulent life and this small, time-polished fossil was like a magic talisman, a sign that perhaps things would be different from now on.

It was late, and the three of them were sitting in the parlor. The curtains were drawn, and Aunt Alice had lit a fire as the night had grown chilly. Now, the children lounged on the wide sofa and sipped hot chocolate.

Jennet looked across at the old lady, whose face glowed in the flickering firelight.

"Shall I tell you the legend of the ammonites and St. Hilda?" Aunt Alice asked them.

Ben pushed himself farther into the cushions and nodded.

The old lady gazed into the fire and began. "In the olden times, when Caedmon was alive, the Abbess of Whitby was the niece of a great northern king. They were dark, severe days, and most of the people were still pagan, worshipping cruel gods on the moors and at the river mouth."

Her quiet voice lulled Jennet's senses, and she began to drift far away. The old lady's words conjured up vivid pictures, and she shivered, imagining the horrible things that must have happened in those savage times.

"Well," continued Aunt Alice, after she had drained her mug, "it is said that the cliff top where the abbey now stands was alive with snakes. They were such a nuisance that the Lady Hilda took up a whip or staff and drove them all into the sea where, by her prayers, they were turned to stone. However, the three largest serpents had escaped her anger, and they rose out of the grass to strike her. Furiously, she hit out first and cut their heads clean off, while their bodies sailed through the air and were embedded in the wall of a house at the bottom of the one hundred ninety-nine steps. They are still there to this day, if you care to look."

Ben groaned—yet another soppy story. He liked the bit about the snakes, though. He examined his fossil once again and hissed softly to it.

Jennet stirred a little but still gazed at the flames through narrowed eyes. "Is any of that true?" she asked. "I mean was Hilda really the niece of a king?"

"Oh, yes," Aunt Alice assured her earnestly. "Edwin of Northumbria was her uncle, though some say father. She was a princess, in any case. Word got around that one of royal blood was coming to Whitby and gossip confused the true facts—rather like Chinese whispers, I imagine. Eventually half the population believed Hilda was a great sorceress, but we actually know very little about the real woman.

The story of the snakes is obviously allegorical, the serpents representing the pagan religion that Hilda overcame. Still, it is a quaint tale.

"Now I think it is time for you both to go to bed. You've had a busy day, and so have I, what with troublesome cats and silly old Tilly."

Jennet dragged Ben from the cushion cave he had made for himself and his pet snake. Hissing like a puncture, the boy ran up the stairs. His sister followed behind him and turned to Aunt Alice, who was carrying the three empty mugs into the kitchen. "Did you go to the real estate agent's?" she called down sleepily.

"Indeed I did," answered the old lady, raising her voice above the sound of the running tap as she rinsed the cocoa dregs away. "The house is not going to be knocked down. A woman has bought it. They weren't going to tell me, but I know the mother of the young man behind the desk. He told me a Mrs. Cooper had purchased the place. Has ideas of turning it into an antiques shop—ridiculous notion. We have far too many of those already, and the house is too far off the beaten track to make it worthwhile."

Miss Boston emerged from the kitchen and smiled up at Jennet. "Well, goodnight, dear," she said.

The next day was Saturday and the beginning of the Folk Week. Early in the morning, the two children raced around the West Cliff, looking at the odd assortment of people who were turning up. They spent an interesting half hour watching cars and vans squeeze through the town while they tried to guess what sort of people were inside.

There were morris dancers, a whole gaggle of bagpipes, long-haired hippies with guitars and peace stickers, a fleet of flutes and penny whistles, a group of mummers dressed in the most outlandish costumes Ben had ever seen, and even two belly dancers.

Whitby was heaving with people. Jennet laughed as she realized how true Aunt Alice's words had been—there were a lot of bearded men, and they all seemed to have the same sort of clothes on. It was like some kind of uniform: a good thick jumper with a clean white shirt underneath, then brown corduroy trousers, and, for the really serious, the ultimate accessory was a pewter tankard, attached to the belt.

A jolly, fat lady with cheeks like two beetroots clambered, with difficulty, out of a beaten-up old car. Then she leaned in once more and hauled out an accordion as big as a coffee table. She beamed at the children as she passed by. Ben stared after her eagerly. This really was the most extraordinary place he had ever been—something always seemed to be happening.

The morning shadows dwindled, and lunchtime drew near. Ben's stomach growled, and he reluctantly agreed with his sister to head back home. The town was seething, its streets thick with enthusiasts, musicians, tourists, and the poor locals trying to do their Saturday shopping. It took an incredibly long time to reach the bridge, and crossing that was another Herculean task.

Jennet sighed with relief as the narrow streets of the East Cliff closed around her, but even here the crowds were phenomenal. She gripped Ben's hand tightly in case he was washed away on the tourist tide and launched herself into the flow.

It was while she was passing the small post office on Church Street that a thought came to her, and she dragged her brother inside. It was jam-packed with people, but if she didn't do this now she would probably forget.

"What are we doing here?" Ben demanded. "I want my lunch."

"I'm going to send Aunt Connie a postcard," Jennet replied, gently pushing through the bodies till she came to the rack.

"Can't I go home now? I'm starved."

Jennet ignored him and studied the collection of cards. It was a picture of the abbey that she eventually chose, and she squirmed with it through to the counter. Strangely enough, nobody else seemed to be buying anything. Jennet put her postcard down and looked through the glass at the postmistress.

"Can I have this and a first-class stamp, please?" she asked.

The woman was about 50. Her graying hair resembled a dilapidated haystack, and the sides of her mouth twitched nervously. Jennet eyed her neat, beige cardigan. There was a crumpled tissue poking out from one sleeve, in case of emergencies. There was no wedding ring on the woman's finger, and Jennet guessed that here was one of the town's spinsters, and she smiled unconsciously.

The postmistress blinked in confusion, not sure why the girl had smiled at her. Up went her ringless hands, fluttering before her like frightened birds.

"A stamp," the woman repeated in a flustered voice as she searched under the counter. "Dear me, no—television license stamps." She twiddled with the chain around her neck, attached to which were her glasses. "Oh fly!" she muttered. "I had them a minute ago."

Jennet smiled again. The woman was a terrible ditherer; how had she ever gotten the job?

"Ah," came a grateful sigh, "there you are, you terrible thing." She pulled a large book of stamps toward her and put on her glasses before wading through it.

"There you are dear," the woman breathed wearily. "That's forty-five pence, please."

Jennet counted out her change, and while the woman waited, the tissue flashed out and dabbed at her nose then was just as speedily consigned to the sleeve once more.

Jennet took her stamp and postcard, thanked her, and looked around for Ben. He was not there. Then from the street came a terrible commotion; a car horn was blowing harshly, and voices were raised in anger. Jennet put her hand to her mouth and ran outside, thinking the worst.

A large old Bentley was attempting to plow down Church Street, and the driver was being none too gentle. Jennet found Ben on the pavement, laughing at the surprised and angry looks of the people who were thrust aside. A girl in a bright orange and purple dress that had little mirrors sewn around the hem shouted equally colorful abuse at the occupants of the car and shook her tambourine at them furiously.

Once Jennet had got over the relief of finding her brother in one piece, she shook him roughly and angrily told him, "Don't you ever, ever do that again! Do you understand?"

But Ben was not really listening. He was still staring at the car, which had pulled up outside the post office. The driver was a bluff Yorkshire man in grubby gardening clothes, but on his head he wore a chauffeur's cap. He got out and walked to one of the rear doors.

"'Ere we are, madam," he said gruffly as he opened it. Both Ben and Jennet peered inside to see who his passenger might be.

A large, flabby lady in a silk print dress and a fur stole stepped heavily onto the pavement. Her hair was a pale peach color, and there seemed to be an inch-thick layer of makeup covering her face. Her lips were smeared a sickly orange to match her rinse, but it just made her look ill. She wore a necklace of pearls, and her pudgy hands were be-jewelled with rings.

Jennet thought she looked like a fat pantomime fairy. Ben began to giggle as the apparition waddled gracelessly toward the post office and brushed past them. Her perfume was incredibly pungent—he could almost taste it.

The woman peered down her nose at the children and gave a peculiar excuse for a smile. Ben scowled. This was one of those phony acknowledgments, the sort the Rodice used to dole out. Jennet nodded at her and shuddered as she wobbled into the post office; there had been lipstick all over her teeth.

"Come on," she said to her brother, "let's go and have lunch."

They found Miss Boston already in the kitchen mak-ing ham sandwiches for them and, as they sat down to eat, they told her what they had done that morning. The old lady listened attentively, clucking now and then in wonder or approval. She laughed as they described the morris dancers and sucked in her cheeks at the disgraceful behavior of the Bentley.

"That Banbury-Scott woman really is too much!" she snorted. "Thinks she owns the town, she does."

"You know that fat lady with all the makeup on her face, then?" asked Ben, forgetting his manners.

Aunt Alice spluttered at this description, pursing her lips and raising her eyebrows to disassociate herself from it. "Yes, I know her," she said. "She just happens to be one of the wealthiest women in the town. Married well, you see—married twice, actually, but both her husbands are dead now. Mrs. Banbury-Scott is a very important person; her home is one of the largest and probably the oldest around here." Miss Boston sighed wistfully and took another bite of her sandwich.

"She's very fat," Ben said again.

Jennet kicked him under the table, but Aunt Alice nodded in agreement. "Yes, she is a bit of a pig," she admitted. "Far too greedy, I'm afraid."

Ben chuckled with surprise and appreciation—he had not expected her to agree with him.

"I didn't like her," said Jennet flatly.

"Not many do," confided Aunt Alice, "but because she's rich, they put up with her. Very useful to have her on the board of this and that if she makes a contribution to the funds now and again. Of course, she's got terribly above herself—putting on airs and graces. She might be able to fool some of them around here with her fancy ways, but I remember what she was like before she got married. Plain Dora Blatchet she was then; father lived in the yard opposite— simple fisherman." She leaned back and stared into space for a moment. "Oh, but she was a lovely creature then—prettiest little thing in Whitby. Another cruel trick of age."

Ben licked the crumbs off the plate and looked around for something else. Miss Boston gave him an apple, but he looked at it woefully; he had been hoping for some chocolate cookies.

"She can't have any real friends, then," said Jennet thoughtfully. "How awful to be liked just because you have money."

"Oh, but she does have friends, dear," Aunt Alice quickly put in. "There's Edith Wethers, the postmistress; Mrs. Joyster; Tilly Droon; and . . ." here she paused, then added guiltily, " . . . and there's me. In fact, Mrs. Banbury-Scott will be coming here tomorrow evening. Our ladies' circle meets once a month."

She cleared the plates away while Jennet puzzled over her words. The way Aunt Alice had mentioned the ladies' circle was strange, as if she was embarrassed and did not want to talk about it.

"Is it a party?" Ben asked with interest.

Miss Boston gave a nervous laugh and shook her head quickly. "Oh no, Benjamin," she said. "Just a collection of dreary old woman like me—extremely dull, I'm afraid."

Jennet looked across at her brother. It was obvious they were not wanted at this meeting, and she wondered what they were supposed to do during it.

By a strange coincidence, Aunt Alice was thinking exactly the same thing. The old lady stuck out her chins and chewed the problem over in her mind. It would never do for the children to find out what happened at these meetings and discover her little secret, she told herself. Jennet watched her and a suspicion began to form in the back of her mind, but for the moment she said nothing.

The rest of the afternoon was spent listening to the various little pockets of folk music that sprang up wherever a clear space could be found. Ben enjoyed this immensely and joined in the clapping and cheering. There was so much to see that the time passed very quickly, and the children were exhausted by the time they eventually clambered into their beds.

Another loud chorus of screeching gulls startled Jennet out of her sleep the next morning. She glanced at her watch: it was half past six. With an exasperated groan, she turned on her side and lifted the edge of her bedroom curtain.

The day was wet and windy, with gulls riding the gusts and circling overhead. Jennet's room looked out on to the yard, but nothing stirred there. She fumbled with the catch and opened the window.

At once, the drizzly Sunday morning crowded into her bedroom. The clamor of the sea birds rang in her ears, and the warm wind blew salt and rain into her face. From somewhere, the delicious and enviable smell of frying bacon tantalized her senses. Quickly pulling her clothes on, Jennet stumbled downstairs to make her breakfast.

In the kitchen, she found that Miss Boston was already up and about. She had evidently just returned from her morning walk, as her white hair resembled the collection of sheep's wool and twigs on the hall table.

"Hello, dear," she said, looking up from the kipper on the plate before her. "Sleep well?"

Jennet nodded. "Yes, thank you." She slotted a piece of bread into the toaster and decided it was time to ask what had been preying on her mind. "Aunt Alice," she began casually.

The old lady pulled a fishbone from her lips and glanced up. "Hmmm?"

"When will your friends be coming today?"

Aunt Alice coughed and hastily covered her mouth. "Gracious!" she exclaimed in a fluster. "I must have swallowed a bone by mistake—tiresome thing!" She took a drink of coffee, wondering all the while what the girl would ask next. "They usually arrive after tea, Jennet dear," she answered eventually. "Why?"

"I just wanted to know if you wanted Ben and me around," Jennet replied as the toast popped up. "We could stay upstairs, if you like."

Miss Boston took hold of Jennet's hands, which by this time were holding the butter knife and the toast. "Oh, do you think you could, dear?" she said gleefully, puckering up her wrinkled face. "That really would be such a help. Some of the circle are not very fond of children, and we do need to concentrate, you see."

"Don't worry," Jennet said. "I'll take Ben on a long walk this afternoon to tire him out. You won't hear a peep from him all night."

"Oh, you are considerate, thank you again." But Miss Boston's face, as she bent her head over her plate once more, seemed far from happy.

The girl turned back to the toast and grinned. She had guessed correctly: the ladies in the circle were secret gamblers.

Nothing titillates old ladies more than gambling for money, be it bingo or bridge. Jennet decided that Aunt Alice was being so furtive because she was too embarrassed to admit it. She crunched through her breakfast and stared out of the window. I wonder what they play? she thought to herself. It must be cards, she decided. Gin rummy or whist, perhaps, or maybe even poker. The thought of all those old women sitting around a table playing poker like cowboys in a Wild West saloon greatly amused her. She imagined Mrs. Banbury-Scott in a 10-gallon hat and nearly spat out the toast with her laughter.

Aunt Alice frowned to herself. Could Jennet have found out somehow? Perhaps it was not too late to cancel tonight's meeting. She took another gulp of coffee and fixed her eyes on the remains of the kipper as though it were to blame in some way. I must make this the very last meeting of the circle, she insisted to herself. It will get too dangerous if the children become involved—especially for Benjamin.

Ben was sleeping soundly with his ammonite clasped firmly in his hand. He had been dreaming of snakes and dragons all night—he was the valiant hero who slew them. The dream was just coming to a ridiculous conclusion, as his dreams usually did, with a grand parade of headless serpents wriggling behind him on brightly colored leads while he fed cat munchies to the heads bouncing around his ankles.

"Ben, Ben," shouted one of the heads, "wake up, you lazy lump!"

He rolled over and pulled his covers higher.

Jennet was in no mood for this today. "Wake up, thick-head!" She dragged the blankets off him and he flapped about like a headless serpent himself. Then he glared at his sister and brought his bottom teeth over his lip to show annoyance.

"You and me are going for a long walk today," she told him sharply. "So come downstairs and help me make a packed lunch."

"Where we going?" he asked, wishing he could stay in bed all day. But she had already left the room.

The drizzling weather was soon blown inland and by midmorning the sky was blue. Aunt Alice waved the children off, but her heart was troubled, and she watched them leave with a guilty look on her face.

It was late when they returned, making their way through the town. The children crossed the bridge to the East Cliff and wearily tramped up Church Street.

"My dears!" Aunt Alice sighed with relief as they opened the front door. "You've been gone an age; I was beginning to worry." The old lady stared at their tired faces and tutted. "My goodness, you are a dozy pair, and look at the state of you both. I'll turn the heater on so there'll be plenty of hot water."

Some time later, Ben lounged in his bed. He had been fed, had bathed himself, and was now reading a brand-new comic book that Miss Boston had bought for him. It was a warm night, so he had only put on his pajama bottoms. The sheets were crisp and clean, smelling of the linen closet, and he felt new all over as he wormed into them, tired and contented. From the bathroom, he could hear Jennet stepping out of the bath, and downstairs Aunt Alice was setting out her best china cups on a tray. She was humming to herself, and the sound drifted up to his room.

Ben's window did not overlook the yard, so he missed the arrival of the old lady's guests. A sharp knock on the front door vibrated through the cottage and startled him. He sat up and listened to see if he could hear who it was as Miss Boston let the newcomer in. A brisk, abrupt voice drifted up the stairs—that must be Mrs. Joyster, he thought to himself. Just then, his own door opened, and Jennet, wrapped in a towel with another turbaned around her wet hair, looked in.

"Was that the army woman?" he asked her.

Jennet glanced behind her and shrugged. "I think so," she said. "Now, have you got everything you want? You're not to go downstairs tonight, do you understand?"

Ben nodded, but Jennet recognized the look in his eyes and waved a warning finger toward him. "If you so much as sit on the top step, there'll be trouble, OK?"

Ben threw himself on his back and raised the comic book over his head sulkily. Jennet closed the door and went to her own room. She heard some more guests arrive, and recognized Miss Wethers' voice and that of Miss Droon.

The postmistress was sneezing and asked for a glass of water. "I just can't sit next to Tilly tonight," came the muffled twitterings. "All that cat fur brings on my—achoo!"

Jennet smiled to herself; the tissue would have its work cut out tonight. She dried her hair and began thinking about the card sharps downstairs. This time she wondered what the stakes were—just how much did the old dears play for? Perhaps it was only 10 or 20 pence. What if it was more than that—a pound or two? Maybe the gambling fever was so strong that a whole week's pension was frittered away in one night. A new idea came to her as she tugged at a tangled clump of hair with her brush. What if Aunt Alice was in league with the others to swindle Mrs. Banbury-Scott out of all her money? Jennet smiled at her own fanciful imaginings and just hoped the cards would favor Aunt Alice tonight. It was probably nothing worse than a game of happy families, she concluded, putting the hairbrush down.

The light faded outside Ben's window, and the shadows deepened in his room. The boy fell into a light, uneasy sleep that was invaded by unpleasant dreams. In them, he was walking down a long, narrow corridor that seemed familiar, but he couldn't think where he had seen it before. His feet were heavy in the dream, and though his legs were moving, he never got anywhere. Beads of sweat pricked Ben's forehead as he turned over, and his breath came in short gasps.

He knew there was something behind him, but he could not turn his head around to look. He could feel its presence dogging his every footstep, its eyes burning into his back; he sensed the tension in the air as it prepared to spring. A howl boomed inside his head, a weird, unearthly sound that slashed the watchful night. With a hideous growl, the unseen beast bore down on him.

The boy whimpered in his sleep, trapped in a nightmare that was rapidly approaching its gruesome end. His face was screwed up in fear. "Go away," he mumbled tearfully, "make it go away!"

But the horror continued. The creature was snapping at his heels, and with a shriek he called out, "Mom! Mom!"

Ben found himself sitting up in bed, drenched with sweat. The room was dark, yet he could make out the figure sitting beside him quite clearly.

"Mom," he whispered.

The figure smiled at him, as any mother might do to comfort her child in the night. Ben put his arms out to embrace her, but she rose and backed away. It was then that he remembered she was dead.

He rubbed the sleep from his eyes and wondered how he could have mistaken this vision for something real. A thread of silver light ran around her outline, flickering like sunlight over water. His mother opened her mouth, but Ben could not hear the words she was speaking. He averted his eyes quickly when he saw the pattern on the wallpaper through the darkness, where the roof on her mouth should have been. He knew there was nothing to fear, but it unnerved him, and he found himself wishing she would leave. Watching his own mother mouthing dumbly like an actress in some crackly silent film was horrible.

The boy hid his eyes and waited for her to disappear—his visitors usually left if he ignored them. But when he looked up, she was still there. She had moved to the end of the bed and was kneeling down with her face turned sadly toward him. She had stopped trying to talk, as if she realized that it was upsetting him. Instead, she shook her head at her son with that gentle smile on her lips that he remembered so well. That was better; Ben smiled back at her. She then inclined her head toward the door, beckoning Ben with her hands.

Puzzled, the boy clambered out of bed and shivered; his sweat had become cold, and he was chilled. Stepping up to the door, he looked up at the shade of his mother and asked her with the expression in his eyes what she wanted.

The figure pointed at the doorknob. Trembling, Ben reached out a hand, slowly opened the door, and peered out.

He was totally unprepared for what was on the other side and gasped in disbelief.

There, crammed on the small landing, was a multitude of "visitors." They were sitting on the banisters and crowded down the stairs. Ben could only shake his head and stare; he had never seen this many together before. The ghosts of over a hundred people were there. There were young faces and old, some wearing old-fashioned costumes and others dressed in clothes more familiar to him. But they all seemed to be waiting for something. A long line of them trailed down into the hall and gathered outside the closed parlor door.

Although Ben did not understand why he saw his "visitors," they sometimes seemed as real and ordinary as the rest of the world—the Rodice's husband had been one of these. But he could tell these forms were phantoms. Some of them were transparent as glass, while others were just indistinct shapes made of gray mist.

As he opened the bedroom door a little wider to get a clearer view, they suddenly became aware of him, and all their faces turned in his direction. For a moment Ben felt afraid, and he pulled himself back into the bedroom. But his qualms disappeared as the light that flickered around the apparitions welled up and illuminated the stairwell from top to bottom with a beautiful radiance.

The blaze lit his face, and he glanced up to find his mother. She was no longer at his side, and it was some moments before he caught sight of her again in the hall below, motioning for him to follow.

Ben stepped onto the landing and instantly regretted it. Every soul rushed toward him. They gathered thickly

around, pressing in on all sides, their eyes imploring him to help them. They wrung their hands piteously before his face, their expressions desperate with the need to communicate with the living. He never actually felt them touch him, but it was suffocating all the same, and he hated it. It was like being surrounded by beggars and knowing you had nothing to give them. The pleading faces were images of sorrow and regret that burned into him, and a claustrophobic panic began to bubble up inside. He had never experienced anything like this, and it frightened him; what were these spirits doing here, and what did they want? It was as if they had been dragged here against their will and were beseeching him to release them.

"I can't hear you," he wailed helplessly. "Stop it! Stop it!" The boy closed his eyes tight shut and struggled along the landing. He had to escape from this clamoring madness, and he groped for the door to Jennet's room. The throng of spirits parted before him like scythed corn.

There it was: the doorknob. He fumbled for a moment, opened his eyes, and flung himself inside.

"What's up?" asked his sister in mild surprise. She was reading one of Aunt Alice's books in bed and had obviously not heard a thing. But once she saw how pale and frightened her brother was, she hastily put the book down and held out her arms to him.

"Oh, Jen!" he howled, throwing himself at her. "They won't leave me alone, Jen; I can't hear what they're trying to say. Tell them to go away, will you? I've never seen so many of them before." He sobbed into the large T-shirt she used as a nightie, and the rest of what he said was unintelligible.

Jennet stroked his hair and tried to soothe him. It was a long time since Ben had had one of his turns, and she wondered that he should have one now—he seemed to be so happy here.

"Are you . . . are you seeing things again, Ben?" she ventured.

He nodded into her shoulder. "Mom's here, too," he cried. "There's so many, Jen."

Jennet pushed him away from her and looked steadily into his eyes. For a moment, all her old suspicions about his visions had flooded back, but no, he was really scared. "Don't worry," she told him calmly. "I'll take a look outside and make sure there's no one there."

She got up and crossed to the door, but Ben sprang past her and slammed himself against it violently. "Don't go out!" he begged. "You'll let them in!"

Jennet was beginning to get worried; he had never been this terrified before. She wondered if she ought to go and ask Aunt Alice's advice. Would she mind the interruption? This certainly seemed urgent enough.

"Don't worry, Ben," she said, pulling him from the door. "I won't let anyone in, I promise."

The boy backed toward the bed as she turned the knob and opened the door. She could see nothing out there—but he could. On the landing, the crowd of souls raised their arms and surged forward. Ben screamed and collapsed on the bed.

Jennet was horrified. She raced down the stairs, calling for Aunt Alice at the top of her voice. Up to the parlor door she ran and, without knocking, thrust it open and charged inside.

A red light fell on her. For a moment, the girl was confused by it, but as she looked around to find its infernal source, the truth of the situation she had stumbled into was revealed.

Seated at the round parlor table was the ladies' circle: Miss Wethers, Mrs. Joyster, Miss Droon, Mrs. Banbury-Scott, and Aunt Alice. They were all holding hands and looked extremely startled by Jennet's entrance. She had interrupted a séance.

For a second, Jennet could only stare back at them. Miss Wethers made an uncomfortable squeaking noise and pulled her hands away from the table to reach for a tissue.

Aunt Alice sucked her cheeks in guiltily. "Oh dear," she began but did not know what else to say.

Jennet was speechless. She watched as Mrs. Joyster tut-ted at her inconvenient arrival and left the table to switch on the main light. Then she leaned over the small lamp that had been fitted with a red bulb and clicked it off. "We'll get no more tonight," she huffed disagreeably and fixed the girl with a withering glare.

Anger quickly replaced the surprise that Jennet had at first felt. All this time, Aunt Alice had deceived her! She felt cheated and used—the old woman wasn't interested in her at all; she just wanted Ben because of his gift. Her resentment welled up until she could contain it no longer.

"I hate you!" she stormed. "You're nothing but a load of old witches!"

She slammed the door shut and stomped upstairs to pack her things and Ben's. They weren't going to stay in this house any longer; she didn't care where they went just so long as they got away.

"Who was that?" asked the fat Mrs. Banbury-Scott, as she reached over to a plate of scones and crammed one into her gaping mouth.

"That young lady has completely ruined the sitting," repeated Mrs. Joyster, snorting in disgust.

Another scone disappeared into the Banbury-Scott cavern. "Most disagreeable child. Mmmmm . . . didn't I see her outside the post office yesterday?" She paused to give her tongue an airing as it came across a most peculiar taste. "What did you put in your jam, Tilly darling—catnip?"

Miss Wethers stared at the closed door unhappily. "Oh my," the mouse whined. "She didn't seem very happy."

Aunt Alice wiped her moist eyes. "No, she didn't, did she?" and the old lady covered her face in shame.

CHAPTER FOUR

THE AUFWADER

Jennet cradled Ben in her arms and held him tightly. The boy mumbled under his breath and opened one bleary eye. Jennet had left the door to her room ajar and over her shoulder he could see onto the landing—it was dark and empty.

"Good," he breathed with relief, "they've gone."

"Are you all right, Ben?" his sister asked gently. He nodded and wiped his forehead. Jennet looked at him to make sure, then pulled her large blue bag from underneath the bed.

"Come on," she said firmly. "We're leaving. Go and fetch your stuff."

Ben stared miserably at her. He had done it again; yet another chance had been ruined by his behavior. He pouted and rubbed his eyes, for he had liked Whitby. "Where will we go now?" he asked in a small voice.

"I don't know, and I don't care," the girl fumed, "but we're not staying here a minute longer."

He ran into his own room, and the tears started to fall. Jennet had not told him what she had seen downstairs, so he assumed she was angry with him.

In the parlor, Aunt Alice was shooing her guests out. "Hurry up," she cried frantically. "No, leave that, Edith—I'll put it away, thank you."

"Adolescent histrionics," Mrs. Joyster remarked dryly as she went into the hall and took her coat off the peg. "Girls like that are only seeking attention."

"Well, I'll make sure she receives some, then," Aunt Alice barked back at her.

"Wasn't worth leaving Eurydice and her little babies," grumbled the whiskered Miss Droon. "Did I tell you she had three of the little beauties?"

"Achoo!" sneezed Edith Wethers as she squeezed by.

Miss Boston shepherded them out of the front door, ignoring the protests and grumbles. She was the undisputed leader of the ladies' circle, and her authority was absolute. Mrs. Banbury-Scott was not at all pleased though, as, scone in hand, she trundled out of the yard and looked for her Bentley.

Aunt Alice closed the front door and gazed uneasily up the stairs—this was going to be extremely difficult.

Jennet emptied the contents of her chest of drawers onto the bed and stuffed her clothes into the bag. Her thoughts were a jumble of confused strands. What was she to do now? Where could she and Ben go? It was all very well to run away if you had somewhere to run to, but they had nowhere. The foster home was out of the question; no way would she go back there. The Rodice wouldn't let them anyway, the mean old crow.

"May I come in?" Miss Boston stood timidly on the landing with her hands clasped to her chest. She looked like a small child waiting outside the headmaster's office.

Jennet continued her packing without looking up. "It's your house," she muttered in a dull tone.

Aunt Alice glanced at the large bag that the girl was filling. She clutched at the door frame and asked fretfully, "But my dear, what are you doing? Are you going somewhere?"

"You lied to me," Jennet snorted. "You let me think you wanted me here. How long would it have been before you involved Ben in your sinister games?" She threw the last of her clothes in the bag and whirled around to face the old woman. "I could report you, you know—tell the Sunday papers or something. They'd love this, wouldn't they? Imagine the headlines: 'Coven of Geriatric Witches Exposed.'"

Miss Boston stared at the carpet, thoroughly abashed. "Yes, I suppose I deserve that," she said meekly. "What I have done is unforgivable—I'm sorry."

"Too late for that now. You frightened Ben half to death."

The old lady raised her eyebrows eagerly. "Really? Why, what did he see?"

"You don't stop, do you?" Jennet gasped incredulously. "You just don't care—he might have lost his mind, and all you're interested in is what sort of ghosts he saw!"

Aunt Alice shook her head. "That isn't true," she denied vehemently. "Of course I'm concerned."

At that moment, Ben appeared. In his arms, he carried a bundle of belongings, and his cheeks were stained with tears. He gazed up at Miss Boston miserably. "Why don't you like us any more?" he asked in a tremulous voice. "I don't want to go."

She yelped as though wounded. "Oh, but I *do* like you Benjamin," she cried, "and I don't want you to leave."

"Give me your stuff, Ben," Jennet said coldly.

The boy looked from Aunt Alice to his sister, his unhappy face betraying his emotions. He was torn between love and loyalty to Jennet and reluctance to leave the one place he had felt at home since the death of his parents. Miss Boston saw his pain and decided that enough was enough.

"Go back to bed, Benjamin," she told him kindly. "We'll sort this out."

Jennet glared at her and was about to speak, but Aunt Alice puffed herself up and spoke in such a forceful voice that for a moment the girl was startled into silence. "Let Benjamin go," she instructed firmly. With one hand on his shoulder, she guided the boy out of the room, then closed the door and turned to his sister.

"What right have you got—" Jennet began.

But now it was Miss Boston's turn to speak. "I have every right," she declared. "I am now legally responsible for both of you, and if you think I am going to let you run off in the middle of the night, you're not the clever girl I thought you were." She jutted her chins out determinedly, daring the girl to disagree.

Jennet sat down heavily on the bed and sobbed bitterly.

Aunt Alice's expression softened, and she sat next to her. "Let me explain, Jennet dear," she said gently. "When I was a young girl, not much older than yourself, I saw things I didn't understand."

"Like Ben does, you mean?"

"Exactly so, but at the time my mama forbade me to mention them. In those days, children were not spared the rod, and I soon learned to save my poor hands from the cane by ignoring what I saw." She stared for a moment at her palms, remembering the welts that had once marred them, then she thrust her hands under her knees. "A gift such as I possessed goes into decline if neglected," Aunt Alice resumed sadly, "and I neglected it for very many years."

"So what were you doing downstairs?" asked Jennet, totally unmoved.

Miss Boston heaved a great sigh. "I do wish you would be a little less prickly, Jennet dear. I'm afraid that what you saw downstairs was one of my attempts to regain the gift. The circle meets every month for what Mrs. Banbury-Scott jokingly calls 'spirits and scones.' More often than not, it ends up as just a little social chit-chat—our dear departed don't always feel inclined to come through, you know."

"You had a good turnout tonight though, didn't you?" Jennet put in. "Practically a full house."

The old lady clucked uncomfortably. "You must believe me, child, I had already made up my mind that tonight's little get-together would be the very last."

"So you say."

"I swear it on my life, Jennet; there will be no more meetings of the circle."

Jennet remained wary and distrustful, but she realized that there were no other options open to her. "All right," she said slowly, "we'll stay—providing there are no more 'spirits and scones.'"

"There won't be." The old lady brightened, confident that the situation had been resolved. "Well, it's time you got some sleep now," she smiled, getting to her feet and crossing to the door.

Jennet did not reply.

As she left, Miss Boston hesitated. "Oh, and by the way," she added, "you need thirteen for a coven, and I prefer the term *wise woman*. Goodnight, dear."

A wild and windy Monday kept most of the tourists indoors, to the irritation of the inkeepers and the profit of the arcade owners. The north wind blasted in off the sea, and even the buildings seemed to shiver and shrink closer into the cliffs.

In the afternoon, Ben went for a walk alone. Jennet was brooding in her room, and he sensed the tension between her and Aunt Alice, but at least they were staying in Whitby. He stood on the church steps and leaned on the handrail. Set into the wall of one of the houses below, he noticed three large ammonites, just above the lintel. Ben grinned—it was just as the story had said.

He looked up at the gulls and stretched out his arms like wings. After drawing a deep breath, he squawked, mocking them as loudly as he could, and tore up the steps. When he reached the top, Ben threw himself on the grass around the gravestones and rolled over so he could see the sky.

A miserable collection of people was wandering around the church, and he heard the dull drone of their voices, although he did not sit up to see them. One of the group was evidently a child—a boy. He was asking questions to someone who Ben presumed was his mother, and she was answering with a voice full of irritation. Curiously, he turned on his side just to make sure.

There they were trailing along the path, a family of three, and all dressed in totally inappropriate clothes for this sort of weather. They were obviously vacationers who had not come prepared for anything other than sunshine. The father was walking a little ahead with his hands thrust into his pockets, and the mother was trying to control her flapping summer dress with one hand while hanging on to her son with the other.

The boy was roughly around Ben's age. He wore red shorts, and his legs looked pinched and cold. An extra strong gust caught the woman unaware, and she shrieked as her skirt blew right up. Her son seized his chance and escaped from her clutches.

Into the forest of gravestones he scampered, and squealing his name at the top of her shrill voice, his mother chased after him. The boy knew his freedom would be shortlived, so he looked around for something to take his temper out on.

"Get lost Dracula!" he bawled, raising his foot and giving the nearest headstone a mighty kick.

His mother screeched as she snatched him up once more. "Don't you ever do that again!" she yelled. "If your father catches you, he'll cripple you. Show some respect!" With that she slapped his legs, and the boy let loose a dreadful howl.

Ben winced; that must have hurt—especially with it being so cold. He lay back in the grass once more and found himself thanking his stars that he and Jennet had never been sent to people like them.

The family passed along the path nearby. The boy stared unhappily at Ben, shamed by the red mark that glowed on his leg.

Chewing a piece of grass, he contemplated the previous night's happenings. He was not exactly sure why Jennet had been so cold toward Aunt Alice that morning, but it must have had something to do with what he had seen. If only he was like everyone else.

The evening was drawing in, but he had no desire to go back yet, especially if the atmosphere had not lifted. He propped himself up on his elbows and looked down on the harbor. A fishing boat was sailing out to sea, defying the rough waves. Ben remembered that he had still not visited the lifeboat museum and promised himself that treat for tomorrow. His gaze followed the progress of the boat as it sailed out to sea; as he turned his head to do so, something startled him.

On one of the tomb slabs sat a small figure. It was silhouetted against the horizon and, until his eyes adjusted to the light, Ben could not make it out. It was as large as a child and wore a dark-blue fishing jersey. A battered canvas bag was slung over one arm and poking out of it was a slimy bundle of seaweed. The head of the figure was hunched deep into its shoulders and the neck of the thickly-knitted garment had been pulled up over its ears. Its back was turned to Ben so he could not see the face. To make identification even more difficult, a black woollen hat obscured most of the head. A thick tangle of brown hair fluttered in the wind below the wide brim of the hat, suggesting perhaps the figure was a girl.

Something buzzed inside his head. Ben shook himself and rubbed his eyes. He was not certain, but he thought it was one of his "visitors." The boy was at once afraid and yet greatly interested. Although he remembered the horror of last night, he realized he had only been terrified because there were so many of them.

Ben continued to stare until curiosity overpowered him. Very quietly, he got up and stretched. With the tip of his tongue pressed over his top lip in concentration, he stepped over the grass toward the tomb where she sat. Closer and closer he crept, his heart pounding. Then, just as he came within reach, the figure moved and turned her face full on him.

Ben froze. He had never beheld anything like it before; the creature was not human. Her face was like soft leather. The nose was large and upturned, with a small mouth shaped like the crescent moon and cheeks burned brown by the wind. Yet it was her eyes that transfixed the boy. They were as big as his fists and as gray as the stormy sea, and the wrinkles that framed them spread about her brow like ripples on the shore.

They faced each other in silence, but the space between them was electrified. Ben gulped.

The other kept her fathomless eyes upon him. She, too, swallowed nervously, but as a cornered animal might. Finally, her lips parted, and she spoke; her voice held the cry of the gulls and the lulling of the sea.

"You see me, human child," she said simply, and something close to a smile hovered about her mouth.

Ben could only nod in reply.

The creature averted her eyes, and he felt as though invisible chains released him. "Never have I met one with the sight," she said, breaking into a grin.

"What . . . who are you?" he stammered at last.

"I am Nelda," she answered teasingly, "but that was not your meaning." She lifted her eyes again, and the sea stirred in the very heart of them. Can a human child understand? she asked herself. For a moment, she considered the situation,

then shrugged. "I am a wanderer of the shore," she told him. "Our folk dwell by the sea and have done so long before your kind came."

Ben frowned. "But why haven't I heard of you before? Nobody's ever mentioned you to me."

Nelda smiled. "That is because man no longer remembers or believes in us. We are figures of legend now, and it is better so." She brushed the wild, unkempt hair off her face and looked down to the harbor. "We fade away," she muttered darkly. "*Aufwader* was the name that once you gave to us. But who now recalls it? Very few, I think."

Ben still did not understand. Shaking his head he asked, "But why have they—I mean, we—forgotten? Surely people must see you when—" Even as he said the words, he realized what she meant: only people like him could see them. "Oh," he uttered slowly.

She laughed, swinging her legs off the tomb and leaping to the ground. "That's right, human child," Nelda gurgled. "No one will believe you if you tell them—they shall think you mad."

The strange creature prepared to leave, but Ben caught her arm. With a shock, he realized she was real and alive, not one of his visitors at all.

"Don't go yet," he pleaded. "My name's Ben."

The aufwader considered him for a moment, and the smile flickered over her face again. "Why should I linger here?" she asked mildly. "Already I have dared much just to speak with you. Our races are apart, Ben—yours is strong and has conquered the world, but the tally of our years might soon come to an end." Nelda stared out to sea and hung her head as if overwhelmed by some terrible grief. "I must go," she said in a husky voice.

Ben did not want her to leave just yet; there were so many questions ricocheting round his head. How many of her kind were there? Where did she come from, and would he see her again?

Nelda began walking down the path, and he could think of nothing that would make her stay. He felt useless and watched helplessly as she approached the steps. Then, as she turned to nod farewell, the boy caught sight of a raw emotion in her eyes and was jolted out of his dumbness. There was something troubling her.

Quickly, he cupped his hands around his mouth. "Won't you tell me what's the matter?" he shouted after her.

The departing figure hesitated on the steps. Nelda lifted her head, and the face that had shown those teasing smiles was now brimming with sorrow.

Ben ran up and put his hand on her shoulder. "Can't I help?" he asked.

Nelda studied him. How could a human child know of her pain, she wondered. Perhaps the elders were wrong, and some of them could be trusted.

"What age do you reckon me?" she asked him suddenly.

Ben shrugged. He was not very good at guessing people's ages, and it usually upset them when he got it wrong. He looked at the network of wrinkles that scored her face. If it wasn't for those he would have assumed she was a child too; she was only as tall as he was. Could she be 50, 60? He decided on the former because it was more complimentary.

"I am seventy of your years," Nelda corrected him. "Yet I am the youngest of my tribe—a mere whelp am I to them. Though I have lived in this world since before your father was born, you and I are probably of similar age to our blood kin."

"I haven't got a father," Ben told her. "He's dead."

A quick succession of expressions passed over Nelda's face. She was wondering whether she could stay for just a little while longer; no one need know. "So be it," she said aloud once the decision had been made. "Let us talk, you and I."

She led him over the gravestones to where the cliff sloped grassily down to the backs of houses; there they sat down. Delicious-smelling kipper smoke came from one of the chimneys, and the wind seized it eagerly, scattering the tantalizing scent over the town. Nelda nuzzled her chin into the wide neck of her jersey and embraced her knees until she was curled up like an urchin.

Ben waited patiently. He was content to just sit there, breathing the kippery air next to the remarkable aufwader. A middle-aged couple trudged up the church steps while he waited. They smiled at him pleasantly as they passed by. Ben bit his lip with excitement—they had not seen Nelda. It was all a marvelous secret, and one that he realized had to be kept. If he told his sister, she might have another argument with Aunt Alice and threaten to leave again. No, he would tell no one about Nelda.

"I fear my father is dead also," she said suddenly.

Ben started and glanced at her. "Don't you know?" he asked.

She put her head on one side and replied thoughtfully, "My heart knows, and that is enough."

Ben did not understand. How could she not know whether her father was alive or dead?

Nelda saw his confusion. "My father has not been seen for over two weeks now," she explained.

"Doesn't mean he's dead, though."

Nelda pressed the fingers of her left hand against her brow and sighed. "Oh," she began, "it does not end there—my uncle is missing also."

Ben nibbled his lip uncomfortably; he was not sure what to say. "I'm sorry," he murmured quietly.

At this Nelda snorted. "Pah! I care not for him; he is nothing to me." She paused to spit on the ground with disgust. "Like the scum that floats now on the water he is!" she said, shuddering. "None like Silas, my uncle. The elders only suffer him for the sake of my aunt. No, my belief is that Silas has done a black deed; I fear he has murdered my father."

There was a silence in which Nelda glared at the sea. Ben opened his mouth in shock. Murder? She must be mistaken. "Are . . . are you sure?" he stuttered feebly. "Can't they just have . . . well, gone away?"

"My father would not have left like that," she said firmly. "On the last day they were seen, they quarreled. No one knew what the argument was about—my father would not tell me. Never had I seen him in such a mood. No, he is dead, I feel it, and my uncle hides in some dark corner—the craven mudworm."

In part, Ben understood what she was going through. Human or not, she still had feelings. "Both my parents were killed in a crash," he said simply, "but at least I knew they were really dead and not just missing. It must be awful not to know."

"Then we are both orphans, Ben," she breathed. "I never knew my mother; she died when I was born—as do all mothers now." Nelda fell silent as though she had said too much, then squinted at the pale sun. It was time for her to go. She got to her feet and said, "I must return to my people."

"Do you have to?" Ben protested. "Can't you stay just a bit longer?"

The smile pulled at the corners of her crescent mouth once more. She liked this human boy—there was an understanding between them. Would it hurt if she met him again? Nelda wondered. But what if such a meeting was discovered by the elders? Mixing with humans was strictly forbidden. The penalty for disobeying one of the prime laws was exile from the tribe and Nelda did not want to risk that. It would be better if she left now and stayed in the caves for a while.

Yet she looked down at Ben and rashly said, "Tomorrow—when the sun is as now." And with a quick, desperate look, Nelda dashed to the steps and sped down them.

Ben stayed where he was. Now that she was gone, he doubted if Nelda had ever existed—had he imagined it all? He remained seated for some time, staring at the harbor. Everything seemed so normal and everyday now, as though nothing out of the ordinary had occurred. But a slow grin spread from ear to ear. He had touched another world that nobody knew anything about. The boy could hardly wait for the next day.

CHAPTER FIVE

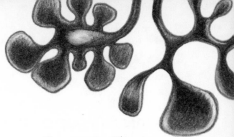

A GRISLY CATCH

The gulls were not yet awake, and the night fishermen were still out at sea. A dismal gray half-light lit the water on the horizon, but inland the shadows were deep and velvety black. All Whitby slept, and the streets were as still and silent as death.

The waves fell softly against the shore, dragging the sand down as they retreated. The tide was going out, and behind Tate Hill Pier, dark and deadly rocks were beginning to emerge. Vicious boulders, they had sunk many unwary ships in their time. They were the teeth of the East Cliff, always eager to grind and splinter timbers.

On the treacherously smooth, slippery shore, three small figures appeared. They seemed to step out of the sheer cliff face, though in the gloom it was impossible to see properly. They were three aufwaders.

Those families who have worked and lived in Whitby for generation after salty generation might recall the old tales of the fisher folk, or the "old whalers," as some called them. They were mysterious beings in legends told to wide-eyed children as they lingered in the tobacco smoke–filled parlors before traipsing off to bed. Creatures from half-forgotten stories brought home by sea-weary fishermen, remembered late in the night, if at all, when the wind howls down the chimney like the wail of the Barguest and the fire burns low. Then these childhood fancies return to haunt the aged and disturb their nodding sleep.

The three indistinct forms clambered over the boulders. Slowly and deliberately, they went, pausing only to peer into rock pools that the tide had left behind and to part the thick clumps of weed washed ashore. They were searching for something.

Nelda's grandfather prodded a loose heap of shale with his staff, as he had done every morning for the past fortnight. His old bones ached, and he grumbled to himself, "Us'll nivver find owt now. Bin too long, as says, them's gone fer good." His face was even more crinkled with age than Nelda's; whiskers bristled over his chin, and his wiry, white hair was tied back in a long hank. The ears of all male aufwaders are large and bat-shaped; Tarr's were no exception. He scratched one with his grubby fingers and stared along the shore at Nelda and Hesper. "Them won't nivver gi' up," he muttered with a groan. "Canna tell them nowt."

Hesper was his daughter. She was also the missing Silas's wife and Nelda's aunt. A kindly soul, everyone liked her—or was it pity they felt? She had married the leering Silas Gull against her father's wishes nigh on two hundred years ago. The more he forbade the union, the more stubborn she had become, and in the end he had relented. But a foul, black-hearted fellow Silas had remained, and nothing Hesper could do would ever change that.

She climbed over the rocks with her niece, a battered old oilskin hat perched comically on her head and her light, sand-colored hair hanging down over one eye as usual. Her face had the texture of a pickled walnut, but the lines that had etched themselves so deeply there were the marks of sorrow and care. To the rest of the tribe, she was a tragic figure, solitary and quiet, speaking to none but her family. Even she did not know if she still loved Silas; whatever had first attracted her to him had quickly disappeared. However Hesper's heart was kept aflame by her true passion: her unceasing search for that which could lift the curse from them forever.

Nelda lifted a thick, dripping curtain of weed, and a startled crab scuttled into the nearest shade. She looked across at her aunt and shook her head. "Nothing," she sighed.

Hesper hitched up the cork lifebelt as it slipped down over her stomach. She was always ready for emergencies: a length of rope was tucked under one arm, two ancient satchels were slung over each shoulder and threaded through the straps of these at her back was a small fishing net attached to a long pole. She wiped her sea green eyes and scanned the rocks and boulders. She had not had a wink of sleep all night, and a wide yawn suddenly split her face in two.

"You should not be out," Nelda told her. "You do too much."

Her aunt scooped up a handful of sea water and splashed it over her forehead. "Someone must keep the vigil," she answered resignedly. "Who else would go out as I? None. There is not one in the whole tribe who will go in my stead."

Nelda smiled gently. "That is because they do not believe in what you seek. To them it is a fanciful tale, nothing more. The doom will never be lifted."

Hesper did not reply. She was accustomed to the ridcule her quest invited, and her faith was never shaken. At this moment, however, she had just noticed a tangled mass of green nylon net in the hollow between two huge boulders. Hesper climbed onto one of the smooth wet rocks and looked down into the untidy mess.

She furrowed her brow and stooped. Was it a trick of the shadows? Beyond the twisted drapes of fishing net and seaweed she thought she saw . . .

Hesper breathed in sharply. "Nelda," she uttered in a fearful voice, "fetch Tarr at once."

Nelda frowned, curious to know what her aunt had discovered. She glanced back along the shore to where old Tarr hobbled along, leaning on his staff, and waved for him to hurry. "What is it?" she asked her aunt, pulling herself onto the boulder.

Hesper's face was pale when she turned around to her niece. "I said go fetch him," she said quietly. "Now."

Nelda's heart fluttered, while her eyes looked past her aunt into the darkness beyond the netting. Hesper grabbed her shoulders fiercely and pushed the young aufwader off the rock. "Don't look," she said in a voice that she was struggling to control.

Frightened, Nelda stared at Hesper, then ran, weeping, to her grandfather.

The net was held down by large, round weights. Hesper leaned over and, with difficulty, hauled some of it away. "Nine times bless me!" she exclaimed and clapped a hand over her mouth in horror. For there, revealed beneath the chaotic jungle of net and weed, was a body.

Tarr strode up as fast as he could. "Shut yer blutherin'," he
snapped at Nelda. But behind a mask of irritation, he too was
afraid. What had his daughter found? he asked himself. As he
drew near to where Hesper was kneeling, he could hear her
cries of despair and saw that she had removed her hat.

"Stay 'ere," he told Nelda when they reached the rock.
"Tha's too young t'look on what she's found." With an effort
he pulled himself up and gazed down into the hollow. "Deeps
take me!" he gasped.

Hesper clasped his hand and squeezed it tightly. "I can't
bring myself to uncover any more," she sobbed. "What if both
are in there?"

Tarr's old face hardened, for he had seen death before.
Anyway, there was not enough time to run back to the caves
for the others. Already the sun was edging over the rim of the
world, and the gulls were waking. "Ah'll see t'this," he said
gruffly. "Get thissen down theer wi' Nelda."

His whiskered jaw was set like granite, and Hesper did
not hesitate. Down the rock she skid and held on to her niece,
waiting for the worst.

With his staff, Tarr cleared the rest of the netting away to
uncover more of the gruesome remains. Grimly, he continued,
though his face was awful to see. Finally, he rocked back and
turned his head from the horrible sight.

"Theer's just the one," he told the others.

Both Nelda and Hesper clung to each other—who was it:
Nelda's father or Silas?

Tarr shook his head at them. "Ah canna tell, 'e's in a reet
state." He shivered and said softly, "'Ed's all battered in, like.
"'Is own mother nivver'd know 'im."

He stretched his legs over the side so that he could drop down beside the body. There was only one way of identifying such a grisly corpse: by the pattern on its jersey. For many years, the jersey—or gansey, as the fisher folk called it—was not merely an item of clothing. The arrangement of the ribs and cables upon each was like a family crest. One close look would tell him who it was.

As he bent down to examine the gansey, Tarr could not help seeing the terrible mess above the neck once again. "Tha's nivver the work o' rocks," he told himself bitterly. "Thissun's bin done in." Ugly images flashed into his head; there must have been a bloody fight between Silas and Nelda's father, Abe. With a trembling hand, he rolled the body over—Abe was his son.

"Nah," he whispered as he inspected the complicated rows, "them's Gull stitches, reet enough." Here then was Silas Gull, the black sheep of the tribe—a rascal descended from rogues. There would not be many, he told himself, who would weep over his loss. Only Hesper, perhaps.

Tarr whistled softly to himself as the significance of this discovery sank in. So it was Silas who had been murdered, and, from the looks of things, by Nelda's father. A fierce scowl formed on Tarr's face. "Tha's in deep, dark waters, Abe lad," he murmured, "an' tha canna hide ferivver."

The heels of Miss Boston's shoes clicked over the beautifully polished wooden floor. She had brought the children to the museum and was thoroughly enjoying showing them around.

Jennet had always grouped museums, art galleries, and exhibitions into a great big yawn-making lump. She had only agreed to come along today because she couldn't bear the tension in the house any more, and she prepared herself for a dull and boring morning.

It was with great surprise, therefore, that she discovered the Pannett Park Museum to be a fascinating place, jam-packed with curiosities and wonders. It was like some magnificent jumble sale of the imagination. Glass cases proudly flaunted their treasures: painstaking models of ships, Victorian dolls, a small Noah's ark with a parade of wooden animals trailing down the gangplank, intricate works in jet, old costumes, a collection of boats in bottles, and a flock of stuffed birds.

Aunt Alice watched Jennet's expressions with satisfaction. They lingered by the display of jet, and the girl was dazzled by the craftsmanship of the tiaras and brooches. The old lady beamed and rubbed her hands together; soon all that unpleasantness would be forgotten. So long as she stuck to her side of the bargain, all would be well. Still, she cast a wistful eye at Ben and sighed: it was a pity the meetings of the circle had to end.

"And here," she began, bubbling with joy, "is one of our most wonderful masterpieces—Dr. Merryweather's Tempest Prognosticator!" With a flourish of her hands, she introduced a grand glass dome that housed a very peculiar mechanism indeed. At the top were lots of little bells, attached to long strings that hung down into small glass jars above the base.

Jennet looked into the jars and grimaced: they contained revolting furry grubs. Aunt Alice saw her and laughed. "Leeches," she informed the girl. "Apparently those slimy little creatures could tell when a storm was coming and would jiggle about in their jars, causing the bells to ring. Isn't it a marvelous thing altogether?" And she clasped her hands together and heaved a great sigh.

"It's disgusting," remarked Jennet. "They could have cleaned the jars out."

On any normal day, Ben would have been fascinated by the moldy remains of long-dead leeches, but he merely twitched his eyebrows and waited for the tour to end. He had stared at all the exhibits without enthusiasm because his mind was crammed too full of his meeting with Nelda. For most of the previous night, he had lain awake, wondering if she would come to the cliff top the next evening as arranged. He could not bear the painfully slow movements of the clock on the museum wall and threw it a suspicious glance to see if it was working properly.

They left Dr. Merryweather's brainchild and wandered around to a scale model of the abbey. Jennet looked at it and realized that something was not quite right. Of course, it showed the building at some earlier time.

Miss Boston's eyes were sparkling as she explained, "This is how the abbey looked before the great west window collapsed in 1794, and the central tower fell in 1830."

"Was anyone hurt?" asked Jennet.

"Bless you, no," Aunt Alice explained. "Why, nobody ever went there much in those days, except artists and dogs."

Jennet frowned. "Dogs?"

"Why, yes. Apparently after the tower collapsed, they discovered the crushed body of a large dog under the rubble."

"How sad, the poor thing."

Some distance away, Ben licked his top lip and stared down wide-eyed. For the first time that morning, his interest was engaged. He had wandered off, leaving his sister and Aunt Alice, for something unusual had caught his eye. In a glass case, all on its own, was one of the most hideous objects he had ever seen: a severed human hand.

It must have been very old, for the skin was dry and gray, but you could still see the fingernails and the wrinkles on its knuckles. A delighted shiver ran down Ben's back. He loved macabre horrors like this.

Jennet and Miss Boston soon joined him. The girl made a face, and the old lady's chins quivered as she explained what the ghastly thing was.

"A Hand of Glory," she uttered in a thrilled whisper. "This unpleasant little item was used as a charm by witches and burglars many years ago."

"What as?" asked Jennet grimly. "A back-scratcher?"

Aunt Alice cackled. "It was believed in those times that this charm, if used properly, could put to sleep an entire household so that a thief could ransack the place without anybody stirring." She paused and waited for encouragement to continue; there was none, so she rattled on regardless. "A true Hand of Glory had to be cut from a man while he was still dangling from the gallows. It then had to be pickled and dried and the fingers set alight—" Aunt Alice stopped in midsentence, for Jennet had baulked and was looking ill. "I'm sorry, dear," she said in alarm. "Did I go too far?"

"I think I'll sit outside, if you don't mind," Jennet said quickly. "I need some fresh air."

Miss Boston blinked and assumed her guilt-ridden face. "Oh dear," she murmured.

"Tell me more about the gallows," asked Ben eagerly.

The old lady coughed. "I think it's time we left too, Benjamin."

For the rest of the day, Ben was restless and fidgety. He drifted about the town like a lost soul, counting the hours till it was time to meet Nelda again. The afternoon dragged on, and he was so out of sorts that he totally forgot about visiting the lifeboat museum.

To celebrate their truce, Aunt Alice and Jennet went into a small café for a cream tea. There they met another of the old lady's friends. Mr. Roper was a soft-spoken old man, smelling of hair oil and mothballs. He pulled his chair over to their table and proceeded to tell them the morning's gossip. Jennet listened to him politely but felt sorry for the old man; he was obviously lonely and had nothing better to do than take part in the scandal-mongering of the Whitby busybodies. Among the useless titbits he divulged was one interesting fact, however—a Mrs. Rowena Cooper had just moved into the empty house on Abbey Lane.

Aunt Alice frowned at the news. Surely the house was far too damp and dilapidated to live in. She stirred her tea vigorously and pondered on the character of Mrs. Cooper, who was quickly becoming a mysterious figure. She sipped her brew in silence and stared over the rim of her cup out of the window at the passersby, in case the focus of her thoughts was among them.

At last, the evening came. With his heart in his mouth, Ben ran up the 199 steps and stared about the graves.

There she was, the youngest of the fisher folk, sitting on the same tombstone and staring at the white-crested waves far below. She turned as she heard Ben running toward her, and the face he saw was marked with worry and pain.

"I cannot stay," she told him at once. "I should not be here at all, but I did promise. Now I must go."

"Wait a minute," gasped Ben. "What's happened?"

She looked away and shrugged. "My uncle has been found," she muttered.

"Oh," he said, "what does that mean? Was he hiding? Had he done something horrible to your father?"

She pulled the woollen hat from her head and let the wind seize her hair. "Silas was dead when we found him," she answered simply. "It was he who had been killed."

For a moment, Ben struggled to understand what she was saying and then it dawned on him. "You mean your father did it?"

Nelda squeezed her large gray eyes tight shut and spoke with anguish. "Never!" she cried. "He is kind and gentle—my father would not harm anything." Then she sobbed bitterly into her sleeve. Ben waited till the emotion subsided and produced a handkerchief from his pocket. Nelda took it and wiped her face. "Already the tribe shuns me and my grandfather. In their eyes, the blood that stains the hands of my father touches us also. I do not know what will befall us. The kin of a murderer must take some of the blame—that is the law, and we must suffer it."

"Sounds like a stupid law to me," Ben remarked.

A slight smile tugged at the corners of Nelda's mouth; she liked this human child and found his company comforting. "I think you are right," she answered, "for the old laws have never brought anything but pain. What use are they now to us wanderers of the shore? The number of our years grows ever shorter. One day, we shall leave both sea and sand forever, and none shall remember us."

A gull screeched overhead, and its voice reminded Nelda that she did not have time to talk at length. "I must go now," she told Ben. "There is much to do, for we send Silas on his way tonight. The black boat has been prepared all day for this, his final journey. I slipped away to see you, but I shall soon be missed. I am out of favor already, I do not wish for any more—"

She was suddenly interrupted by a shocked voice. "NELDA!" It shrieked.

The aufwader jumped off the tombstone as though stung and stared around in terror. Coming up the grassy slope was her aunt.

Ben was overjoyed to see yet another of the strange creatures. This one looked quite comical, and delightedly he drank the sight in: the oilskin hat, the cork lifebelt, the satchels, the fishing net on the pole. . . . Then he remembered Nelda's words. If any of her tribe were to discover that she was talking to a human, she would be severely punished. He held his breath as he saw the stern expression on the new-comer's face and waited for her to clamber up. Nelda shrank back against the tomb as her aunt approached, wondering how she would react toward Ben.

Hesper was waving her arms about like a demented wind-mill, and her wrinkled face had turned a peculiar shade of purple. "A human child with the sight!" she squealed in panic as she ran to her niece, skirting around Ben as though he were a bomb that might explode at any moment. "Nelda, I thought you were wiser than to mix with such creatures. And today of all days!" She pulled up the lifebelt that had fallen around her knees and continued. "Come away this instant; the prayer is ready to be spoken."

"Don't blame her," Ben piped up. "I made her talk to me."

Hesper's crinkled face studied him distastefully for a moment before turning back to her niece. "Give thanks it was I who found you," she said. "Old Parry desired to come, and you know what a barbed tongue she has. Return with me now, and we shall speak of this no more."

Nelda threw her arms around her aunt's neck. "You mean you won't tell? Oh, thank you."

Hesper gave a little gasp as she struggled to get free. "Come away! Words must be said by all the tribe over the black boat before it burns."

"Won't I see you again, then?" Ben asked miserably.

Nelda shot a hasty glance at her aunt. Hesper pursed her lips and shook her head firmly. "Our worlds must not mix," she said with force. "Tragedy has ever occurred when such attempts are made." She gripped her niece's hand and squeezed it urgently. "Would you have the curse tighten ever more about us?" she asked. "Is the doom that awaits us not enough, that you would seek more?"

Nelda hung her head and prepared to say farewell to her human friend. She knew Hesper was right—it was wrong for her to hope to see Ben again. And yet . . .

A strange feeling swept over her, like nothing she had ever experienced before. Her head swam, and the light of the setting sun faded to darkness. Nelda's eyes opened wide, and they were blacker than jet, black as the pathless voids into which her thoughts voyaged. Out of her body she drifted, and visions of things to come flashed past her. She saw a white,

billowing shape high on the cliff top and heard the beat of
pagan drums. A glowing form shimmered from the depths
of the sea, and she uttered a cry of astonishment when she
recognized . . . With a sickening lurch, the scene was snatched
away, and her blood turned to ice. A huge, gaping maw
rushed toward her. She heard the vicious hatred in its voice as
a nightmarish growl issued from the scarlet throat.

Nelda screamed and tumbled backward, waving her arms
before her face to fend off the evil that attacked her.

Hesper and Ben knelt down by the aufwader's side.
Hesper rummaged quickly in one of her satchels and produced a leather flask. "A little liquor distilled from limpets,"
she explained to Ben as she poured it into her niece's mouth.
In her concern, all suspicions about the boy were forgotten.

"What happened?" asked Ben fearfully. "Will she be all right?"

Even as he spoke, Nelda's eyes flickered open. Hesper
examined them; they were soft and gray once more. "All will
be well," she said, nodding with satisfaction. "It is the strain
taking its toll, nothing more."

Nelda choked back a cry, and she clutched her aunt's arm.
"I have seen!" she exclaimed frenziedly. "I saw it, Hesper, out
under the waves. The time is near—you were right all along."

Hesper caught her breath and leaned back. "What did you
see?" she asked in a trembling voice, not daring to hope.

Nelda took hold of her shoulders and shook her joyfully.
"That which you have sought so long—the moonkelp!"

Hesper gawped at her in disbelief for a second, then let
loose a terrific squeal of glee.

Ben covered his ears and wondered why they were so
excited. Finally, Nelda remembered him and hurriedly told her
aunt, "I know not how this vision came to be, but I am sure

this human child is caught up in our plight. Hesper, do you not see? It is written for him to play a part in this. Do not ask me how, but my heart knows his life is entwined with that of the tribe. Spurn him now, and the curse will engulf us all."

Her voice and her words were powerful, and Hesper did not doubt that Nelda had been shown a glimpse of the future. The wisdom of the cold deeps had touched her for a moment. "Then we must tell the child of our woe," she said simply.

Hesper struggled to her feet and looked at Ben. "Listen to me, unhappy man-pup," she told him soberly. "All that you hear from this moment on must not cross your lips into another's hearing—you understand?" Ben mumbled that he did, not sure if he was prepared for what she was about to tell him.

Hesper pulled the oilskin hat further over her eyes so that they were lost in its shadow. She gazed into the distance and began. "The land has changed since our remote grandsires first harvested the waters here and wandered by the shore. It was wild hereabouts; the rocks were sharper, and the cliffs reached further into the clean sea. Your kind was scarce then, I believe, but there were many tribes of our folk." She faltered, regretting that she had not been born in such a time. "But all things must change," she continued. "The stones of your dwellings were laid here and more of your folk made their way over the moor and over the water to settle at the river mouth. It is said that when first they came, our tribes welcomed them, but the two races were never at ease with each other. There were quarrels and fights. Never was there a more frightened creature than Man—like a rabbit he is, afraid of anything that walks under the moon."

At this point, Nelda interrupted. "It was decided that we should withdraw from your world, Ben," she said. "The tribe elders asked the advice of the Lords of the Deep, and so the prime laws were made." A frown crossed her face as she wondered how much he needed to know.

"If he is to aid us the child must be told all!" Hesper muttered gravely.

Nelda swallowed and resumed the tale. "For many years, my people obeyed the strict rules of the elders and Man forgot us, or we were consigned to stories for the amusement of children. All was well, and we prospered, but not as quickly as you. How crowded became the harbor and how tall became your ships. Yet you knew nothing of the sea; though you girdled the world, still you learned naught. You were ignorant of the mysteries that lie in the deeps, of the Lords who could end everything if they so wished. Yes, your kind grew strong, but your might was used for bloodshed and conquest, as you slaughtered all who dared to oppose you. Our forefathers were glad indeed that they had retreated from your race."

"Until that fateful day," Hesper broke in, "that day which all rue now."

"What happened?" asked Ben overawed.

"The two races mingled," Nelda answered darkly. "A fisherman with the same sight you possess took to wife one of our kind, and a child was born."

"A creature that did not belong in either world," said Hesper sadly. "The moment it breathed its first breath, the Lords of the Deep were aware of it and knew the laws that they had made had been broken. When the fisherman next set sail to cast his nets, they rose against him and dragged his boat under the waves. On hearing this, the child's mother became mad with grief. She threw herself off this very cliff and was dashed to pieces on the rocks below."

"There is more," said Nelda. "Cheated of their revenge, the Lords vented their wrath on all women of our race. We were cursed, and the fate of our kind was sealed."

"What did they do?" ventured Ben.

"Our doom is a grim one," said Hesper tearfully. "Nelda's mother was one of the many who have fallen victim to it."

Ben did not want to ask any more questions, but it was Nelda herself who explained. "The curse of the Deep Ones is thus, Ben: they condemned every female of our kind to die in childbirth. A bitter vengeance it is, that destroys love."

Hesper laid her hand gently on Nelda's arm. "Now you see why we are doomed, for we cannot prosper and our future is bleak. Our tribes dwindled in number, and now only one remains. A time will come when the last black boat blazes over the sea—but who will make it and oversee its departure, I wonder?"

Ben stared miserably at the ground. It was a horrible story and one he wished he had not heard.

"Do not grieve yet," Nelda cried, "for there is hope, although before this night I had not believed in it myself. Only my aunt had faith, and so it is right that she should tell you of it."

A dreamy look stole over Hesper's face. "The moonkelp," she murmured longingly. "That which haunts my wak-ing hours and invades my sleep—the moonkelp. For most of my life I have suffered ridicule because of my faith in it. It appears in one of our many legends, the saga of Irl in the darkness. I heard that story by the fireside when I was younger than Nelda. Oona was a great teller of tales. Very wise she was—in many ways, save the one. All my weed and shell lore I learned under her guidance. She too believed in the moonkelp, the treasure of the Deep Ones that was stolen by Irl from their dark, cold realm. Only once in nine hundred years does it bloom and then for one night only, when the moon is brightest in the sky. It was Oona's favorite tale and mine also."

"But how does that help?" said Ben, shaking his head in confusion.

"Because whoever finds the lost treasure of the Lords of the Deep may ask of them anything that is in their power to give," blurted out Nelda. "Do you not see? If we can discover it we could ask them to lift the curse."

"I see," Ben whistled. "But how can I help?"

"Just how you are involved I am not certain," Nelda told him excitedly. "But for an instant back then I saw the moon-kelp and . . . and you were holding it, human child!"

CHAPTER SIX

CREAM CAKES AND DEATH

The following few days were extremely busy. Ben secretly met Nelda and Hesper, and together they searched the shallows for the moonkelp. Jennet began to wonder what he found to do between tea and supper, but all inquiries yielded no clues. She even offered to go with him, but these suggestions were always firmly refused. Jennet was mystified but too tired to press him any further, for she had not been sleeping at all well lately. An animal was howling in the night, keeping her awake. It was a horrible sound, and she shivered in her bed, remembering the legend of the Barguest that was supposed to roam the midnight streets.

Jennet would have talked about it to Aunt Alice, but the old woman seemed to be having problems of her own. After she had swept the ladies' circle out of her parlor on the night of the séance, Miss Boston had been confident that such an action would quickly be forgiven. However, some of the others were not inclined to forget the incident so readily.

Mrs. Joyster did not harbor a grudge; she dismissed the whole affair in her usual military manner. She had no time for such petty grudges and greeted Miss Boston cordially when they next met in the street. Miss Droon was another who forgot the whole affair, although her motives were totally different. She was far too busy fussing around Eurydice and the kittens to harbor any ill feelings, especially as Eurydice was already showing signs of restlessness and lack of interest in her offspring.

No, it was Mrs. Banbury-Scott and Miss Wethers who were snubbing Aunt Alice. Mrs. Banbury-Scott swore never to set foot in that house again, for she had had to suffer the indignity of walking home that night: her chauffeur had driven the Bentley back to the rambling old house for a quick bite of supper. Miss Wethers, the postmistress, was also in a twist with herself about Alice's behavior. The furthest she came to showing her annoyance, though, was a pert and aloof manner when Miss Boston ventured into the post office for her pension. But for dithery Edith, that was a pretty powerful declaration of annoyance.

Aunt Alice felt her position as leader of the circle was under threat. Things would no doubt calm down eventually, and they could all settle back into the routine of visiting one another for an afternoon cup of tea. That is what she had hoped—until the arrival of Rowena Cooper.

Speculation raged over the best china during the next few days. How could the newcomer bear to live in that terrible damp mess of a house? Surely there was a mountain of work for decorators and builders to do, yet the word was that none of the local contractors had been approached. The whole thing was very intriguing and fueled the gossips for some time.

Miss Boston rammed the old shapeless hat onto her head and threw the sage green cloak over her shoulders. "I'll see her today, by God!" she fumed passionately.

Everybody, it seemed, had met the confounded Mrs. Cooper except her. For some reason, she always missed the wretched woman, and what a fuss they all made over her. It seemed the newcomer was a paragon in every respect: she had already made large donations to the church fund and the hospital appeal, and everyone she met described her as a warm and sincere individual. Even Aunt Alice's neighbor, the disagreeable Mrs. Gregson, had succumbed to Mrs. Cooper's charms. It was maddening to hear all these tales secondhand, without actually having met the heroine of them. More than that, it was becoming positively embarrassing, as though some conspiracy was at work to deny her access to this marvel.

With the front door slamming behind her, Miss Boston crossed the yard and strode determinedly toward Church Street, a bloodhound expression on her face.

"Morning, Alice," Mrs. Joyster saluted briskly.

Miss Boston shook herself out of her thoughts and returned the greeting. "Hello, Prudence," she said. "Might I have a word?" If there was anyone in Whitby who would give her an unbiased opinion, it was Prudence Joyster. She led her aside, out of the hustle and bustle of the tourists, and came straight to the point. "Prudence, dear, what do you make of this Cooper woman?" she demanded.

Mrs. Joyster clasped her handbag with both hands and clicked her heels together, as though brought to attention by some superior officer. "Don't really know, Alice, to tell you the truth," she replied. "Only saw her the once yesterday and that was brief." She knitted her brows as though trying to remember. "There was something . . ." she began slowly. "No, it's gone—sorry."

Miss Boston sighed. "Pity," she said.

Mrs. Joyster glanced at her watch and scowled at the time. "Expect I'll remember this afternoon," she said. "Must dash now—lots to do before then."

"This afternoon?" echoed Miss Boston. "And what is happening then?"

Prudence was already marching away. "The ladies' circle," she called. "We've all been invited to Mrs. Cooper's for tea."

Aunt Alice's mouth dropped open. So this Mrs. Cooper had asked the circle—*her* circle—to tea, without inviting her. This was tantamount to a slap in the face, and she would be a laughing stock in the town. Was this woman deliberately trying to provoke her? With her jaw set and all her chins trembling, Aunt Alice stormed back to her cottage.

"Damn the creature!" she yelled, as the front door smashed into the frame once more. Even though she had not yet met Mrs. Cooper, she had built up a violent dislike toward her. "The audacity," she raged, "the sheer—"

An envelope on the floor suddenly caught her eye; it must have been stuck in the letterbox and her slamming of the door had sent it fluttering to the carpet.

The letter was addressed to her, but she did not recognize the confident, flowing script. Curiously, she opened the envelope and raised her eyebrows as she read its contents.

Dearest Miss Boston,
I hope you will not think this letter intrusive, but I have heard
so many interesting and curious things about you and as yet we

have not been introduced. You must be the one person I have not met. Everybody is so welcoming in this amusing little town of yours, I feel quite at home already. Would you do me the honor of joining myself and a few friends for tea this afternoon, say a quarter to four?
Sincerely yours,
Rowena Cooper

"Good gracious," muttered Miss Boston in surprise. "A most peculiar invitation, to be sure." She read it again and exclaimed, "What does she mean, 'interesting and curious things'? She makes me sound like a pet monkey." The more she studied the letter, the more incredulous she became. "The 'few friends' must be the rest of the ladies' circle, yet she mentions them as though they were strangers to me." Aunt Alice crushed the piece of paper in her hands. "I've a good mind not to go! That will show her—tiresome woman!"

At half past three, Miss Boston's cloaked figure trundled up Abbey Lane. The desire to see Mrs. Cooper for herself, and the knowledge that her absence would be grist to the mill for certain tongues, had conquered her resolve not to go.

The dark bulk of The Hawes reared before her, and the old lady held her breath in astonishment. It could have been a different house, so drastic was the change. The jungle of weeds and nettles had been transformed into a neat garden and the ground floor window, which only last week was boarded up, had been replaced and now bore the words "Cooper's Antiques," in large red and gold letters. Miss Boston peered through it and blinked in bewilderment. Inside, all looked immaculate; various well-polished tables and chairs, old paintings, and silverware were on display. She could not understand how Mrs. Cooper had managed it all in such a short time.

"Alice," an awkward voice called. It was Edith Wethers, waving half-heartedly from the rear of the house. "This way," she mumbled into her tissue. It was the most Miss Wethers had said to her since the séance.

Miss Boston trotted down the path to the kitchen, where she noticed that the door had been replaced too. Edith shuffled back inside. "Rowena's busy with the tea upstairs," she explained dutifully, "so she sent me down to guide you in—the front's for business only. This way."

Aunt Alice stepped over the shining linoleum; the kitchen was dazzlingly unreal. Pans of decreasing size gleamed from hooks on the wall, and everything was spotless.

"Except for this, all the ground floor is the shop, and Rowena lives upstairs," Miss Wethers prattled as she led her into the hall.

Miss Boston shuddered as she followed Edith up the stairs. There was something creepy about the place: everything was in order and yet . . .

They had reached the landing and Miss Wethers pushed open the door of what had once been a bedroom. "Here she is, Rowena," the postmistress declared. "Alice Boston."

The old lady entered the room. It had been tastefully furnished to serve as a parlor, and sitting on the plush armchairs were all the ladies' circle—and Rowena Cooper.

She was a striking woman, tall and slim, with short, strawberry blonde hair and pale, almost translucent skin.

Late 40s to early 50s, Aunt Alice guessed. She wore a loose purple sweater with black slacks; her feet were bare, and the toenails painted a garish red.

"Delighted," Mrs. Cooper cooed, rising from her seat and stretching out her arms theatrically. "At last we meet. I feel we shall be such friends, you and I."

Aunt Alice managed a smile, although she instantly disliked this gushing woman. "That would be . . . lovely," she found herself saying.

"Marvelous," breathed Mrs. Cooper. She pressed her hands together as though in prayer, then placed her two forefingers between her teeth as she studied Miss Boston. "You're such a darling antique," she said, with a laugh in her voice.

The old lady stared at her incredulously. Nobody had ever called her that before. She unwrapped her scarf. "I beg your pardon?" she asked.

Mrs. Cooper rushed forward, her bare feet padding over the swirling blue carpet. "Do let me take your things," she begged. "What a quaint cloak! I had no idea people still wore these—how funny and sweet."

Miss Boston looked around at her friends for support. Prudence leaned back in her chair and shook her head with disgust—she hated silly women. Tilly Droon was on the sofa next to Mrs. Banbury-Scott, absorbed in a book on the psychology of cats that Mrs. Cooper had lent her. Mrs. Banbury-Scott was still ignoring Aunt Alice and pointedly diverted her attention toward a mouth-watering array of goodies on the coffee table. Her fat ringed fingers hovered over the meringues, but swooped down on the cream cakes and snatched up a chocolate éclair. Edith Wethers sidled past Rowena, drinking in her words as she squeezed by, and sat as far away from the cat-haired Miss Droon as she could manage.

"You must call me Rowena," Mrs. Cooper oozed to Miss Boston as she hung up the old lady's hat and cloak, "and I shall call you Alice. Do sit down and have some tea." Her voice was level and precise, breaking into little girlish laughs now and then that, to Miss Boston's ears, sounded false and strangely chilling. Nevertheless, she did as she was bid and took up the cup provided.

"Dora was just telling me about her delicious house," Rowena drooled in an envious tone. "Do continue, please. I long to know *everything* there is to know." There were no seats free, so she sat on the arm of the sofa and rested her chin on her hand, while playing with an amethyst ring on her finger.

Mrs. Banbury-Scott patted the corners of her mouth and gave a little amused cough. "My Bobo left it to me," she said thickly, as her voice was still clogged with chocolate. "He was my second hubby, you know. It had been in his family for years, one of the oldest around here."

Rowena shivered ecstatically. "Sounds *gorgeous*. How I've always wanted a house like that—you must invite me around to see it some time."

Miss Boston let the flow of conversation wash over her. She drank her tea quietly and exchanged despairing glances with Prudence; both longed for the ordeal to be over. Rowena and Mrs. Banbury-Scott dominated the talk, the one shame-lessly flattering the other.

"You must tell me who does you hair," Rowena said cloy-ingly. "That peach tint suits you so well."

Mrs. Banbury-Scott fluttered her false eyelashes and giggled coyly as she reached for another éclair.

"Do you like the chocolate on those?" Rowena asked. "I must admit I'm a real chocoholic, too. Sometimes I think I've got cocoa in my veins instead of blood." She waved her fingers excitedly and cried, "Don't move; I must let you have one of these. Excuse me a moment, everyone." Mrs. Cooper slipped out of the room.

When she had gone, Miss Boston let out a great sigh. "Preposterous!" she snorted indignantly.

Miss Wethers sniffed and turned her head to one side. "Well, I think she's very nice," she observed acidly.

"So warm, so friendly," added Mrs. Banbury-Scott. "What do you think, Tilly?"

Miss Droon dragged her eyes away from the book and peered at them over her thick glasses. "Seems pleasant enough," she replied mildly. "Done wonders with this place."

Prudence was staring into space. There it was again, that strange feeling. Try as she might, she could not define her suspicions, but in the back of her mind, a little whisper of disquiet was nagging at her.

"Here we are." Rowena came bursting back into the room, carrying a small, gold cardboard box. "I have a friend in Belgium," she explained, "who sends me these, knowing my passion for them."

She handed the box to Mrs. Banbury-Scott. The fat pig-woman took it greedily and peered inside.

"Handmade chocolates," Rowena informed the others. "Frightfully expensive but absolutely heavenly. Do help yourselves." She hesitated and looked at Mrs. Joyster. "Prudy, I do believe you are staring. Is there something the matter?"

Prudence pulled herself together. "I'm so sorry," she stammered. "Not like me at all, but for a moment I could have sworn . . . Never mind, it was nothing."

"Wonderful!" Mrs. Banbury-Scott declared, with her mouth full of truffles and coffee creams. "These are sublime."

Another painful hour crawled by. Mrs. Banbury-Scott hogged the chocolates and wolfed them all, but Rowena did not seem to mind. Miss Boston was bored and stared dismally out of the window. Rowena lounged on the chair arm, laughing at all the fat woman's feeble jokes. Edith Wethers watched her pathetically, like a dog waiting for scraps to be thrown its way.

Prudence, meanwhile, scrutinized Mrs. Cooper through half-closed eyes, as though she were trying to see what the woman might have looked like 20 or 30 years ago.

Finally Miss Boston decided it was time for her to return home and see to the children's tea. She rattled her cup impatiently onto its saucer and said to her hostess, "A most enlightening afternoon. So glad to have met you, but I really must get back and see to Jennet and Benjamin."

Rowena looked at her blankly for a moment as if she had forgotten she was ever there. "Must do this again, Alison," she said, swinging her legs off the chair arm and stretching.

"Don't bother to see me out," Miss Boston said, ignoring the mistake and taking her things down from the coatrack.

At that moment, Prudence Joyster rose to leave also. "Yes, a very . . . interesting time," she muttered distractedly. "Are you coming too, Tilly?"

Miss Droon thanked Rowena for the loan of the book and made her farewells.

"But Dora, dearest," cried Rowena to the Buddha-like figure that dwarfed the sofa, "say *you'll* stay. Don't abandon me as well; promise you'll stay just an eensy teensy bit longer." Mrs. Banbury-Scott agreed amiably.

Miss Wethers would have stayed too if Rowena had not suddenly said to her, "Darling Edie, how nice—do come again." So the postmistress reluctantly put her coat on as well.

Rowena padded out to the landing after the four departing ladies. Miss Boston looked up at the hole in the ceiling that led to the attic while the others made their way downstairs.

"Must get that seen to," Rowena said quickly, following her gaze. "Afraid my little home is nowhere near as nice as Dora's."

"Strange," murmured Miss Boston, her eyes still fixed upward, "thought I saw a movement up there. Have you got bats?"

The change in Rowena was immediate and startling. The smile vanished from her face, and she almost snarled at the old woman. Quickly, though, she regained her composure, yet her voice was more false than before. "Don't alarm me so, Alison, dear," she cried with a thin, harsh laugh. "I shouldn't get a wink of sleep if I thought that."

Miss Boston uttered a last farewell and turned to go down the stairs. That was most interesting, she thought to herself. *I wonder what she has up there she doesn't want anyone to know about? Very suspicious indeed.*

In the lane, she walked alongside Mrs. Joyster. "Well, Prudence," she said, arching her brows, "what did you make of that?"

"I don't like it, Alice," her friend whispered, so that Miss Wethers could not hear. "There's something decidedly wrong about that woman. I don't know what it is but . . . No, it's gone again."

Aunt Alice pursed her lips in concentration. "Curious," she observed softly, "how Mrs. Cooper likes to give the impression that she is a stupid creature. All those ridiculous affectations—she called you 'Prudy,' for heaven's sake. Nobody talks like that—most bizarre and perplexing. And yet for all this, or perhaps in spite of it, I believe that she is a very clever woman. Was it all an act, I wonder? But if so, then for whose benefit? She must have something to hide. I think that is a distinct possibility. Do you know anything about her husband—is he dead, or are they separated?"

Prudence brought herself to a standstill and clasped her handbag to her chest. "Husband!" she repeated. "Of course, the husband!" Her face clouded over, and she became very troubled indeed.

"Whatever is it?" inquired Miss Boston.

"I can't say," Prudence replied. "I'm not certain yet, but . . . Well, it just won't do if I am right about this."

Prudence Joyster headed for home. She lived in one of the houses behind the railway station on the West Cliff. It had belonged to her late husband's sister, who had left it to them in her will. A perfect place to retire to, although it had taken some time to get used to the bracing sea air after the hot winds of Kenya.

She turned the key in the front door and marched past the spears and shields made of stretched zebra hide that decorated her hallway. Into the dark study she strode and cast her handbag aside fretfully. Still wearing her coat, she knelt by a panel of shelves and ran her fingers along the spines of the books. She knew it had to be there; this was the one thing of her husband's she had made a point of keeping.

"Ah!" Prudence grunted. "There you are." She eased out a leatherbound book and turned the first page.

"Diary of Major Howard Joyster—1959 to 1967," she read quietly to herself. Prudence held her hand in front of her face, momentarily breathless. It had been a long time since she had dared to open this. It was enough just to know its reassuring presence was there on the shelf—a comforting relic of their blissful time in Africa.

"The hours you spent writing this, dear," she said aloud to the spirit of her husband that she felt sure was always with her. Page after page of well-ordered, disciplined handwriting flicked beneath her searching fingers. Oh, if she could only remember the correct year.

The time wore on, and outside the light failed. Prudence rubbed her eyes as they strained in the gloom, and when she looked at the clock was startled to discover it had turned nine.

The diary brought it all flooding back. Although she had meant to skim through it to find the page she wanted, odd paragraphs or just sentences seemed to leap out at her, and she would end up reading the whole passage. All those memories, places, and people she had not thought of for many years.

With the study lamp switched on, she continued. Days long gone unfolded before her; she almost felt the sun burn the nape of her neck and heard in the far away of her mind the rumble of the jeep as it bounced over the hot red earth and the loud buzz of the crickets in the evening. And then the diary yielded its secret at last.

Monday, July 12. Came across old Natty Pelridge this afternoon—chap who left the regiment to go native. Tells me the Maasai are uneasy and could I do anything about it. Seems that couple who were chased out of Nairobi have started up again. Drove to the Maasai village with Pru but only saw the wife. Nasty piece of work, that, and mouth like a sewer—damn near struck the blasted woman. If I believed just half of what people say about them I would have brought her in there and then. Don't know why the Maasai haven't chased her and her God-awful husband out already, but Natty tells me they're too scared of them. Can't under-stand it—just hope I've warned them off. Came back and there's more of this dratted paperwork to do. The job isn't what it was . . .

Thursday, July 15. Bad news. Middle of the night, Natty comes over, white as a sheet and shaking like a leaf. Never seen him like that before, and it put the wind up me. Terrible busi-ness at the village, he tells me, after I give him some brandy. That ruddy couple have got half the Maasai involved in some foul ceremony. Seems those stories were true after all. Drove over with a small show of force, but by the time we arrived, it was all over. Never heard such a commotion and the wails of the women is a sound I shan't ever forget. Glad I never brought Pru this time. Why the villagers allowed it is a damn mystery; can't get any sense out of them. They keep talking about a big dog or some-thing—scared to death they looked too. I'll have to start a full investigation, but it looks like the birds have flown. Not a sign of that hellish pair. They won't get far though; I'll get a message to the neighboring commissioners. Nathan and Roslyn Crosier deserve to hang for this.

Mrs. Joyster laid the book on her knee, feeling sick. Roslyn Crosier—that young, evil woman she had met all those years ago—was none other than Rowena Cooper!

An angry look crossed Prudence Joyster's face; she thought of what they had done, and her hands trembled with fury. Slamming the diary on the floor, she stormed out of her house.

Her intention had been to go to the police station, which was not far away, but as she strode down Windsor Terrace, the emotion that was seething inside her took charge. Past the police station marched Mrs. Joyster, up the New Quay Road, and over the bridge to the East Cliff. The pubs were just closing as she hurried up Church Street to the 199 steps. Grimly, she began to climb. Her face was like thunder, and she felt ready to burst.

A mist was coming in off the sea, drifting over the churchyard and shrouding the lamps, softening the light that lit her way up the stone stairs. Finally, she reached the top and purposefully made for The Hawes.

There were no lights on in the ugly house; for a second it seemed to shimmer and the renovations disappeared. Tangled weeds overran the garden once more, the front window was boarded up, and a smell of damp and decay greeted Mrs. Joyster as she pushed the rusted gate open. Then suddenly it was back to normal. It was as if she had caught the house off-guard momentarily. The window displayed its red and gold letters, and the lawn was neat again.

Prudence took no notice. It would take more than nighttime imaginings to cool her temper. She went briskly to the kitchen door and hammered violently on it. A light snapped on upstairs, and she heard footsteps coming down the hall.

"Prudence!" exclaimed a surprised Mrs. Cooper. "What can I do for you? I was just about to go to bed."

"You can stop pretending!" snapped Mrs. Joyster furiously. "I know who you are—Roslyn!"

Mrs. Cooper's face froze. "Rowena," she corrected coldly.

"Don't bother denying it," spat Mrs. Joyster. "I knew there was something—you and that devil of a husband, wherever he is." Her pale-blue eyes were like two frosty diamonds that glinted and shone in the darkness.

Rowena ground her teeth together, and an unpleasant sneer curled her mouth. She realized it was useless to deny anything now. "I thought you might have forgotten," she said. Her voice was totally different from that of the person she had been that afternoon. It had a cruel, malicious edge, harder than steel and more bitter than death.

"Forgotten!" blazed Mrs. Joyster. "How could I forget what you and your husband did! I don't know how you live with yourself, you evil creature!"

Rowena smiled wickedly, and her teeth gleamed. "What will you do now?" she asked with calculating calm. "Have you called the police?"

Prudence glared back at the woman. "Not yet," she said, "but I shall, and don't think you can escape this time."

The smile on Rowena's face widened into a harsh, menacing grin. "You had better do your duty like a good citizen should," she growled as her lips pulled back even further.

Mrs. Joyster pointed a steady, assured finger at her. It would take more than that to frighten her. "I'll wipe that smile off your face, your remorseless—abomination!" she cried defiantly. She whirled around, and her sensible shoes rang over the path as she left.

Framed in the doorway, Rowena heard the older woman's footsteps disappear into the mist. She threw back her head and let loose a horrible laugh. "Run, Prudence!" she called wildly. "Hurry home—if you can."

Mrs. Joyster heard the muffled shrieks seeping through the fog. "Woman's unhinged," she told herself, but then she would have to be.

The ruins of the abbey rose out of the mist to her left as she approached the churchyard. The gravestones were like little islands poking up from a smoky sea as she strode by. The police station was her goal now. It would probably take some time to convince them, but fortunately she was well-respected in the town.

The 199 steps trailed into darkness below as the fog swirled about her ankles and concealed the streets of Whitby. She might have been standing on the roof of the world, for all she could see. A shudder ran down her spine, and she glanced back nervously.

"Pull yourself together," she scolded herself. It was unlike her to be afraid of the dark; she was far too practical for such ridiculous fancies. Resolutely, she began the long descent. It was tough going, for the fog lay thickly over the steps and made it impossible to see them. With one hand, she gripped the rail tightly, and she covered her throat with the other.

The night was cold, yet Mrs. Joyster's forehead dripped with perspiration. She felt afraid; someone was watching her. It was as if a sharp blade was being pushed between her shoulders. Countless times, she looked around nervously up to the top of the steps to try and catch a glimpse of whoever it was. But there was always nothing there, which seemed to make it worse somehow.

Her heart pounded in her breast as she neared the half-way point. It thumped like the drums she had heard in

Kenya, tribal beats that echoed into the night. Prudence was breathing hard; the blood in her temples pumped in time to the drums, and her footsteps faltered.

There it was again, that uncomfortable feeling at her spine. With an overwhelming sense of dread, she turned and looked back once more.

"No!" she cried in terror. "No!"

But it was too late. There on the topmost step was the most horrifying sight she had ever witnessed. Under the dim glow of the lamp, she saw an immense hound. It was as large as a calf, blacker than midnight, and its red, fiery eyes burned into her.

Prudence screamed as she tore down the steps as fast as she could. With a blood-freezing growl, the monstrous hound bounded after her. Streaming breath issued from its huge nostrils, and its mighty jaws slavered viciously.

"Help! Help!" Prudence shouted at the top of her voice. But there was no one to hear her.

The demon dog took the steps five at a time and bore unerringly down upon the petrified woman. Prudence felt its hot breath on the back of her legs. She spun around to face it. The infernal eyes crackled and blasted toward her.

"Nooooo!" she wailed, raising her arms before her face as the beast snarled and prepared to spring.

Its muscular shoulders tensed, then the creature launched itself straight at her. With a last, piteous cry, Prudence Joyster fell back into the fog.

CHAPTER SEVEN

THE FIGURE ON THE CLIFF

Miss Boston sat down and mechanically sipped the hot sweet tea Jennet had made for her. "Poor Prudence," she said shakily.

The body of Mrs. Joyster had been discovered early that morning. She had evidently lost her footing while descending the steps in the fog the previous night; at least that is what the police thought. There was nothing to suggest otherwise, and Doctor Adams wrote "accidental death" on the certificate.

Aunt Alice saw the ambulance drive down Church Street on her pre-breakfast walk and heard the terrible news from a burly police sergeant.

There was a great deal to be done. Miss Boston telephoned the only relative Mrs. Joyster had, a nephew in Halifax, and assured him that she would look after everything until his arrival. Then she went around to the dead woman's house. Some time ago, Prudence had given her a spare key, and she used this now to let herself in. Oddly enough, the police had been unable to find any keys on Mrs. Joyster's person.

Miss Boston found the house just as her friend had left it the night before. The lamp in the study was still on, and the old diary lay sprawled on the floor. "Curious," the old lady murmured as she examined the book. I wonder what Prudence was doing reading this—it used to upset her so." She recalled how strange Mrs. Joyster had been yesterday when they parted. There had been something troubling her—something to do with Rowena Cooper. If only she had said more at the time. A nasty suspicion was forming in Miss Boston's mind. The steps were on the way to Mrs. Cooper's house; perhaps Prudence had paid a second visit to the dreadful woman last night. She stuffed the diary into her capacious handbag to read later, deciding there had to be some sort of clue in there. One thing was certain—Prudence Joyster had not died in any accident.

"I don't care what the police say," Aunt Alice told Jennet when she was sitting in her own kitchen once more. "Prudence was far too sensible to go out in a fog for no good cause—she was never one for solitary walks."

"What do you think she was doing, then?" the girl asked.

Aunt Alice flattened her chins against her chest and muttered mysteriously, "Confrontations."

Jennet looked puzzled.

"Prudence could never bottle things up," Miss Boston explained. "She would always tell you exactly what she thought. I can still hear her barking voice . . . unbelievable to think that it has been silenced forever. She was a good friend to me, you know." Jennet held out her hand, and the old lady took it thankfully. "I'm so very glad you and Benjamin are here," she said.

The rest of the day was spent visiting the rest of the ladies' circle to share with them the grief and sense of loss. Edith Wethers was beside herself and had to take the day off work. Miss Droon was sitting with her, handing out the tissues. She was so upset she never mentioned Eurydice or her offspring at all. It was an unpleasant time, but all appreciated one another's company.

"I think I had better go around to Dora's now," said Miss Boston, swinging her cloak over her shoulders. "I don't know why she isn't here."

The other ladies, one whiskered, one sniveling, feebly waved good-bye.

The comical figure of Miss Boston on her rickety old bicycle rode to the outskirts of the town.

Mrs. Banbury-Scott's house was a solid, grand building. Nobody knew exactly how old it was, although architects had squabbled for years over its probable age. The gray stones were mottled with moss and lichen, and the west-facing walls had been totally claimed by ivy.

Miss Boston waggled from side to side as she pedaled up the gravel drive. In one wobbly movement, she dismounted from the bicycle and rested it against the porch. The iron bellpull jangled in her fingers, and she waited patiently for admittance.

Mrs. Banbury-Scott kept three servants: Grice, her gruff chauffeur and gardener; Mrs. Rigpath, the cook; and a dumpy little maid called Rachel Turner. It was the last who opened the door.

"Oh, hello, Miss," Rachel said brightly on seeing Aunt Alice. "Come in. Madam has got a visitor, but I shouldn't think she'd mind if you joined them. They're in the morning room."

Miss Boston removed her outdoor things and made her way down the oak-paneled hall. "And how is your mother,

Rachel dear?" she asked the maid chattily. "Still devoted to her garden?" They exchanged a few pleasantries before Aunt Alice asked, as they stood outside the morning room, "By the way, just who has she got in there?"

"Why, Mrs. Cooper, Miss," Rachel replied. "Didn't I say?" She knocked and opened the door while the old lady winced and made a disagreeable face—she had not expected this.

"Miss Boston, Madam," announced Rachel.

The morning room was comfort itself; it had a general air of doziness about it, a perfect place to nod off. The chairs were of old, worn leather, and the pile of the rugs was soft and deep. The curtains were heavily embroidered and very thick, to shut out the cold winter nights. Miss Boston had spent many a cozy afternoon in this room. Now, though, she was ill at ease and braced herself for this meeting. Her suspicions about Rowena Cooper gnawed at her as she entered.

There in the snug armchair was Mrs. Banbury-Scott. Her small, piglike eyes were puffy and red—she had been crying. Rowena perched on a cushion in front of the hearth, soaking up the fire's heat. She was feeding the fat woman chocolates from another of those gold cardboard boxes.

"Alice," burbled Mrs. Banbury-Scott anxiously. "Poor Pru . . . Prudence," and she descended into a fit of hysterical tears and woeful grunts.

"Such dreadful news," Rowena Cooper broke in. "I was deeply shocked when I heard and rushed straight around to Dora's. She is such a sensitive soul; she feels this loss most deeply. Why, when I first arrived she was inconsolable."

Miss Boston sat down and eyed the blonde woman shrewdly. All she said had a false ring to it. She puckered her lips, and the question that had been burning her tongue leaped out on its own. "Did Prudence visit you last night, Mrs. Cooper?"

Rowena fluttered her eyelashes and answered smartly—and rather too readily—"Why, no. Why should she do that?"

Mrs. Banbury-Scott lowered the handkerchief of Nottingham lace into which she had been wailing and spitting chocolatey phlegm. "Rowena's been marvelous, Alice," she breathed hoarsely. "I feel quite ill myself now. I don't know what I would have done without her." She took the box, and her pink, sausage-shaped fingers rooted about in it.

"More chocolates?" murmured Miss Boston mildly. "My goodness, you do seem to have an inexhaustible supply, Mrs. Cooper."

"If they comfort dear Dora then they are a small price to pay," she replied with sickening humility.

An idea suddenly struck Aunt Alice. "And what do you think of her house now?" she asked abruptly.

A momentary look of distress appeared on Rowena's face. "Why . . . it's a darling residence," she eventually cooed. "I am green with envy."

The inconsolable Mrs. Banbury-Scott stuffed another chocolate into her face and waved the hanky again. "I shall show you around," she told Rowena gratefully.

Miss Boston got up to leave, feeling as though she was intruding upon the pair of them. She was surprised at how quickly Rowena had ingratiated herself with Dora. But then, the fat woman had always been prone to flattery.

"Well," she said, "now I must be going. I only came to see if you'd heard the news."

The others hardly turned around to see her go. Miss Boston hesitated at the door and took one last look at Rowena as the woman threw back her head and laughed too loudly at something Mrs. Banbury-Scott had said. Just what was she up to?

Jennet rammed her hands into the deep pockets of her coat. The town of Whitby lay behind her, and she scanned the beaches for signs of Ben. He had gone out directly after tea again; it was a most annoying habit of his. She had no idea where he got to, but he usually came back in time for supper. Tonight, however, he had not returned. It was now half past ten, and she was worried. Aunt Alice had gone over to Miss Droon's some time ago, and she had not come back either, so Jennet went out to look for her troublesome brother alone.

The wind was cold, and she wished she had a thermos of hot soup with her. She walked along one of the piers that stretched, pincerlike, into the sea. From here, she thought she would be able to see a good deal of the coast, but it had grown too dark now; even if Ben was on the beach, her eyes could not penetrate the gloom.

Whitby twinkled before her. The lights of the amusement arcades sparkled and the street lamps were like tangled necklaces of fiery gems. Jennet turned her head to the East Cliff and gazed at the abbey. Her eyes wandered to the church, and then she gasped.

Fluttering among the gravestones was a figure in white. Jennet wondered if Ben had taken a sheet from his bed and was playing ghosts up there. She was furious. After all that had happened to him, Ben was still drawn to phantoms and

the supernatural? Jennet hurried back along the pier and ran to the steps.

The wind was stronger on the cliff, and as Jennet entered the churchyard it snatched her breath away. She glanced around, but there was no sign of the white figure; it must have moved behind the church. Great arc lights were positioned on the ground to illuminate the building, and, as she made her way between the tombs, her shadow was flung against the great stone walls. It was a monstrous, distorted shape, and in the corner of her eye she could see it mimicking her movements. Jennet shivered. It was extremely creepy up here at night. Beyond the blinding lights there were impenetrable wells of darkness where anything could be hiding.

"Ben must be mad to come here," she said to herself.

She followed the narrow path around to the far side of the church and scanned the expanse of headstones for her brother. There it was—the figure in white. Jennet stared at it for some moments before she realized that it was too tall to be Ben. A sudden urge to discover more gripped the girl, and, as quietly as she could, she crept closer and crouched down behind a gravestone.

The figure was near the cemetery wall, staring out to sea with the wind tugging at its white robes. The garment was oddly familiar, but as it flapped in the wind it was difficult to be sure. Suddenly, Jennet bit her lip in surprise—the stranger was one of the sisters from the convent!

What was one of the novices doing up there in the dark? the girl wondered. Breathlessly she watched, motionless and silent in the shadow of the gravestone.

The novice lifted her downcast head and turned it slightly to one side. Her face was extraordinary—not pretty, yet too unusual to be plain. Her eyes were almond-shaped, and the moonlight danced in them, but her mouth was too wide—it almost went from one side of her face to the other. Then the head was turned away once more, the shoulders drooped, and the novice rested her elbows on the wall. She lowered her head and covered her eyes. Very quietly, she began to weep.

The soft whimpers floated into the night, and in her hiding place, Jennet felt miserable. She had never heard such a sound before; it wrenched at her heart and tore into her soul. The absolute desolation of those pathetic sobs left her feeling empty and cold.

The anguish was unbearable; it was as if the grief of centuries came pouring out in one fierce torrent of despair. Jennet trembled as the novice's voice rose, and the weeping became a horrible scream. Every terrible emotion was contained in that hideous wail.

Images of grief filled Jennet's mind. She thought of her parents and remembered the day of the funeral. The ghastly, raw hurt she had felt then returned in a vicious rush. The girl hid her face and covered her ears, until she could bear it no longer.

"Stop! Stop!" she cried suddenly.

The woman whirled around in surprise, her face stricken with fear. She watched Jennet come out of her hiding place, and her eyes were wide with fright.

"It's all right," Jennet said gently. "Don't worry, I won't tell anyone."

The novice flattened herself against the wall as the girl approached. She said nothing, but stared about wildly.

"I only want to help," Jennet assured her.

But before she could say anything else, the sister darted away. Through the maze of graves she ran, as though a demon were after her. She fled past the arc lights, and in their glare, the white habit blazed as if it were on fire. Her billowing, dazzling shape resembled that of a moth that had fluttered too close to a candle flame. And then she was gone, vanished into the darkness as if the light had consumed her.

Jennet found herself shaking, whether from the cold or from nerves, she couldn't say. Shivering, she walked home. There, she found Ben and the old lady finishing off their cocoa in the parlor. Jennet did not mention the novice to Aunt Alice, for she was not proud of the way she had spied on the poor woman. After she had drunk the steaming cup of hot chocolate that was waiting for her, the girl wearily went straight to bed, without even asking Ben where he had been.

The room was pitch dark when she awoke, and for an awful moment, Jennet thought she had been buried alive. But gradually her eyes adjusted and could make out the walls of her bedroom. She sighed with relief but twitched back one of the curtains to make sure. Moonlight poured in, and she squinted sleepily at her watch—it was two in the morning.

Jennet knew why she had awoken in the middle of the night. She vaguely remembered the dream she had been having and pulled up the bedclothes to dispel the unpleasant memory. A dark shape had been stalking her. Its cry was terrifying, and she was glad to have escaped the nightmare.

"I don't know what's the matter with me," she muttered to herself. "Can't seem to sleep properly any more."

She rolled onto her side and stared at the stripes and flowers on the wallpaper. They made her feel comfortable and safe, locked cozily inside Aunt Alice's house, where no evil thing could enter.

From the moonlit world outside, there came a sound that banished all such thoughts. A dreadful howl boomed into the night, shattering the illusion of calm.

Jennet jumped to the window—it was the sound she had been hearing in her dreams. A sickening fear gripped her stomach as she realized they had not been nightmares after all. There *was* something prowling the streets of Whitby at night.

Peering over the windowsill, she gazed down on the yard below. The light from one of the lamps on Church Street slanted in through the narrow alleyway, its pale tip just touching the sleeping geraniums by the front door. Jennet stared over the rooftops. Somewhere in the dark, narrow lanes, the creature howled again. It was closer now.

Jennet felt very afraid. She tried to tell herself that she was being stupid and that it was probably just somebody's dog crying to be let in. But deep down, she knew it was more than that.

All at once, the light in the yard was cut off, eclipsed by a large, black shape that blocked the alley. Its shadow stretched into the yard—it was that of an enormous hound. The beast paused and, as Jennet watched, the huge nostrils of the shadow sniffed and quested the air. For one awful moment, she thought that it was searching for her, hunting for her scent, and preparing to strike.

The shade grew blacker and larger as the beast crept further into the alley toward the yard. In that narrow tunnel of darkness, two points of red light glimmered malevolently. Jennet stepped back and clasped her hands tightly over her mouth to stop herself from screaming.

The shadow lengthened, flowing over the doorstep and up to the lock. But when it reached the curious stone that hung above the lintel, it halted abruptly.

A deep growl vibrated through the air. Jennet shrank back and so did not see a faint blue radiance pierce the yard. The round, hollow stone over the front door was madly dancing on its thread, jerking and banging against the wall as if trying to get free. Small sparks of blue fire crackled from the hole at its center and splashed down onto the threshold of the cottage like a waterfall of flame. The green door was lit up eerily, and the solid darkness of the shadow suddenly fractured.

The eyes retreated back down the alley, and a hideous snarl reverberated about the yard. The calm returned, broken only by the distant sound of claws as they clattered up the abbey steps.

The screeching of the gulls heralded a new morning. Miss Boston tiptoed down the stairs, careful not to wake the children.

She gazed at her reflection as she put on her hat and tutted; she was feeling her age today. All this sad business about Prudence had unsettled her. She felt sure she ought to have come across some clue as to how her friend had really died, but all her efforts had been useless. She had read some of the diary though it was extremely boring; she had pestered

Doctor Adams in case he had missed anything, but he had just been very rude to her; she had even questioned Prudence's neighbors to see if they knew why she had gone out that night—but it was all to no avail. Prudence Joyster was being buried tomorrow afternoon, and Miss Boston knew she had failed.

There was, of course, one other avenue she had not pursued, and it was the most promising of them all. If only she could get the circle together and hold just one more séance. What better person to ask than Prudence herself? Miss Boston was sorely tempted to try, but the promise she had made to Jennet did not allow it.

Sighing with resignation, she slung the cloak over her shoulders and opened the front door.

"Great heavens!" she exclaimed.

The doorstep was covered in a fine coating of ash and cinders. The old lady looked up to where the stone had hung, but only the thread remained, and that was black and charred. Her face became grave. "I see," she said in a whisper. "So that is what I am dealing with. I should have guessed as much."

Aunt Alice swept the mess from the step before she went on her walk. There was hardly a breeze that morning, which was a pity, as she felt she had a great many cobwebs that needed blowing away. As she passed the spot where Mrs. Joyster had died, she paused. "I wish I knew what was going on, Prudence dear," she sighed.

"Alice! Alice!" called a voice.

The old lady looked heavenward and a great smile lit her wrinkled face. "Prudence?" she asked with delight.

Alas, it was not the spirit of Mrs. Joyster, only the grisled reality of Matilda Droon. She came panting down Church

Street with a worried expression on her whiskered face and a well-chewed toy mouse in her hand. "Alice!" she cried again.

Miss Boston hid her disappointment and noticed that Tilly had not bothered to get dressed properly. Her cardigan was buttoned incorrectly, and she was still wearing her old slippers. She raised her eyebrows curiously but waited for her to come closer.

"Tilly, dear," Aunt Alice said, smiling indulgently at her friend, "whatever is the matter? You don't usually get up this early."

Miss Droon was out of breath. She waved Binky, the toy mouse, and puffed, "She's gone, went off just like that. How can she leave her babies? She's a terrible mother!"

Aunt Alice wearily rolled her eyes. "Eurydice?" she ventured.

Tilly nodded anxiously. "Whatever shall I do?" she asked unhappily.

"Don't worry, dear; she won't have gone far. You know all her favorite haunts—try one of those."

"I suppose I could," Tilly said slowly. "But where to start?"

"Well, what about the last place we found her?"

Miss Droon's face brightened at once. "Of course—Mrs. Cooper's house. I shall go there at once." And she immediately began to climb the abbey steps.

Aunt Alice frowned. "Be careful, Tilly dear," she called after—but Miss Droon took no notice.

Miss Boston was in no mood for her walk now. She sauntered back along Church Street but didn't take the alley that led to her cottage. She was troubled and walked with her eyes fixed on the ground as though it might yield up some clue to the mystery of Prudence's death.

The old lady crossed the bridge, wrapped in thought. She was not aware of the direction she was going, but when she looked up, she found herself outside the police station. It seemed to be exceedingly busy inside for this early hour. Miss Boston pushed open the door and went inside.

"Good morning, Constable," she said to the young man behind the reception desk.

He looked up and wished he was on duty elsewhere— everyone in the station knew Miss Boston. "Morning, madam," he said civilly. "Is there anything I can do for you?"

Aunt Alice was looking at all the coming and going behind the glass doors to the left. "I say," she inquired, "has something exciting occurred?"

Constable Mayhew liked a quiet life. He knew that if he pretended he had not heard the question, the old dragon would only ask it again and make a nuisance of herself. Besides, it wasn't confidential business. He leaned forward and whispered, "Burglary last night at Pannett Park."

"The museum?" gasped the old lady. "Good heavens— what was stolen?"

"Only one exhibit was removed from the premises, madam—The Hand of Glory."

Miss Boston said nothing, but her face was a picture of bewilderment that gradually changed to one of concern. "I see," she said quietly.

Constable Mayhew allowed himself a little smile. Really, these old ladies were so nosy. That was obviously all she had come in for—to see if there was anything interesting to gossip about. He picked up a sheaf of papers and tapped them tidily on the desk like a newsreader, to appear busy. "If that's all, madam," he said briskly, "I do have work to do."

Miss Boston nodded and made for the door but turned around again when she reached it. "Oh, Constable," she began, "how did the thieves break in? I do hope nothing was damaged."

"Actually, no," he replied. "The locks weren't forced, and the alarm never went off—it's as if the thieves had a set of keys to the place."

"Oh, but they did," the old lady said mildly, and with that she left.

CHAPTER EIGHT

KNIFE AND TOOTH

That afternoon Miss Boston was sitting in Tilly Droon's little sitting room, a cup of tea in one hand and a half-eaten bonbon in the other.

It was a poky little place, cluttered further by the sleeping cats that seemed to cover every available surface. There were tabbies on the chair arms, tortoiseshells underfoot, and a fat marmalade specimen squatting before the fire, glaring at two black felines who were getting dangerously close. Everything was covered in hair; the carpet had long since disappeared beneath the sea of countless molts. There was precious little left of the chair backs, either; they had been used as claw sharpeners for years.

The worst aspect of Miss Droon's house, though, was the smell. She always swore blind that she could not detect any odor, but this opinion was challenged by her lack of human visitors. Only Aunt Alice and Mrs. Joyster had ever ventured in more than once. Mrs. Banbury-Scott did promise to return one day, but there was always some excuse. Miss Wethers was more honest about it and refused even to peep through the letterbox.

"Move over, Chunky," Tilly told the marmalade cat. "Let Inky and Jet feel the fire." She eased herself into a tattered armchair and slurped her tea. "That Cooper woman," Tilly said, resuming the story she had begun before pottering into the kitchen to make the tea.

"Oh yes," Miss Boston murmured, with interest.

"Well, you should have seen her face when I went over this morning to find Eurydice. Never seen anyone so put out and unpleasant." She chewed on a rather stale bonbon before continuing. "She wouldn't let me go and find her myself, but darted upstairs like a bullet. Anyway, five minutes later, she brings Eurydice down, and the poor dear was petrified. She didn't like the woman one little bit—terrible state she was in."

"At least she's safe now, Tilly," Miss Boston remarked. "And what was this other news you dragged me in to hear?"

Miss Droon licked her moustache. "Well, it was about lunchtime, and I hadn't a tin of cat food in the house, so I dashed out to the shop, and who do you think I saw?"

"Haven't a clue."

"Kenneth Grice!"

Miss Boston put her cup down. "Dora's handyman—what is so curious about that, dear?"

"Well he stopped me. Made a point of it, he did, crossed the road especially."

"Really? How strange; he's such a rude, gruff man as a rule. What did he say?"

"Dora's not well. Told me Doctor Adams had been to see her that morning."

Miss Boston shook her head. "But she always has some illness or thinks she has—she likes to be fussed over. Where's the news in that?"

"But that's just it, Alice. She isn't faking it this time, there really is something wrong with her."

"Poor Dora. Whatever's the matter?"

"Grice said it was something to do with her heart, high blood pressure—not as strong as she was. He said the doctor was quite concerned."

"Oh dear," tutted Aunt Alice. "We shall have to go around and cheer her up. She must be feeling very low."

Tilly banged her fists on the chair arm in frustration and in doing so, knocked a startled tabby to the floor. "No, no, no," she cried. "That's the point, you see; that's why Grice came and spoke to me. He says Dora's not to have any visitors for a few days—doctor's orders. She needs complete rest. So she'd told him to tell us." She leaned forward and lowered her voice. "Thing is, though, Grice wasn't very happy because after telling me that, he said he was to go and fetch Mrs. Cooper. Seems Dora wants to see *her* in spite of what the doctor said."

"But that's outrageous," said Miss Boston, flabbergasted. "Do you mean to say that she can't see old friends like us but is quite capable of having visits from that Rowena person?"

"Exactly! Grice thought it was dreadful, too—never seen him look so awkward before."

Miss Boston's chins wobbled in annoyance. "I think we have been snubbed, Tilly dear," she said. "And I believe Dora will live to regret allowing that woman into her house."

The baked potato was still too hot to touch. Jennet could feel the heat from it radiate through the lining of her coat. The girl had been thinking about the previous night all day long. She could not forget that tragic figure in white pouring out her grief in the churchyard. It had had a profound effect on Jennet. She knew what it was like to suffer and grieve, but at least she had Ben. The poor woman obviously had no one. She hoped the novice would return tonight. There had to be something she could do to help. The woman might not be so frightened this time.

The stone of the tomb slab was cold, and she shifted uncomfortably. She had come armed against the pangs of hunger: in one pocket there was the baked potato and in the other, one of Aunt Alice's forks. It was dark now, and only the pubs around the harbor seemed alive, all the tourists having deserted the streets for cozier entertainments. It was going to be a cold night; there was a musty, autumn scent in the air. Jennet shivered and decided it was time to eat.

Wisps of steam curled out of the potato as she broke its brown, papery skin with the old silver fork. It smelled delicious, and she waited for a moment before digging in. It was still hot, and Jennet had to suck in the cold night air to prevent her mouth being burned.

The sea lapped against the cliff face; all was calm, and the waxing moon rose above the few dim clouds that reached over the horizon. Jennet finished the last fragments of baked potato and returned the fork to her pocket. She felt better for that and was marvelously warm inside. It was ten o'clock, and she was all alone in the graveyard.

A seabird flew overhead and was caught in the beams of the arc lights. Jennet watched it falter and then regain its balance. When she lowered her eyes, something white caught her attention.

There she was, the sister from the convent. Just as she had done the night before, the woman crossed the cemetery and stood by the wall, where she gazed out to sea.

Undetected, Jennet rose and began to walk over to her. She could see the woman's shoulders shaking with emotion as the miserable weeping began; the pitiful whimpers filled her ears.

Suddenly Jennet dropped to the ground—someone else was there. A figure dressed in black had emerged from the darkness, strode quickly over the graves, and grabbed the novice by the wrist.

Jennet scrambled behind a headstone and waited. She was confused. What was happening? And why should she feel the need to hide? It was ridiculous; she wasn't doing anything wrong, yet she felt it would be safer if she were not observed.

A voice drifted over the tombs to her dark sanctuary. It was a wheedling, fawning voice but one that contained a hidden power that might erupt at any moment. For some reason, Jennet was afraid. The sound of that voice made her shudder; it was ugly and menacing. She wiped her forehead and plucked up enough courage to peer around the stone.

By the wall, the white form of the novice was trying to pull away from the intruder. Her small, frightened face was screwed up in misery as she tugged to release her arm.

Jennet reared up a little higher, for she could not quite see the other person. A little more and there, dressed in black, with her short blonde hair gleaming under the moon, was Rowena Cooper. Jennet had never met the woman before, but Aunt Alice had given her a perfect description. It could be no other.

The two women struggled with each other, but Rowena was the stronger, and she laughed triumphantly. "You don't get away that easily, my little mule," she sneered.

Jennet was fascinated. All her instincts warned her, and tiny alarm signals jangled in her head, but she had to find out what was going on. Ignoring her better judgement, she crawled through the grass and drew closer.

Ben trudged to the bridge, yawning and stumbling. Another evening had gone by, and still there was no sign of the moon-kelp. He hated leaving Nelda and Hesper to continue the search without him, but what would Aunt Alice and Jennet say if he stayed out all night?

He had enjoyed the past week. Once they had gone out in a tiny rowing boat, and Hesper had told him a great many things. She had warmed to Ben, and, although the threat of discovery by the rest of the tribe still caused her to panic every now and again, at other times she would chatter to him quite freely.

The boy was learning a great deal about the fisher folk. He knew that they honored the sea and were keepers of great mysteries. They guarded the secrets of the magic tides and had once been able to consult the Lords of the Deep, who lived in the dark, cold realm under the water. Hesper told him many old tales: of the Weathercharmers who controlled the winds and waves by singing the Song of the Moon, of the Shorebrides who rejected tribal life and became solitary coast wanderers, and of the Gullspeakers who knew the tongues of all sea birds. To Ben's delight, she also told him of the hideous serpents and other monsters that used to inhabit the waters around Whitby.

While Hesper was telling him of the Weathercharmers, a salty tear trickled down her nut-brown cheek. They were out in the small aufwader boat, and she stopped rowing and gazed dreamily into the distance.

"Oona was the mightiest of these," she said. "It was only the women folk who practiced the art. Very great in all lore was she, and the Song of the Moon was never sung better than when it issued from her lips. Her talent excelled so that no others could compete against it, and the craft was forgotten by all save she. Oona might have been a tribal elder if she had had a mind. All respected her—some were even a little afraid—but she was a gentle creature and did not crave to rule others." Slowly Hesper dipped the oars into the water and continued the tale sadly.

"A Shorebride Oona was close to becoming, and though I was young, I can remember the light in her eyes when she spoke of the moonkelp, and I knew that she yearned to find it. I believe she knew when and where it would bloom, but they were secrets she kept to herself. Not even I was entrusted with that knowledge."

"What happened to her?" Ben asked. "It's a pity she isn't here now."

Hesper bowed her head and said no more. It was Nelda who explained to him. "But if Oona was here," she said, "then there would be no need to find the moonkelp. For she it was who fell in love with the fisherman and bore the half-child. It is through her that we are all accursed."

Ben's head spun with all he had learned. He was too tired to take most of it in, and his feet dragged beneath him. Crossing over the bridge, he headed down Church Street for home. When he came to the alleyway, something caught his eye.

He turned around, and, through the gap between the houses opposite, he looked down on the sands of Tate Hill Pier.

A figure was crouching on the shore; although it was dark, it was unmistakeably an aufwader. The boy grinned. His excitement expelled all traces of weariness, and he hurried over the road and sped down the steps that led to the beach.

The aufwader had his back to Ben. He was dressed pretty much the same as Nelda: a woollen hat, a gansey, and an old worn pair of oilskin waders. Ben could hear him muttering but could not make out the words. The tone, however, did not sound pleasant.

He was not sure if he wanted to meet this aufwader after all. What if he had been spying on Nelda and Hesper and was going to tell the elders of the tribe? Ben might make it worse if he went right up to him and introduced himself.

"Garr!" spat the guttural voice of the stranger as a wave rushed in unexpectedly and covered his feet. Ben didn't like the sound of him. He stopped in his tracks and prepared to turn back, but it was too late. The aufwader spun around and saw the boy.

He was an ugly character. A great sneer scarred his face, and his large ears were ragged and torn from many fights. His side-whiskers were black and wiry, framing his leering head like the legs of a huge poisonous spider, and his large dark eyes slid slyly from side to side in the shadow of scowling brows.

Ben backed away, but he could not stop staring at the creature. Even in the dim light of the street lamps, he could recognize the pattern on the gansey—it was the same as Nelda's. This evil-looking creature was her father!

The aufwader paced to one side, not sure if the child could see him. The sneer widened, however, when he saw Ben's gaze follow him. He opened his wrinkled, tobacco-stained mouth and hissed, "A human whelp wi' the sight, is it?"

The black eyes glinted, and as Ben looked into them, he felt invisible bonds tighten around him, just as they had when he had first met Nelda. He was unable to move, caught in the aufwader snare—a restraining power that froze his tongue and turned his feet to lead. He could only watch as the foul figure crept ever closer to him.

The creature took a sharp knife from his belt and held it up to the boy's face. "Come to pry again 'ave ya, landbreed? Always poking yer nose in where it's not wanted, ain'tcha?" The deadly blade touched Ben's cheek, and he shuddered with fear. The aufwader cackled menacingly. "Ain't no cats round 'ere fer yer to rescue, laddie."

Then Ben remembered his experience in The Hawes, when he had gone upstairs to find Eurydice. He was now facing the thing that had dropped from the opening to the attic.

"Know what I does wi' smart little brats like you?" the aufwader asked, bringing his face closer to Ben's.

The boy tried to turn his face away from the stale breath that stank in his nostrils, but the snare held him fast.

"I don't like bein' seen by maggots like you!" snapped the creature. "And to make sure ya won't nivver make that mistake again, I'm gonna poke them charmed little eyeballs out fer ya!"

He clasped the handle of his knife even tighter and drew his hand back to strike. Ben tried to call out in terror, but his voice was stuck in his throat.

The glittering blade sliced down.

"Deeps damn her!" bellowed the aufwader suddenly. His blow went astray, and he turned his head toward the cliff, apparently having heard something that Ben had not. His concentration was broken, and the hypnotic snare destroyed.

Ben seized his chance. He kicked the aufwader in the stomach, and his knife spun through the air as the creature doubled up in agony. Grabbing a handful of sand, the boy flung it into his opponent's gasping face. Then he scrambled back over the beach for dear life and did not stop until he was safely indoors and in a startled Aunt Alice's arms.

Jennet squashed herself against the headstone and listened.

"I can help you," said the voice of Rowena Cooper.

The novice made no reply. She tried to pry the other woman's fingers from her wrist, without success.

"I shan't release you until the bargain is made," Rowena growled.

The novice stopped struggling and eyed her suspiciously.

"That's better," cooed Rowena. "There's nothing to fear— yet." She gave a sharp little laugh, then smiled, showing all her teeth. "I know a great many things," she said. "I know who you are, and I know why you come here every night to weep and bemoan your fate." With her free arm, she made a grand, sweeping gesture to the sea. "I know why you ache for the water and why you dare not go near it."

For the first time, the novice spoke; it was a fragile voice full of fear. "Who are you?" she asked. "How could you know such things?"

Rowena's eyes opened wide. "It is my business to discover secrets," she declared importantly. "Forbidden knowledge has always been my passion. That is why I can help you. There are ways around your predicament, my dear. Allow me to assist in easing your burden." Her words were coaxing and full of promises; they seemed to reach out and subdue the will. Even hiding some distance away, Jennet felt the power of that voice as it oozed and persuaded.

"Tell me what I need to know," Rowena's honeyed tone continued. "It cannot mean anything to you now. Tell me where I may find what I seek, and we shall both profit by it."

"There is nothing you can give me," replied the novice coldly. "I must live with my sins."

Rowena showed signs of displeasure. "Tuh! I do not believe there is such a thing. How long will you cower like an insect in the miserable life you have chosen? I don't think you could have picked a more pathetic role." She threw back her head and laughed in mockery. "What a fool you are! Anything could have been yours—you are unique. But what do you do? You hide yourself away all this time, hoping to escape from that which awaits you. But the years rolled on, didn't they? You grew weary of running, and so here you are at last. The wanderer has returned."

She twisted her lip in scorn and shook the novice's wrist harshly. "Tell me what I want to know, or I shall be forced to compel you."

"There is no torment you can inflict upon me that I have not already suffered a thousand times over," the novice answered defiantly. "Now let me go!"

She pulled her arm back sharply, throwing Rowena off balance and making her tumble backwards. Released from the iron grip, the sister fled away, past the church and down the steps. Rowena picked herself up from the grass where she had fallen, her face white with rage. She marched over to the edge of the cliff and called out impatiently.

Jennet was cold and frightened. She had understood very little of what had passed between these two, but one thing was certain—Rowena was the vilest person she had ever heard of. She just hoped she could make her way back to the steps without being seen by that awful woman. She began to wriggle along the ground as silently as she was able.

"Where have you been?" Rowena demanded angrily. "Why were you not here?"

Jennet pressed herself into the grass. Surely Mrs. Cooper wasn't speaking to her? Quickly, she squirmed around to see.

Rowena's imposing figure was silhouetted against the night sky, but she was not looking in the girl's direction. She appeared to be having a conversation with herself, or at least that is how Jennet perceived it.

"I don't care if you were seen," Rowena snorted. "A human child with the sight can do no harm. Just be sure you obey my instructions tonight. The novice told me nothing. We shall have to proceed with the original plan—" She broke off as though interrupted. "You don't have to tell me that; I know it could take days to find . . . Well, if we don't, my husband will have to deal with it, but I am loath to involve him more than necessary."

Jennet was intrigued. Was the woman mad? Just who did she think she was talking to? The girl raised her head a little to make sure that somebody wasn't hiding over there.

At that precise moment, Rowena looked around and spotted her. "Who's there?" she screamed furiously.

Jennet did not stay to tell her. Like a hare, she leaped over the graves and charged toward the steps.

Mrs. Cooper's face was a mask of rage. She stormed over to where Jennet had been hiding and said coldly, "The girl has heard too much." Something rustled through the grass and seemed to stop beside her. "She's not for your knife," Rowena told the unseen companion. "There is a more . . . appropriate way of silencing her."

Jennet shielded her eyes from the fierce glare of the arc lamps as she ran past the church. It was not far to the steps now, and she hurried over the graves to reach them.

"Aagh!" the girl cried as her shin struck the sharp edge of a tomb, and she fell. Her arms flew out to save herself, but it was too late; she cracked her knees on the stone, and the top layer of skin was scraped from her hands.

Frantically, Jennet sat up and nursed her bruised knees. Her palms felt as though they were on fire, and she blew on them in panic. She did not have time to cry, even though it hurt like mad. The girl turned her head quickly—where was Rowena? She staggered to her feet and looked about cautiously. Nothing; only the grass stirred between the headstones. It was too quiet.

Suddenly, a terrible howl rent the night air. Jennet breathed faster as the sound of her nightmares thundered through the darkness. She whirled around but still could not see anything.

The howl went up again. Jennet began nervously limping toward the steps, and the shadows closed in on her. The light from the arc lamps crackled and flashed like lightning. With a loud crash, the bulbs exploded, and glass splintered out onto the path. The cliff top plummeted into total darkness.

"Oh, no. Oh, no," Jennet muttered to herself. "This isn't happening; it can't be happening." She hurled herself forward,

but in her fear the headstones seemed to rear up before her, barring the way to the steps. She dodged one way and then another.

A third fearsome howl cut into the night—it terrified Jennet so much that she ran blindly. In the dark, Jennet did not realize she was going in the wrong direction. She had totally lost her bearings, and when she stopped running found that she was in the center of the cemetery, completely surrounded by graves.

She leaned against one of the stones and tried to quell her panic. The church now lay between her and the steps, but the nightmare creature could be anywhere. Jennet's stinging hands trembled as they automatically clenched into fists; the breathing of a large animal was drawing nearer.

To her horror, Jennet saw two gleaming red eyes appear in the deep dark ahead. The full glare of their malice was focused on her, and she felt faint at their baleful stare. The eyes came closer and then vanished behind one of the head-stones: the creature was circling her. She caught glimpses of those hideous, fiery points as it stealthily stalked around, preparing for the kill. Jennet whimpered, and the beast stole into view.

It was the worst moment of her life; her heart leaped into her mouth. The enormous black hound bared its teeth, and its growl rumbled like an earthquake through the cliff. It shifted the weight from paw to paw and tensed itself.

Then it sprang.

Jennet screamed as loudly as she could. The beast slammed into her, and the defenseless girl was thrust backward over a gravestone. The world tumbled upside down, and she could not move, pinned mercilessly to the ground by the hound's tremendous weight. Its claws dug deeply into her shoulders.

Jennet tried to struggle. She flailed her arms and kicked with her feet, but it was no good. Her efforts were puny and ridiculous set against that huge bulk. It lowered its head and the hellish eyes burned into her. Hot breath steamed down on her face as the hound snapped its frothing jaws together.

A trickle of saliva dripped onto the girl's cheek, and she made one last attempt to escape. It was useless. The hound snarled and pressed its wet snout against her throat. Jennet waited for the end, and her fists uncurled. Something cold and metal touched her outstretched fingers. It was the fork, which had fallen out of her pocket.

The hound reared its head and opened a slavering mouth as it lunged for her neck. Jennet swung her arm up and stabbed the fork into its jowls, ramming it as far in as she could.

The reaction was incredible. The beast yelped and fell back, lurching awkwardly and yammering in pain. Jennet could not believe her eyes; it was impossible for her to have inflicted so much pain on the creature. It spun around, whining in agony and pawing at its cheek till the fork fell to the ground. As soon as it was free, the hound leaped away and disappeared into the darkness, yelping madly as it went.

Shaken, Jennet got to her feet. On the ground, the fork burst into blue flames and vanished. The girl tore to the steps and ran home.

CHAPTER NINE

"BUT A LITTLE TIME TO LIVE"

Ben and Jennet sat on the sofa in Aunt Alice's cozy parlor. The old lady stood in front of the fireplace with her hands clasped behind her back. She had dressed the girl's cuts and bruises and given them both a hot cup of tea with cookies. When she had made sure they were comfortable, she made them tell her exactly what had happened.

Ben had been reluctant to explain why he had come rushing back in such panic; it would mean telling her about the fisher folk. For awhile, he stared miserable at the floor, but Aunt Alice was insistent—he had never seen her in this mood before. Slowly Ben mumbled about meeting Nelda and Hesper and how they were searching for the moonkelp. Finally, he got around to the evil creature he had met on the beach that night.

Miss Boston stood stiff and stern throughout his tale. Her face was scrunched up in such a way that it was impossible to tell what she was thinking. Jennet, however, gawked at her brother as though he had gone mad. She had never heard such a load of old rubbish. Fisher folk, indeed!

Aunt Alice now turned to her. Jennet guiltily told how she had spied on the novice in the churchyard the previous night and how she had gone out that evening with the same intention. Aunt Alice's brows raised a little on hearing this, and she pursed her lips in disapproval. Jennet then related the events that had led up to the appearance of the hound and described how it had attacked her. When her story was over, the girl kept her eyes fixed on Aunt Alice. She realized her tale sounded almost as ridiculous as Ben's—would the old lady believe her?

Miss Boston studied them both for a few moments. Ben was dejected about breaking his promise of silence, and Jennet looked unhappy.

Aunt Alice cleared her throat and rocked on her heels. "A most perilous time you pair have had," she said eventually. "I must say that I am rather disappointed in you both for having kept these things to yourselves."

Neither of the children made an answer. They both felt awful.

The old lady stooped to pick up the poker and gave the dying fire a few irritated and vigorous thrusts. "There," she said when that was done. Her mood had changed back to normal. "Now the main thing is, what are we to do about this situation?" She rubbed her hands together excitedly. Both Jennet and Ben looked at her, bewildered.

"First of all," Aunt Alice began, "I must tell you, Benjamin, that you haven't really betrayed a trust in telling me about your aufwader friends. You're not the only one who can see them, you know. Of course to me they're a little blurred, as my gift is not as sharp as it should be. I have seen them many times, although I have never had the courage to go up and actually speak to them, as you did. Do close your mouth, dear, or you'll catch a fly in it." She chuckled to herself at the expressions on the children's faces. Ben was amazed, but his sister was annoyed.

"You don't mean you believe all that twaddle about goblins on the beach?" Jennet asked incredulously. "I don't understand you at all. Why let Ben go on imagining things—isn't it bad enough already?"

Miss Boston glared her into silence. "Really, I'm surprised at you, Jennet," she remarked. "I thought you had accepted the fact that Benjamin could see things you do not. There are many things in this world that are hidden from us, and the fisher folk are just one of them. Tell me, if you close your eyes now, do you think we have disappeared? Of course not. You know that we are still here; your common sense tells you that. Benjamin merely has an extra sense that most people do not possess."

Jennet was still doubtful, until suddenly she remembered the way in which Rowena had appeared to be speaking to thin air. "Then Mrs. Cooper has the sight as well," she cried suddenly. "It wasn't herself she was talking to, it was—"

"The disagreeable aufwader who tried to murder your brother," Miss Boston put in. She sucked her cheeks and murmured thoughtfully, "I am afraid that Rowena Cooper is a very dangerous person indeed."

"Do you think that dog was hers?" the girl asked. "You ought to tell the police Rowena needs locking up."

Aunt Alice shook her head. "The constabulary would laugh at us, my dear," she said. "You must remember that Mrs. Cooper has made herself very popular in the town—who would believe that she threatens nuns and keeps a huge, mad dog?"

Jennet could see that, put like that, it did sound rather silly. "And as for whether the dog is hers," the old lady concluded, "I'm not too sure about that either."

"But it must belong to her!" the girl protested.

Aunt Alice did not reply. She looked across to Ben, who had fallen fast asleep on the sofa, and checked the time. It was very late. "We can discuss this tomorrow," she said to Jennet, "but right now, I think you ought to get some rest. You've had quite a harrowing ordeal."

A little while later, Miss Boston tucked Ben into bed. She was dying to learn more about the fisher folk and their way of life, but that would have to wait till another time. "Sleep well, Benjamin," she said softly before closing the door. "Dream not of darkness." With that, she made a curious sign in the air, which she repeated outside Jennet's room.

Later that night, on the outskirts of Whitby, mysterious lights flickered behind the windows of Mrs. Banbury-Scott's grand house and a foul smell laced the air. A terrible series of crashes and bangs rang through the old building. But in her pink, chiffon-curtained bed, Mrs. Banbury-Scott slept soundly.

Miss Boston had a very busy day ahead of her. Prudence was to be buried that afternoon, and she had taken it upon herself to do all the baking for the small buffet that was to be held in the late woman's house after the service. The nephew from Halifax had arrived the day before, but he was such an incapable man that she decided it would be best if he left it all up to her.

By the time Jennet and Ben came downstairs, she had already baked sausage rolls and two trays of scones and was taking a cake from the oven. The children's mouths watered, but she told them that they had to have a proper breakfast.

Ben eyed the sausage rolls greedily as the milk from his cereal dribbled down his chin and onto his shirt.

"Can I help, Aunt Alice?" Jennet offered when she had finished hers.

"Thank you, dear. Yes, you make the sandwiches, if you like. I need that loaf buttered. Oh, botheration! I used the last of the butter to make the cake. I shall have to dash out to the shops as soon as they open."

Jennet played with the spoon in her bowl. She turned it around and around before saying quietly, "Do you want Ben and me to come to the funeral this afternoon?"

Miss Boston smiled. "That isn't necessary, dear; you never really knew her. Besides, I think you have been to enough of those sad occasions, don't you?"

Jennet nodded. She didn't know if she could have coped with it, anyway; it would have reminded her too much of her parents' death. She stared into her empty bowl for some time and then said, "You think Mrs. Joyster was murdered, don't you?"

Aunt Alice was not at all startled by this statement. She took off her oven gloves and calmly replied, "Yes, I do. I think Prudence found something out and had to be silenced."

"Something about Rowena?"

"Yes—but what can I do about it? As I said last night, one can't go around accusing people without proof. I shall just have to be careful, that's all."

At half past nine, Miss Boston ventured out to buy some butter. On passing the post office, a little squeak caught her attention.

Miss Wethers was in the window, waving madly at her. "Come in," she mouthed through the glass.

"Whatever can she want?" muttered the old lady in surprise.

The postmistress came to the door and dragged her inside. "You'll never guess," she cried. "The most wicked thing has happened."

"My dear Edith," said Aunt Alice, "are you quite well?"

"Burglars!" Miss Wethers babbled hysterically. "Vandals and hooligans! Ripped the carpets, tore the books from the shelves, kicked in the paneling!" She blew her nose and fiddled with the top button of her gray cardigan.

"Edith you're not making any sense," said Aunt Alice. "Are you saying that you've had burglars?"

The flustered woman wrung her hands in distress. "Not me," she gabbled. "Dora! It's her house that was ransacked— a shocking mess by all accounts."

At once, Miss Boston became very serious. She took hold of Edith's shoulders and gripped her firmly. "Now start at the beginning for heaven's sake."

The postmistress took a deep breath and began. "Well, about ten minutes ago, I was just opening up when Mrs. Turner goes by in a terrible state. Of course, I asked what the matter was, and she tells me that there's been the most dreadful occurrence at Mrs. Banbury-Scott's house, where her daughter Rachel works. Rachel telephoned her just after she had called the police."

Miss Boston interrupted. "But why? You still haven't told me what has happened."

"I was coming to that," Edith sniffed indignantly. "Some time last night, one person, maybe more, broke into Dora's house and wrecked it from top to bottom. They smashed that lovely old wooden mantelpiece into splinters and ripped up some of the floorboards."

"But why weren't the police called in sooner?" Asked Miss Boston, horrified.

"Because nobody heard a thing! They slept through it all. It's quite unbelievable, isn't it? Mrs. Turner was very concerned, and I'm not surprised. There's something fishy about the whole business, if you ask me. I hope the police get to the bottom of it—I won't feel safe in my bed until they do. Burglars crashing about making a din, and no one hearing them! It's not natural." She broke off and dabbed her nose reassuringly.

"Nobody heard a thing," repeated Miss Boston thoughtfully. "How curious. There must have been a dreadful racket going on." She rubbed her chin and then gasped, "But what about poor Dora? She must be horribly upset."

Edith nodded. "I think Mrs. Turner said Doctor Adams had been called out. It must have been a terrible shock."

"I think we should go and see how she is," Aunt Alice declared.

At this, Miss Wethers stiffened. "No need for that," she said with bitterness. "Rowena came by just as Mrs. Turner left. Apparently Dora had phoned and asked her to come. When I offered to close the post office and come along too, that woman had the temerity to suggest that I would only upset Dora all the more."

Miss Boston could not help but smile at the way Edith's devotion to Mrs. Cooper had completely dissolved. "Dear me," she clucked, "yet another rebuff. I wonder if we shall see Dora at the funeral this afternoon?"

"Well, I shall be there at any rate," said Miss Wethers. "Poor Prudence."

Aunt Alice patted her hand as she took her leave. Before she reached the door, she asked, "By the way, Edith, was Mrs. Cooper carrying anything when you saw her?"

Miss Wethers frowned. "Why yes, she was. She had a little square box in her hand. I couldn't see what it was because she had wrapped it up—said it was a gift for Dora. Why do you want to know?"

"Oh, no reason. Good-bye."

The children had the afternoon to themselves. It was a bright, warm day, and Jennet was glad to feel the sun on her face. The dark horrors of the night seemed an age away. She and Ben were together in Whitby, and that was all that mattered. She was in such a good mood that she told Ben he could have the pick of the day. This was a game they had played when they were younger: one of them had the honor of choosing what they were both to do for the whole day.

Ben was thrilled. It was not often he could boss his sister about, but under the rules of the game, she had to go along with him. As they wandered through the town he scratched his head and tried to think what he would most like to do.

"Oh, look," said Jennet suddenly. "It's that Banbury-Scott woman."

The Bentley was bullying its way down the narrow road. As usual, Grice was driving and in the back, heavily veiled and festooned in black mourning, was the fat woman. The car drove slowly by until the weight of traffic forced it to stop altogether. It was now directly opposite the children.

The obese shape in the back popped something into her mouth and, as she moved her arm, a second passenger was revealed beside her. It was Rowena Cooper.

Jennet pulled Ben into a shop when she saw her, but Mrs. Cooper did not seem to notice them. She was too busy talking to Mrs. Banbury-Scott.

"Banbury-Scoff, Banbury-Scoff!" chanted Ben rudely as he saw the pudgy fingers return to those orange lips and stuff something else inside. His words faltered, however, when he caught sight of the second passenger. He had never seen Rowena before. She leaned further forward and said something to Grice, and in doing so he saw the side of her face. Four jagged streaks of silver light were shining on her cheek. They were so bright that they actually lit up the inside of the car.

The Bentley pulled away once more, and Ben stared after it. "Jen," he asked, "who was that woman with the scar?"

"She doesn't have a scar, Ben," Jennet told him. "That was Mrs. Cooper."

The boy said nothing.

The Bentley disappeared around the corner. "I suppose they're off to the funeral," said Jennet. "Anyway, Ben, have you decided what we are going to do?"

A wide grin split the boy's face.

The lifeboat museum was contained in one large room. Dominating the whole length of it was one of the old rowing lifeboats, and in front of this was a counter that sold souvenirs and booklets. Against the rear wall was a roll-a-penny game, and beside that was a finely detailed model of a sinking ship. The mast was broken, and the waves pounded over the half-submerged deck. Around the display were yellow news-paper clippings of the time that told the whole story. Ben wished he was better at reading.

Jennet was not really interested in boats, sinking or other-wise. She gazed at the souvenir counter and looked in her pockets for some change to put in the collection box. After that, she was rather bored.

Ben moved around the cases. He longed to be able to make a model ship like one of these. He loved the pains-taking detail of the intricate rigging and all the tiny brass fittings, and dawdled past each and every display. Just when he thought he had finished, something else grabbed his attention.

The exhibit was like no other. It was a large stump of wood that, when Ben drew closer, he could see had been carved. But the sculpture was an alarming piece of art. Drowning men floundered amid the wooden waves while above them, a capsized lifeboat rode the churning sea. Ben shivered when he saw the terrified faces of the lifeboatmen, and he resolved not to get into the little aufwader boat with Hesper again.

"'Tain't pretty, is it, lad?" said a voice.

Ben turned around. A red-faced, stout man with white hair was standing behind him.

"Know what that is?" the man asked.

Ben shook his head.

"It shows the lifeboat disaster of 1861," said the stranger. He crouched down to the boy's level and pointed at the carved curling waves. "It were a bitter February," his rum-bling voice went on. "A raw gale had been blasting in for nigh

on a week. Three times the lifeboat was launched that day, battling into the storm-mad waters, defying the devil's tempest. Three times the lifeboat returned, safe with the rescued crews of dying ships." The man's eyes bored into the sculpture as he told the tale, while Ben pictured the horror of it all in his mind.

"In the early afternoon," the man continued, "The schooner *Merchant* was hurled ashore. Tired from their earlier valiant efforts, the lifeboatmen doggedly launched their rescue boat for the fourth time. The gale ravaged down, and the sea rose against them. Two great waves collided beneath the boat, overturning it and throwing the crew into the seething waters."

The man put his hand on Ben's shoulder and whispered somberly, "Of the thirteen souls that set out in that lifeboat, only one came back."

It seemed to have grown very cold, and Ben rubbed his goose pimply arms. The man chuckled to himself and left the boy to shiver. Ben thought how horrible it must be to feel the freezing water fill your ears and close over your head. He drew his breath in sharply.

Jennet had been watching all of this. She smiled to herself and silently crept up behind her brother. "BOO!" she shouted.

Ben jumped. "That's not funny," he yelled. "Just you wait till I catch you!"

Jennet ran laughing out of the museum.

Miss Boston sat back in the pew and closed her hymn book. "Jerusalem" had always been a favorite of Prudence's. She wiped the tear from her eye and bowed her head in silent prayer.

It had been an admirable service, and the church was nearly full of those wishing to pay their last respects. The vicar had paid tribute to Mrs. Joyster most commendably, mentioning her involvement with the Whitby Heritage Committee and her sterling work for the Literary and Philosophical Society of the Pannett Park Museum.

Miss Boston half-closed her eyes and pondered these remarks. Yes, Prudence had been a leading light of that particular society. She had even had a set of keys to the museum, which she kept on the same ring as those to her house. The very same bunch of keys that the police had been unable to find.

The service was coming to an end, and Miss Boston looked at the man sitting on her right. It was the incapable nephew, a dull, colorless man of about 50. He sat bemused and awkward on the front row next to her. He hadn't really known Prudence, and Miss Boston recalled that in her turn Prudence had never been very fond of him.

The rustle of coats and the shuffling of feet soon followed the coffin down the aisle. Into the sunlight the congregation trailed.

Miss Boston fell in place behind the nephew, and after her came others of the ladies' circle.

Miss Wethers covered her face with a handkerchief, no doubt fearing that a simple tissue would not stand up to the rigors of her grief. Miss Droon was holding on to her arm, and for once the postmistress showed no signs of sneezing. Behind them came the gentle Mr. Roper to whom Prudence had been so kind when his beloved Margaret had passed on. With him came the assorted worthies of Whitby: the mayor,

Doctor Adams, the curator of the Pannett Park Museum, and the chief inspector of police. Prudence Joyster had been held in high esteem by many.

A fitful bout of sniffling rose from the rear of the group. Out of the church came Mrs. Banbury-Scott, her face hidden by a veil and a sable coat hanging from her shoulders. Her ample bosom heaved under the black drapes of her dress as she wept emotionally into a dainty square of lace. Rowena Cooper was beside her. She wore a neat suit of black silk and projected an image of serene elegance; not a trace of sorrow could be seen on her cool, dispassionate face.

The mourners gathered at the graveside and watched as the coffin was lowered into the ground.

"Good-bye, Prudence dear," whispered Miss Boston softly as the vicar gave the final farewell.

Edith Wethers leaned heavily on Tilly Droon's arm and wrung her hands. "It's just like when Mother went," she uttered miserably.

Miss Droon stuck out her hairy chin and clenched her teeth to keep from crying.

"Oh, oh, oh," whined Mrs. Banbury-Scott, "it's too much. I can't bear it." She put a hand to her chest, and her lips trembled. It had been a dreadful day for her, starting with waking up from that unpleasantly heavy sleep and discovering that her house had been vandalized. She did not feel at all well; the stress was tremendous, and her face looked ill even through the thick layers of makeup.

Doctor Adams shot her a professional glance. He had warned her against coming here this afternoon—she was just not up to it.

Rowena Cooper bent her head and pretended to mourn
for Prudence Joyster. She even managed to squeeze out a
solitary tear. For the first time that afternoon, Miss Boston
managed to get a good look at the woman. She rubbed her
eyes and looked again. On Rowena's cheek something was
faintly shimmering. It was like glimpsing a fine beam of light
through a very dense fog. Miss Boston squinted at the hazy
blur, which seemed to be some sort of scar. She sucked her
teeth and nodded to herself; that was no ordinary mark, and
she knew that nobody else present would be able to see it.

Rowena put her hands together—a deft, graceful movement that allowed her to discreetly check her wristwatch.
It would probably not take too much longer, she thought
to herself.

Miss Boston cast some earth into the grave. Edith and
Tilly did the same, followed by the mayor and the other
mourners. Only Mrs. Banbury-Scott abstained; she did not
feel capable of stooping to pick up some soil. She flapped the
lapels of her sable and fanned herself with her handkerchief—
why was it so warm suddenly? Beads of sweat appeared
through the makeup on her forehead, and the powder began
to slide off her face. She found it increasingly difficult to
breathe, and there was an awful tightness in her breast.

"Help!" she croaked, throwing off her furs and bending
double with the pain.

"Dora!" cried Rowena smartly. "What is it?"

"Let me through, let me through," called Doctor Adams.

Everyone watched him ease the fat woman onto the
grass, where he banged her chest with his fist. Aunt Alice
shook her head in disbelief as Mrs. Banbury-Scott gasped

on the ground like a fish out of water. She could not bear
to witness any more and dragged her eyes away. How pale
everyone had become—everyone, that is, except Rowena.

Mrs. Cooper had stepped back from the main group and
was studying the sky as though nothing out of the ordinary had occurred. Aunt Alice scowled, her temper boiling.
Rowena gazed down at her shoes and tutted at a smear of
mud on them, before looking back to where Doctor Adams
fought for Mrs. Banbury-Scott's life.

An expression of genuine concern crossed her face, but
that was soon dispelled when Doctor Adams raised his head
and said slowly, "I'm sorry. She's gone."

CHAPTER TEN

EURYDICE AGAIN

A week had passed since the sudden death of Mrs. Banbury-Scott. Surprisingly enough, her demise aroused less emotion than that of Prudence Joyster—business seemed to get in the way of grief. The numerous civic bodies of which she had been a member missed her donations more than herself, and the dead woman's lawyers were kept very busy sorting through her affairs. Mrs. Banbury-Scott had no relatives, so the bulk of her estate was to be divided between the various charities she had been fond of. Grice, her handyman and chauffeur, was left a small amount of money in her will, as were her cook and Rachel Turner, the maid. What surprised most people, though, was the revelation that she had left her house and its entire contents to Rowena Cooper.

As soon as she heard this outrageous news, Miss Boston stormed furiously over to Doctor Adams's surgery, demanding he investigate the cause of death more fully. The doctor chased the old woman out of the building. Mrs. Banbury-Scott had died of a heart attack, he shouted at her. There was absolutely nothing suspicious about it whatsoever, considering her age, weight, and lack of exercise. But Aunt Alice was undeterred. She strode straight to the police station, announced that Dora had been murdered, and asked what they were going to do about it. The police were kind but suggested that she go home and have a nice cup of tea.

The grandfather clock ticked dully in the corner of the parlor. Miss Boston gave it a withering glance and drummed her fingers on the chair arm. It had been a very trying day, and she had been sorely tempted to knock the policeman's helmet off. It was a pity that he had not been wearing one.

She felt useless. First Prudence and now Dora—she was sure that Rowena had had a hand in both deaths. "Oh, if only I had proof of some sort," she grumbled. "But where am I to get it?"

Miss Boston rose and took a book down from one of the shelves: the diary of Howard Joyster. Once again, she attempted to read the regimented handwriting, and once again, she was forced to put it down after several minutes. What a dull, humorless man he had been.

She sat glum and despondent. Perhaps Doctor Adams and the police were right, and she was a silly old woman who ought to mind her own business and not go stirring up trouble. The children had gone out for the day as the past week had been so wet and bleak that they had been forced to stay indoors. She could have done with their company right now. The house was extremely quiet, and she could almost feel the silence settle in, layer upon stifling layer.

"How empty it is without those two," she said to herself. "I've never noticed it before. Strange to think that only a few weeks ago they were not a part of my life, and now they belong here more than I do, in some ways." The silence was beginning to get on her nerves.

It was quiet as the grave—but that comparison jolted the old lady out of the dismal humor she had been wallowing in.

Pulling herself up smartly, she said, "Come on, Alice, apply yourself! Don't give in because everyone else tells you to." She threw on her hat and cloak once more and strode determinedly out of the front door.

The office of the Mother Superior was rather like that of a headmistress. It was a small room, painted an antiseptic green, containing a wide desk with neat piles of paper arranged on one half and a black wartime telephone dominating the other. An old plastic radio nestled in one corner beside a large potted plant and on the sill of the tiny window stood a plaster figure of Our Lady.

"Please sit down," the Mother Superior said kindly. She was a small woman, in her late 60s, with buttonlike eyes that peered through her spectacles with the keenest interest at whomever or whatever she was addressing. The strength of her faith was indomitable. To her, the cares of the world were there to be conquered; her chief weapon for this was often humor. She was one of those rare people with an intense zest for life, and she inspired the same in those around her.

Sitting behind the desk, she studied the old lady opposite with benign interest. "What can I do for you, Miss Boston?" her warm voice asked. "Is it something spiritual or do you want to offer your services for the rummage sale tomorrow afternoon?"

Aunt Alice settled herself into the seat provided. "Er, no, not exactly," she said.

The little black buttons peeked through the lenses curiously. For a moment, she seemed confused, but then her expression changed, and she smiled with glee. "Marvelous!" she cried. "At long last. I always knew you would take the veil one day. What a glorious nun you will make!" she clapped her hands together and then said soberly, "You have joined rather late, though."

Miss Boston was never sure when the Mother Superior was joking; she really had a most disconcerting sense of humor sometimes. "That isn't what I came for either," she stammered with embarrassment.

The Mother Superior waved an apologetic hand at her. "Forgive me," she chuckled, "couldn't resist it. Now, tell me what I can do for you."

"I was wondering if I might have a word with one of the novices here," Miss Boston asked.

"But of course," the Mother Superior replied. "That is, if I can find her. Which one is it? If it is Sister Clare or Sister Agnes you are after, I'm afraid you will be disappointed. Both are visiting the sick in hospital this afternoon."

Miss Boston gave an awkward cough. This was the difficult part—she had no idea who Jennet had seen on the cliff. "No, I don't think it was either of those two," she said slowly.

The Mother Superior smiled at her patiently. "Then who? Surely not Sister Frances—nobody ever wants to talk to her, not even me."

But Miss Boston was in no mood for this whimsy today. "I believe you have a novice staying with you who is not of your order," she said. "Would I be right in assuming she has not been here very long?"

"I find time a very difficult thing at my age," the Mother Superior breathed wistfully. "Before I know where I am, the year seems to get pulled from under me. I had no idea it was nearly September—it seems only last week we were celebrating Easter." She laughed and thumped her hands on the desk. "Are you sure you don't want to help with the rummage sale? The white-elephant stall still has no one to organize it, and Sister Frances refuses point-blank to abandon the raffle to run the dreadful thing."

Miss Boston watched her in surprise. Why was she avoiding the question? She asked it again.

The Mother Superior could not ignore it this time. "Not been here very long?" she repeated. "I don't thing there is . . ."

"You must be mistaken," snapped Aunt Alice, with force. What was the woman hiding? Did she know something of this business?

All the merriment left the nun's face; it was useless to pretend any longer. She pushed herself away from the desk and looked at the old lady warily. "Yes . . . there is one newly come among us," she answered in a cautious voice. "Sister Bridget."

"May I speak with her?" Miss Boston asked.

There was pause, and the small woman frowned as she solemnly considered the matter. She had not expected this. She had hoped her guest would have gone undetected. What if it all reached the ears of the bishop? The Mother Superior looked up to the window as if for inspiration, then, with her hands laced together, she stared at Aunt Alice and said softly, "Of course, I cannot forbid you to see Sister Bridget if that is what you wish, but may I know what the matter concerns?"

This was difficult. Miss Boston could hardly tell her what she suspected—and yet maybe the Mother Superior knew more about it than she did. "Shall I just say that it is of the gravest importance," she said. "I hope I shall not have to go to a higher authority."

A look of understanding passed between them, and the other sighed. "How much do you know of this?"

"A little," answered Miss Boston, "but I have also guessed a great deal."

The nun laid her hands on the table. "Let me explain before you confront her," she said. "Sister Bridget is a timid, frightened creature. I took her in because she needed my help—she has always needed our help."

"Always? Has she been here before?"

"Sister Bridget once lived in this convent, though long before I came here."

"But you've been here for forty years!" Miss Boston exclaimed.

"Yes," smiled the small woman, "but our records mention her." She gazed up at the window again, and the soft light fell on her face. "I recall that the previous Mother Superior warned me—very insistent she was—and sat me down in this same office to tell me. What an earful I had that day; she was a tough old bird, but she had the heart of a saint, and I have never forgotten what she said to me."

She closed her eyes and repeated, word for word, what she had been told all those years ago. "There are many wonders in this world, glories and miracles abound, yet there are also the unfortunate ones: the sick, the poor, and those who need our help. Surely these souls deserve our greatest love and care.

It is your sworn duty to give mercy and protection to any creature, however strange the circumstance."

The button eyes opened again and the smile returned. "I don't think I really understood what she was trying to tell me back then, but it was as if she were preparing me. Only now do I understand fully. I told you of the records, Miss Boston. Our files date back to 1738 and in the earliest of them—a tattered old thing it is, too—a Sister Bridget is mentioned."

"But surely it cannot be the same woman?"

"I am certain that it is," the nun said firmly. "I now know the whole of her tragic story." She shook herself and rose from her seat. "Come, then," she said, "let us see if we can find her."

She led Miss Boston out of her office and through the refectory hall, then into a corridor that smelled of floor polish. There were many doors on either side of the passage and these led to the small bare cells of the sisters.

When they reached one of the doors, the Mother Superior halted and raised her hand to knock. "This is the cell of Sister Bridget," she explained.

Miss Boston put her hands behind her back and waited for her to tap on the door. But instead the nun said, "Perhaps I have erred in taking her in again, but I did what I thought was best." She looked steadily at Aunt Alice. "Are we not all creatures of God?" she asked.

"Indeed we are," said Miss Boston gently, "and I'm sure it was the only Christian thing to do."

The Mother Superior gave a weak laugh. "So now I am her guardian, like all those before me."

Miss Boston rubbed her chin thoughtfully. "Do you know why she has returned?"

The small woman seemed about to speak, but she checked herself. "That you must ask her," she said and raised her hand once more. She knocked and entered the room beyond.

"It's all right, Sister," she said reassuringly to the figure in white who backed away, startled. "There's someone here who would like a word with you, that's all."

The novice looked fearfully over the Mother Superior's shoulder to see who the visitor was. When she saw that it was only an old lady, she relaxed and the hunted look left her face.

Miss Boston entered the room. It was so small that three of them were quite squashed inside it. It contained the absolute minimum of comforts: a bed, a wooden chair, and a table. There was a Bible open on the table, and Aunt Alice cast her eyes over the passage Sister Bridget had been reading.

And God created the great whales and every living and moving creature that the waters brought forth, according to their kinds, and every winged fowl according to its kind. And God saw that it was good.

"Shall I leave you two alone?" asked the Mother Superior.

The novice glanced at Miss Boston curiously and then nodded.

"Very well then, I'll be just outside."

The door closed.

Miss Boston smiled. "I'm afraid we haven't been introduced," she said. "I know that you are called Sister Bridget. My name is Alice Boston—delighted to meet you."

The novice did not respond. She eyed the stranger doubtfully then sat down, motioning for the old lady to do the same.

Miss Boston perched on the hard bed. The woman was obviously still very unsure of her, but then the feeling was mutual. Now that they were alone she looked at the novice with undisguised interest and realized just how strange she actually was. Those almond-shaped eyes glittered like nothing she had ever seen before, and the curiously wide mouth was hardly human. But that was not all. Aunt Alice blinked and took a second look. A faint green light surrounded the woman, so pale that at first she thought it was her imagination. No, it was definitely there—for those who could see.

"May I ask you some questions?" she inquired politely.

There was no reply; the novice merely stared dumbly at her.

It would take more than that, however, to put Miss Boston off. She cleared her throat. "I think I know who you are," she said.

The woman made no answer.

"I should like to know why you have come back to Whitby after all this time," continued the old lady, "and I should also like to know what Rowena Cooper has said to you."

Again there was nothing, but the novice had tensed on hearing that name.

"You see," Miss Boston carried on, "I believe you know who she really is and what she is looking for—she has come to Whitby to find something, hasn't she? Would that be the same thing you are seeking? I hope you are not planning to help her." She leaned forward and the loose flesh under her chin quivered with passion. "Rowena is a dangerous woman," she said. "Two of my friends are already dead. If there is anything you can tell me that will prove her guilt, you cannot withhold it. Rowena must be stopped before anyone else perishes!"

The novice lowered her eyes. "I cannot help you," she said quietly.

"There is no such word as *cannot,*" Aunt Alice retorted. "Say what you mean, tell me that you will not! Let me hear you condemn another poor soul to Rowena's cruelty."

The novice shrank back from the force of the old lady's outburst. Her whole frame shook with fear, and she hid her face. "I cannot help you," she wailed.

Miss Boston regained her self-control and puffed out her cheeks. "I'm sorry, my dear," she apologized. "I did not mean to frighten you." She realized that further conversation was useless; the woman was too afraid to talk. Wearily she crossed to the door. "I hope you can live with yourself when all is done," she said.

In the corridor, the Mother Superior asked nervously, "Did she tell you what you wanted?"

"No, she told me nothing."

"I am sorry," she said earnestly. "Perhaps it has all got out of hand. Things are not as simple as once they were. I'm terribly afraid for Sister Bridget—the danger she faces increases every day. The good Lord alone knows how she managed to return here without being discovered, the poor creature."

Miss Boston slung her scarf around her neck. "I fear that there are many in danger because of her refusal to speak. I don't know what I am to do now. There is evil at work in this town, and it is steadily growing in strength."

The Mother Superior clasped her hands together. "God go with you," she said.

Aunt Alice received the blessing gravely. "I believe I may need all the guidance He can give," she said.

She was not under the chair, nor hiding on top of the wardrobe as she sometimes did. She was not even in the airing cupboard. Miss Droon was exasperated with the bothersome animal and threw Binky down in disgust. It had happened again. Eurydice was missing.

Tilly had only nipped to the post office to have a word with Edith, but unfortunately one of the windows in the kitchen had been left open. Miss Droon knew at once that Eurydice had made a dash for it, but that did not stop her turning the house upside down just in case.

Her little sitting room was a hopeless wreck, the threadbare cushions had been yanked off the chairs, the contents of the cupboards were strewn over the carpet, and the tall pile of wildlife magazines that had once towered in the corner now resembled a colorful volcano.

The rest of Miss Droon's menagerie knew enough to get out of her way when this frenzied panic seized her. Under the table cowered a dozen felines, their squabbles momentarily forgotten. Their green and golden eyes watched the whiskered woman dart in and out until, finally, she threw herself at the cushionless couch.

From the upstairs bedroom, pathetic little mews wailed.

"Oh, the poor darlings," cried Tilly. "How could she leave them again?"

The truth of the matter was that Eurydice would have needed the nose of a tracker dog to find out where her newest offspring were. Tilly was continually moving them. Either it was too cold in the kitchen at night, or she was afraid of jealous attacks from the others if they were left unsupervised in the sitting room. The poor, bewildered kittens had seen every inch of her poky house by now, and Eurydice had given up trying to discover where they had been deposited. Every time she got out of the basket to have a drink or something to eat, Miss Droon came along and whisked it away.

Now the kittens were in the bedroom, and in her frantic search for their mother, Tilly had completely forgotten about them.

"All God's little fishes!" she cried as she galumphed up the stairs to rescue the little dears from their loneliness.

The small, furry bundles huddled together in the basket when the bedroom door flew open and the Droon whirlwind gusted in. She scooped up the kittens in her arms and rubbed her furry cheeks against their little bodies.

"There, there," she said dotingly, "don't you worry now, Aunt Tilly's here." After a few minutes of her suffocating cuddles, she returned them to the basket and decided it ought to be moved downstairs once more.

The kittens peered dizzily over the side of the basket as she carried it down to the kitchen. "You must be starving, poor darlings," Miss Droon purred at them. She heated some milk in a saucepan and waited for it to cool. Then she rummaged in a drawer for an old eyedropper that she used to feed them in these emergencies.

It was a long, laborious business, and most of the milk went everywhere except in the kittens' mouths, but in the end, they seemed satisfied enough. Her inept feeding technique had exhausted them, and one by one they fell asleep.

Miss Droon was pleased with herself. "That's right, darlings," she whispered. "You get forty winks, my darlings."

She eyed the basket uncertainly. Perhaps it would be warmer
in the bedroom after all. Before she could make up her mind,
she became aware of a faint scratching sound. It was coming
from the front door, and, with a scowl, Miss Droon strode
into the hall—she knew exactly what that noise was.

She opened the door and sure enough, there was Eurydice.

"You wicked thing!" Tilly exclaimed. "Just where have
you been?"

The three-legged cat darted between her feet and ran into
the sitting room.

"Oh no you don't, my girl," blustered Miss Droon. "You
don't get off that easily. I've looked high and low for you."

Eurydice leaped into one of the open cupboards and curled
around with her back to the world. She was carrying something in her mouth and now she put it down to have a good
sniff and inspection. What an afternoon it had been—she
had got no peace anywhere. Even her favorite refuge was no
longer safe, for the smell of dog was strong there. Still at least
she had managed to find this intriguing little tidbit.

"Got you! You little madam!" Miss Droon's strong hands
closed about her, and she pulled the cat out of the cupboard.

Eurydice mewed in protest, but Miss Droon took no
notice.

"You bad girl!" she scolded. "It's time you lived up to your
responsibilities. From now on, I'm going to lock you in my
room with your babies."

She began taking the squirming cat out into the hall, but
then she noticed the strange object that had fallen to the floor.

"What's this?" she murmured, stooping to pick it up. Eurydice's trophy was extremely unusual. It appeared to be a weirdly shaped piece of wood and parchment that had been dipped in wax at one end and set in a small pewter holder at the other. The whole thing was very small and light. Miss Droon examined it thoughtfully. She assumed that the wooden part was a carving of some kind that had been covered in parchment, for some reason, and perhaps had held a candle. Now though, it was all a mangled mess, except for the ring of metal fixed around the base. Hammered into that were symbols and hieroglyphs that made up a bizarre pattern.

She glared accusingly at the cat under her arm. "Where did you find this, you naughty girl?" she demanded. Of course there was no answer. Suddenly Tilly gave a little shriek. "Did you go to Mrs. Cooper's house this afternoon? Is that where you got it?"

What was she to do? The artifact was probably a valuable antique from Mrs. Cooper's shop.

"Oh, Eurydice," she said, "just look at it—you've spoiled the ruddy thing." Miss Droon was very worried: if Rowena noticed that it was missing she might phone the police. "I'm an accessory to theft," she moaned, and visions of tall policemen knocking on her door flooded through her mind. She would have to go to court. What if they suspected her of training Eurydice especially for crime?

"Matilda Droon, head of the cat burglars," she mumbled idiotically.

Eurydice wriggled to free herself, and her desperate movements brought Miss Droon to her senses.

"I must take this back to Mrs. Cooper at once," she said to herself. "Maybe I could offer to pay for it. I hope it wasn't too expensive."

She went into the kitchen, where she stuffed the troublesome cat into the basket with her kittens.

"I'm going to lock you in my room," she said as she pounded up the stairs with her precious cargo. "Now you just stay in there and look after your babies." Tilly slammed the door. "And behave!" she added.

Wearing her dark blue, cat-haired sweater, Miss Droon ran out of the house and made for the 199 steps.

She hated toiling up the wretched things. Halfway up, she had to rest and sat on one of the benches to regain her breath. The steps were quite busy just now. People in bright anoraks swinging cameras were descending and gave the panting figure on the bench pitying looks as they passed by. It was nearly teatime, and everyone was returning to the main part of town to find a shop or restaurant. Tilly watched them go by, keeping the strange little artifact tucked under her jumper where no one could see it.

When her breather was over, she hauled herself to her feet once more and resumed the uphill slog.

"Never again," she spluttered, once the summit had been reached. "That cat will be the death of me."

Miss Droon trotted through the graveyard and out into the car park behind the abbey. The chill of evening wrapped around her as she hurried along the lane to Rowena's house.

The Hawes looked blank and dreary as she approached. It was a cheerless, uninviting place, and she wondered how Rowena could bear to live in it. She opened the gate and crossed to the large window of the antique shop. With her hand shading her eyes as she pressed against the glass, Miss Droon stared inside.

Nothing stirred; the shop was closed. She pattered around to the kitchen door and knocked loudly, waited for a minute or so, then knocked again.

"She must be out," Miss Droon muttered, disappointedly. She took a few steps back and looked up at the first-floor windows. A movement at one of them caught her attention; a net curtain was swinging back into position as though it had just been released. Was someone in, after all? Were they peeking out to see who had been knocking and stepped back suddenly when she looked up?

Miss Droon stroked her moustache. "Should I knock again?" she wondered. "Maybe Rowena was having a nap, and I've disturbed her." She knew how annoying it was to be woken up—Eurydice often jumped on her stomach in the middle of the night. "Yes," she decided, "I've come all this way up them perishing steps. She'll just have to come down."

She took the object out from beneath her sweater and tutted at the fluff that was now stuck to it. "Damn it," she cursed.

Expecting Mrs. Cooper to open the door at any moment, Miss Droon hastily began picking off the fluff. She was none too gentle at the task, for, as Alice Boston had often said, she really was ham-fisted. Then it happened. As she dug her nails into the wax to remove a stubborn hairy bundle, she pulled too hard. There was brittle "snap" and a large fragment flew over the garden fence.

"Blast!" she yelped. "What have I done?" She brought the thing up to her face and lifted the black-rimmed spectacles off her nose to get a better look at the damage.

A wide section of parchment had been torn off, revealing more of the wooden carving beneath. Miss Droon shook her head and groaned. "You idiot, Matilda!" she hissed.

But then the recrimination died in her throat. She peered closer and her eyes opened wide. Tilly nearly screamed as she recognized at last the foul thing in her hand.

What she had assumed to be carved wood was in fact finger bones and the parchment was dried human skin. The object Eurydice had brought out of Mrs. Cooper's house was the stolen Hand of Glory!

There was very little of it left. Most of the fingers were missing and it was almost unrecognizable. With a sickening shock, Miss Droon realized that it must have been used. She remembered how Mrs. Banbury-Scott's house had been ransacked the night before her death, although no one had heard a thing—this grisly charm was the reason why.

She threw it down in disgust and glanced nervously at the kitchen door. "My God," she breathed, "it was Rowena!"

Tilly ran down the path and out of the gate. Her mind was in a turmoil of fright and confusion. What was she to do? Everything seemed to fall into place now. Rowena's interest in Mrs. Banbury-Scott's house and the way she had ingratiated herself into the fat woman's affections all snapped together. Hidden in that old house was something that Rowena was prepared to steal. Miss Droon gasped. Not only that: Rowena had probably killed Mrs. Banbury-Scott after that night of desperate searching had failed to yield what she was after.

Tilly stumbled down the lane, horrified at these sudden revelations. Rowena had even persuaded Mrs. Banbury-Scott to change her will, and so she had signed her own death warrant in the process. Just what had been in those special chocolates Rowena had force-fed her with?

"Damn, damn," Tilly wailed. "Alice was right all the time!"

At The Hawes, a short figure with an evil, leering face slipped out of the kitchen and hurried after the elderly woman. She had reached the steps and was striding down them. "I must tell Alice," she wheezed to herself. "She'll know what to do."

Dusk had crept up over Whitby. There was no one about now; all had gone in search of food. In the town, the cafés were alive with light and the happy chatter of contented families, but the streets were deserted.

Tilly was nearly at the bottom of the steps. She took the last three in one jump and set off down Church Street. Her bristled face showed her fear, and her footsteps were quick and nervous. Miss Boston's cottage was not far, just through this opening and—

Miss Droon halted, turned her head and listened. What was that?

Above the heaving of her breath, a plaintive whine echoed down the street. It was a high-pitched wail, like that of a small child. Tilly uttered a cry of pity—that was no child; it was the sound of a cat in pain.

The pitiful mewling continued and Tilly's heart ached as she recognized the voice. It was Eurydice! Somewhere her beloved Eurydice was suffering. It was as if someone was deliberately torturing the poor animal.

"Eurydice, darling!" she shouted. "Stay where you are, Mommy's coming."

Forgetting everything else, Miss Droon hurried up the road, tormented by the dismal shrieks that beckoned her on.

Tears sprang to her eyes. How could anyone hurt a small creature like this? It was horrible to hear.

"Leave her alone!" she bawled as the cries became more urgent. "Stop it, you bully, she hasn't done any harm."

The cat was almost squealing now. Miss Droon could not bear it; she hurried along into Henrietta Street with her hands over her ears.

On she sped toward that hideous screech, down the narrow street that ended at the cliff edge. The unnatural, piercing sound drew her forward; it had reached inside and taken command of her reason. Nothing could hold her back from finding Eurydice, not even the wire fence that prevented the unwary tourist from straying too near to the sheer drop.

Tilly pulled herself through this obstacle. She was sobbing with anguish for her loved one and did not feel the wire rake through her hair and scratch her legs. Only the life of Eurydice was important—she simply had to save her.

The wind was strong on the cliff edge, buffeting against her, and Miss Droon swayed back unsteadily. Desperately, she cast around for any sign of her cat but could only hear the crashing of the sea far below and the rushing of the wind in the grass. The crying had stopped.

"Eurydice?" she called. "Eurydice?" But there was no answer. She wept into her sleeve. The madness that had spurred her to this deadly spot was ebbing away now, and she glanced around miserably. There was nowhere for the cat to hide: the grass was short, and there was no cover anywhere.

Miss Droon was puzzled. Why had the noise stopped? There was no sign of either Eurydice or her torturer. An awful thought crept up on her: what if the poor creature had fallen?

In her panic, Eurydice might have fled away from her attacker and not realized until too late that . . .

It was too terrible to contemplate. Anything that fell from that dizzying height would be smashed to pieces on the jagged rocks below. Tilly felt ill, and the strength left her legs. Her sobs choked her as she plucked up enough courage to peer over the edge, preparing herself for the distant sight of a small, furry body floating on the water.

The ground was treacherously soft and spongy as she stepped up to the precipitous brink. The wind sang in her ears and tried to drag her back, but she had to know. Standing on the very edge of the cliff, Miss Droon stared down.

"No!" she screamed.

Directly beneath her, clinging to the vertical cliff face like a spider on the wall, was Rowena Cooper. It was impossible for anyone to do that. No human being could hold on so effortlessly, so casually. Tilly stared at her, stricken with horror.

Rowena threw back her head and looked up. "Meow," she cried mockingly, and the voice was identical to Eurydice's.

Tilly whimpered as she tried to understand. Eurydice must still be safe at home. Rowena had impersonated her to lure Miss Droon to the cliff edge—but why?

Even as the question formed in her mind, Rowena scuttled further up the sheer cliff and stretched out a clawlike hand. It grabbed Tilly's ankle and gripped it fiercely.

"No, no!" she cried in terror.

Rowena laughed into the wind. "Fool!" she scorned, and Tilly knew she was finished as the evil, derisive laughter cut through her.

"Look what the cat's dragged in!" cackled Rowena as she pulled viciously.

Tilly's leg was snatched from under her, and, with a last shriek, she toppled over the cliff and plummeted downward. Far below, the pounding waves surged and crashed, but the air above was filled with raucous, uncontrollable laughter.

CHAPTER ELEVEN

THE HALF-CHILD

Rachel Turner anxiously surveyed the morning room; it was the best she could do until the workmen arrived. The house of the late Mrs. Banbury-Scott was still in chaos, for the damage wrought by those mysterious burglars had not yet been repaired. The large holes in the floor had been temporarily covered with boards by Grice, the scarred oak paneling had been cunningly hidden by pictures and tapestries, but the beautiful old fireplace was ruined. It had taken an awful lot of elbow grease to make the place even remotely habitable again.

The terms of Mrs. Banbury-Scott's will were plain: Rowena Cooper inherited not only the house, but also the servants if she desired. So far she had shown no sign of wishing otherwise.

Rachel patted a cushion into place and went to join Mrs. Rigpath in the hallway. Ayleen Rigpath was a stout woman who bustled about her kitchen with her sleeves rolled up and her face covered in flour, jam, or whatever it was she happened to be making. For twelve years now, she had cooked for Mrs. Banbury-Scott, and she was not happy at the prospect of a new employer. She was not one to try out fancy new recipes; her menus had stayed the same for as long as she had been there and if this Mrs. Cooper didn't like them, well, she would have to find someone else.

"I can't do no more in there," Rachel said.

Mrs. Rigpath sniffed impatiently. "Grice has been gone a while; he ought to be back with her by now. How much longer do we have to stand here?"

Rachel sighed. "I've been dreadin' this, you know. I'm not sure if I like that Mrs. Cooper—don't know what the Madam saw in her."

Ayleen puffed out her chest and folded her arms. I'll give her three weeks," she said dryly. "If she hasn't shaped up by then, I'm off. I'll have enough to retire on, what with the money I have left."

"You're lucky—I didn't get very much."

"I'm not lucky," Mrs. Rigpath replied bitterly. "Just look at me: fifty-three years old, no husband, no kiddies, and no home to call me own—some luck that is."

Rachel had often wondered how someone with Mrs. Rigpath's talent for making delicious desserts could be so utterly sour for most of the time. Such questions had to wait, however, for at that moment both women heard the sound of tires on gravel.

"About time," grumbled Ayleen. "S'pose we'd better get on with it."

The Bentley pulled up outside the great, gray house, and Grice dutifully stepped out to open the door for its passenger. Rowena Cooper wore one of the widest smiles he had ever seen. She had been grinning on the back seat all the way from The Hawes.

"Thank you," the woman murmured as he helped her out. For a moment, Rowena stood quite still. At last, she thought to herself, this ugly pile of stone belongs to me. With a satisfied smirk, she crossed to the front door, where her new staff was waiting to greet her.

"Welcome, Mrs. Cooper," began Rachel cheerfully. Rowena eyed both her and Mrs. Rigpath icily. "I wish to see you all in the morning room in ten minutes' time," she said. And with that she pushed past them and strode down the hall.

Mrs. Rigpath stared after her, open-mouthed. "Well, I never did!" she exclaimed. "I might not give her those three weeks' trial after all."

"Expect she's nervous," said Rachel. "Probably never had staff before."

Grice slammed the door of the Bentley and came indoors. "Bad accident down by the cliffs," he told them. "Ambulance and police were there."

"What happened?" asked Rachel.

"That Miss Droon—found her body this mornin', they did. Seems she fell off the edge some time last night."

"Poor soul," said Rachel sadly. "She was dotty about them cats of hers, wasn't she? I wonder what'll happen to them now."

Mrs. Rigpath, however, was considering a different mystery. "Didn't Mrs. Cooper bring no luggage, then?" she asked curiously. "Is she not staying tonight?"

In the morning room, Rowena positioned herself in front of the covered fireplace and glanced around. "Somewhere here," she whispered. "I know it has to be here! I don't care if

I have to demolish this vile place and sift through the rubble, I *must* have it. Somewhere in this disgusting relic, concealed for centuries from prying eyes—"

"Excuse me, Mrs. Cooper."

Rowena turned around, startled. "Yes?"

Rachel smiled at her from the doorway. "Ten minutes has gone, Madam."

Rowena nodded coldly. "Come in."

The three staff filed into the morning room.

Rowena began loftily, "What I have to say is merely this: I'm afraid that I have decided against keeping you all on. Now, I know that you were all provided for in dear Dora's will, so this news will be no real blow—I'm sure you will all manage quite admirably."

There was a stunned silence. Rachel stared around at the room she had spent the past few days clearing up and shook her head in disbelief. Grice rubbed his frowning forehead and muttered to himself, while Mrs. Rigpath bristled and her chest inflated as she prepared to give vent to a tirade of abuse and a mighty dollop of her mind. Before she could let loose one single syllable, however, Rowena raised a hand and delivered another devastating piece of news.

"Naturally I shall not expect you to remain here. You must vacate your rooms by tomorrow afternoon, at the latest. Now you may go."

"Tomorrow?" spluttered Rachel, and Mrs. Rigpath was too shocked even to protest.

"I believe that is reasonable," said Rowena. "After all, I have no contract with you to uphold. Now I think you had better start packing. Good day."

Later that afternoon, Rachel struggled down the stairs with her suitcases. She wasn't going to spend another minute in that house. Mrs. Rigpath was still in her room, wondering where she could go, and Grice was sitting in the shed, dolefully gazing at the gleaming tools he must leave behind.

The cellars of the old house were filled with the accumulated junk of centuries: armchairs, lampshades, picture frames, empty tea chests, bundles of newspapers bound with string, hideous jugs, cracked vases, a moldy leather flying helmet complete with goggles, a metal gauntlet from a suit of armor, and many other bits of useless rubbish.

A naked lightbulb glared from the vaulted ceiling, throwing stark shadows onto the walls, but Rowena had no time to notice them. With a torch in her hand, she peered into the dark corners and pulled boxes and papers roughly aside.

Cobwebs netted her short blonde hair, and the disturbed dust glued itself to the fine, sticky strands. The grime from years of neglect streaked down her face as she drew her grubby hands over her brow. Insects who had never seen the light fled in terror as the fierce torch beam shone into their dark territories. Brittle beetle backs crunched beneath Rowena's careless feet as she waded deeper into the junk mounds, swearing, and shrieking with impatience.

"Where is it?" she screamed. "Where?"

With unrelenting violence she flung everything aside, then began tapping the walls with the handle of her torch. For an hour, she paced about the cellar, picking at the bricks with her broken fingernails and clawing at the mortar to see if there were any hidden doors or passageways.

When she was satisfied that the walls and floors were solid and free of any secret openings, Rowena stomped up the cellar steps. "It must be somewhere here!" she growled.

In a wild fit of temper, she threw herself against the paneled walls of the hall and snatched down the tapestries and pictures that were hiding the damage from the break-in. She scraped her fingers down the splintered wood and peered into the space between it and the bricks beyond. But the holes were too few and too small for her to see properly.

"If I have to demolish the vile place . . ." Her own words returned to haunt her, and she dashed outside to the shed.

The unquestionable kingdom of Grice was an outbuilding situated against the rear wall of the garden. It was a small stone hut, probably as old as the house itself, with one narrow window. The solid oak door was hung on rusting iron hinges and needed a good shove to open.

Grice was still there when Rowena forced her way in. She stared at him for a moment as if she had forgotten there was anyone in the world apart from herself. And in his turn, Grice stared at her: she looked as though she had been having a dust bath.

"Axe," she demanded. "Give me an axe."

The ex-handyman had never lent his beloved tools to anyone before, but then, they didn't really belong to him any more. Garden shears, hammers, and rakes hung, clean and polished, in tidy rows on the plastered walls. Every conceivable implement was there, and he took a great pride in keeping them all in mint condition.

"What fer you want an axe?" he asked slowly.

Rowena drew herself up. "That is none of your concern," she snarled. "Give it to me!"

Grice removed the gleaming axe from its hook on the wall and passed it over in silence. Rowena snatched at it and charged back to the house. With a crazed yell, she brought the axe blade crashing down into the oak panels. Fragments of splitting wood filled the air as she hewed and chopped. A mad light was in her eyes, and she was consumed by the desire to destroy.

"It will be mine!" she cried. "It must be mine!"

In her room, Mrs. Rigpath the cook heard the terrible noise and changed her mind about not wanting to leave. "Perhaps it is for the best after all," she told herself. "That Cooper woman's definitely off her rocker."

Ben stared out of his bedroom window. It looked down on Aunt Alice's little garden, where a fat blackbird was stealing the raspberries that grew against the cottage wall. Beyond, the steep grassy slope of the cliffside reared up over the rooftops and melted into the afternoon haze.

The boy rolled over onto his bed and glared at the primroses on the wallpaper. He was bored and in a foul mood. Ever since that night on the beach when the evil aufwader had attacked him, Ben had been forbidden to go out after dark. Of course, he had complained and protested—what about Nelda and Hesper? He had an important part to play in the hunt for the moonkelp, for, according to Nelda's vision, without him they would be unable to find it. Miss Boston, however, had stood firm on this; on no account was he to leave the house at night—it was far too dangerous out there now.

So Ben had suffered indoors all this time, without even a chance to tell Nelda about her father. In the daytime, he had roamed along the shore and searched on the cliff top but had not been able to find her. It was so unfair; they probably thought he was deliberately avoiding them.

Miserably, Ben sucked his top lip. At first, he had appealed to Jennet to help him slip out, but that had been a big mistake, for she had immediately told Aunt Alice. After that, they doubled their efforts to keep him indoors at night, making sure that when he went to bed he stayed safely in his room. It was like being a prisoner when the evening fell, and he hated it. He could not even go to the toilet without one of his jailers keeping an ear open.

He pushed his hand under the pillow and fished out the ammonite he had found. Idly, he turned it over in his fingers. "Poor Nelda," he murmured. "She must think I don't care. What if the moonkelp has bloomed while I've been stuck in here? They'll never get the curse lifted if that's happened."

The door to his room opened, and Jennet looked in. "Aunt Alice isn't back yet," she told him, "so what do you want for tea?"

Ben shrugged. "Nothin'," he mumbled.

"Fine by me," his sister answered. She was fed up with his sulks—he had to learn that he could not go off on his own any more. She closed the door and went downstairs. The boy stuck his tongue out at the closed door and muttered rebelliously to himself.

Jennet returned to the parlor where she had been reading a book on the history of Whitby. She didn't feel hungry either. It had been a sad, quiet day. They had heard the tragic news about Miss Droon the first thing that morning, and Aunt

Alice had wept a great deal. Nearly all her friends were gone now, and Jennet felt very sorry for her. After a while, Miss Boston went around to see how Edith Wethers was taking the news, and they mourned their loss together. Whitby had become a very sad place since the arrival of Rowena Cooper.

With a sigh, Jennet sat back in the armchair and picked up the book once more. The hours passed slowly. She stifled several yawns and tried to keep awake. The book waded stodgily through names and events over the centuries, from Hilda to Scoresby, Caedmon to Cook, listing them all with dry detail. Wearily she flicked through its pages, skipping over Whitby's whaling days and a horrible account of the lifeboat disaster. A small passage told how the abbey had been damaged in World War I by two German cruisers that opened fire on the town, but there were no pictures to enliven the dreary text, and Jennet's eyelids slid down heavily. Into the subconscious murk of dreams she sank; whales burst out of the sea and exploding shellfire lit the sky.

With a jolt, Jennet snapped awake. The light outside had failed, and the parlor was filled with shadow. She looked at the grandfather clock: she had been asleep for nearly two hours.

An empty rumble echoed through her stomach, and she decided that it was time to eat. "Ben must be starved," she tutted as she went into the hall.

"Do you want your tea now, Ben?" she called up the stairs. There was no reply. "Stop sulking," she shouted. "I'm doing some beans on toast if you're interested." There was still no sound. Jennet was suddenly suspicious. She ran up to his bedroom and flung open the door. It was empty.

He must have gone out when I was asleep, she told herself. Just wait till I catch him! But she was more afraid than angry. Somewhere, Ben was alone in the dark.

Jennet charged down the stairs, plucked her coat off the hanger, and dashed out of the front door. She had no idea where Ben could be, but she ran to the beach and called his name. Only the rush of the incoming tide answered her. The shore was empty of people, so Jennet ran over the bridge to the West Cliff and searched in all the amusement arcades. It was no good—Ben was nowhere to be found.

The girl left the deafening roar of the amusements and sat on one of the benches at the wharf. The fishing boats bobbed on the black, calm water below, and a group of gulls rode the gentle waves. Jennet watched them in despair. What if her brother had met that evil aufwader again? She raised her head to look at the floodlit ruin of the abbey and the squat shape of the church. Then she blinked and looked again; in the cemetery stood a shining white figure whose robes blazed like flames.

Jennet rose. For a moment, the legend of St. Hilda flitted through her mind. Aunt Alice had told her that sometimes the bright outline of the abbess could be seen in one of the abbey windows, but this figure was in the churchyard.

Suddenly Jennet realized that she was looking at the novice up there. Sister Bridget was deliberately standing in front of the arc lights. It did not make any sense; Jennet could not imagine why that timid, frightened woman should draw attention to herself like that.

The distant, radiant figure stretched out her arms. The glare of the arc lights bounced off her robes and dazzled the girl far below on the wharfside.

"She's beckoning to me," Jennet murmured in astonishment. "She wants me to go up there. Perhaps she knows what's happened to Ben."

Jennet ran to the bridge and sped over it. She was excited yet afraid, knowing that the novice had left the safety of the convent that night, not to weep at the sea but to speak to her. Maybe it was a warning; perhaps Rowena had threatened her again and let slip something about Ben. Jennet tried to forget the terror she had felt the last time she had gone to that churchyard in the dark. But the image of the hound as it pounced on her was ingrained in her mind, and the nearer she drew to the 199 steps, the clearer that memory became.

She hurried down Church Street where the usual well-fed tourists were wandering happily before the darkened shop windows—a last stroll to aid their digestion and tire the children. What a pleasant time they were having, blissfully unaware of the evil that haunted this picturesque town by night. Their smiling faces annoyed Jennet. They saw only what they came to see; the sinister side of Whitby did not interest them. Even if they had been disturbed by the chilling cries of the Barguest as it howled into the night, they chose to ignore it and rolled over in their cozy guesthouse beds, dreaming of kippers for breakfast.

Jennet became impatient as she squeezed between the chatting families who idly gabbed and blocked the road. If only they knew; if only they had seen those hellish eyes.

"Excuse me," she said, pushing through the crowd. "Excuse me."

It seemed that everyone had decided to pop out that evening and dawdle about on Church Street. Jennet grew anxious. What if the novice could not wait for her?

A particularly tight knot of people barred her way to the steps. She tried to dodge in between, but it was very difficult, and she was forced to push quite roughly to get by.

"Do you mind!" snapped a woman whose heel she had just stepped on.

Jennet plowed on, oblivious. She wormed and elbowed her way to the steps, and just as she began to climb the steps, a hand caught her arm.

"Where's the fire?" demanded a voice.

The girl turned around, and there was Aunt Alice. The old lady looked tired, for it had been a long and dismal day for her. Those birdlike eyes were red and swollen, a testament to her grief over Tilly's death. She had spent most of the afternoon with Edith Wethers, then had gone to feed Miss Droon's ravenous cats, and had had an argument with a policeman on the way. Nobody wanted to investigate poor Tilly's death— to the police and Doctor Adams, she was just another old woman who had missed her footing. Miss Boston had grown very angry and retorted in the doctor's face, "That's three old women in as many weeks. Doesn't that arouse the slightest suspicion in you, for heaven's sake, you dithering old quack?" Needless to say, she was guided to the door.

To cool her head and sort out her thoughts, she had decided to walk to the cliff before returning home, and that was when she saw Jennet rampaging through the crowd like a bull elephant.

"Whatever is the matter, Jennet dear?" she asked. "What's the hurry, and where is Benjamin?"

Jennet was so relieved to see her that she threw her arms about the old lady's neck. "Ben's missing," she said quickly.

"I fell asleep, and when I woke up, he had gone. I looked everywhere for him—on the beach, in the arcades—and then I saw the novice."

"Sister Bridget?"

"Yes, she's up there now. She was standing right in front of the lights and I'd swear she was beckoning to me."

Miss Boston frowned and looked up the steps. "Most peculiar," she said. "I wonder if she has changed her mind? Come, let us see if she can throw any light on Benjamin's whereabouts."

Together they began the long upward climb. The full moon appeared from behind the scudding night clouds and bathed the graveyard in silver. The headstones were edged with the pale, milky light, and Jennet wavered on the edge of the cemetery—it looked more ghostly there than ever before. What if the hound appeared again? She gulped and held back; to cross the path and enter that place needed more courage than she thought she possessed. But the plump figure of Aunt Alice trotted on ahead, and the sight of her spurred Jennet forward.

The church of St. Mary seemed to fill the night. The arc lights gave to its solid, square walls a warm, golden glow that made it look like a magical, gilded fortress.

Miss Boston shielded her eyes from the bright lights and glanced around. Sister Bridget was nowhere to be seen. "Are you sure she was here?" she asked Jennet.

"Yes, I'm positive."

The old lady chewed her lip. "Maybe she was afraid to remain in the light for too long," she said thoughtfully. "Unless, of course, she was seen by someone other than yourself."

"You mean Rowena?"

Aunt Alice merely raised her eyebrows. "Who can tell?" she said. "Perhaps a group of visitors walked past and startled her." She rubbed her eyes and wandered down the path. "Come out of those blinding lamps, child," she said. "I do not wish to be seen either."

They walked around the church and left the arc lights behind. For a while, colored swirls danced before their eyes until they became accustomed to the dark once more. Jennet halted and stared out to sea. There, by the cemetery wall stood the novice. She nudged Miss Boston, and the old lady squinted keenly.

Sister Bridget was looking straight at them. Her hands were clasped tightly before her, and the look of worry on her face lifted only momentarily with the relief of seeing them. She took a few hesitant steps forward and then stopped to look around nervously.

Aunt Alice and Jennet approached slowly, careful not to frighten her. The novice looked warily at the shadows beyond and put her hands to her mouth. "Hurry!" she called. "There is little time!"

Jennet and Miss Boston were surprised by her uncharacteristic outburst and wondered what she had to say.

"I must talk with you," Sister Bridget told them urgently.

"Do I take it that you have changed your mind?" asked Miss Boston.

She nodded. "You were right—forgive me. When I heard about the death of your friend this morning, I knew that I could keep silent no longer. I do not want the blood of innocents on my hands. Too many have already died, and the toll will rise if she finds what she seeks."

"I presume you refer to Mrs. Cooper?" said Aunt Alice.

Sister Bridget shuddered and turned her head to be sure they were alone. "Listen to me," she whispered in a rush. "That woman is dangerous. Beware of her, shun her in the street, have nothing to do with her. I have looked into her heart and found it black and rotten, while pure evil courses in her veins."

Jennet did not like this sort of talk. She felt uncomfortable when the novice's eyes fell upon her; the urgency and dread in them was alarming. Silently she took hold of Aunt Alice's hand.

Miss Boston listened to Sister Bridget's words but rejected her warnings. "I have no intention of skulking about," she declared. "The time has come to confront Mrs. Cooper. If the police refuse to listen to me, I shall have to do it myself. She must be stopped!"

The novice took hold of the old lady's shoulders. "You must not cross her!" she cried. "It is perilous to allow even so much as her shadow to touch you. She is too powerful an adversary for one such as you."

Aunt Alice took a deep breath. "I might just surprise her if she tries to do away with me," she snorted. "I haven't lived ninety-two years for nothing, you know."

"Hear me!" shouted Sister Bridget. "I am aware that you are not like others, but whatever talent you may think you have, whatever source you draw from, know now that Rowena Cooper is beyond your strength. She has transcended her human flesh and surrendered humanity to the powers of the dark. Take my advice, old woman: leave her to those best suited for such a task."

Miss Boston stroked Jennet's hair as the girl pressed closer to her. "Are you referring to yourself?" she asked with a laugh in her voice. "I'm sorry, but so far you have not shown much aptitude in that direction. Besides, I have faith in my gifts."

The novice lowered her eyes. "I have found that faith is not enough," she murmured. "Not for me, at least."

Aunt Alice smiled and said gently, "Did your trust in God fail, I wonder, or was it faith in yourself that you lacked?" She touched Sister Bridget's downcast face and asked, "How long have you hidden yourself away, little one? How many years have you wept alone? A convent is no place for a child to grow up. What a wretched life you have led."

A tear sparkled on the novice's cheek, and she hastily wiped it away. "Then you do know my history," she said. "Who told you?"

"Well, I confess that Benjamin told me some of it, but I guessed the rest."

"Benjamin?" repeated Sister Bridget. "That is the boy child's name? He searches with the aufwaders along the shore, does he not? Have the prime laws altered? Do humans consort freely with the fisher folk now? Was all my suffering in vain?"

Jennet pulled herself away from the folds of Aunt Alice's cloak. She did not understand. Did Sister Bridget have the sight, too? "What do you know about my brother?" she asked. "Have you seen him tonight—is he with those things again?" Miss Boston tried to shush her, but Jennet would not be kept quiet. "One of those creatures tried to kill him. If you know where he is, you must tell me."

The corners of Sister Bridget's mouth twitched into a slight smile. "I do not know where your brother is," she said.

For some reason Aunt Alice began apologizing to her. "I'm so sorry," she said hurriedly. "Jennet does not know. I'm sure she would not have—"

The novice held up her hand and broke in. "It is nothing. I have heard worse descriptions and from those with wiser heads on their shoulders."

Jennet looked at Aunt Alice, confused by all this—had she offended the woman in some way?

Sister Bridget smiled at her. "The time has come to cast aside all pretense," she said. "I shall hide no longer. If Rowena Cooper succeeds, then such secrets are useless. The world that remains if we fail will not care who I am."

Miss Boston put her arm around Jennet and drew her back a little. The novice raised her hands and methodically removed the pins that kept the white veil in place. She threw them to the ground and, with a great, glad sigh, she tore the veil from her head.

Jennet gasped in amazement while Miss Boston clapped her hands gleefully. "Welcome back," she said.

Sister Bridget stretched out her arms and let out a cry like nothing the girl had ever heard. Centuries of torment and fear roared into the night, released at last. The hair that she shook loose was a thick tangle of dark green that grew far back on the top of her head. She swept the heavy, seaweed-like hanks over her shoulders, and as she did so, Jennet saw the scales beneath her scalloped ears glisten in the moonlight.

"You . . . you're not human!" she stammered.

"Tut tut, Jennet," chided Aunt Alice. "Don't be so rude."

"Do not be afraid, child," assured the novice. "I will not harm you."

"Of course she won't," said Aunt Alice. "Remember that story Benjamin told us—the one about the aufwaders?"

Jennet could not think clearly and shook her head.

"I stand before you the first and last of my kind," Sister Bridget told her. "My father was a fisherman. A good soul, yet cursed with the sight. Cursed because it ruined his life. He saw and fell in love with an aufwader, and together they defied the wishes of the Lords of the Deep." She turned and stared out to the calm black sea. "I was the result of their union," she said. "The sin of my parents was born out in me. A freak of nature I am, a hideous crossbreed that should never have been allowed to draw breath."

"Well, I think you look marvelous," piped up Aunt Alice, unable to conceal her enthusiasm any longer.

The novice shrugged. "Then you are the only one," she said. "Even Oona, my mother, could not bear to see me once my father was taken to the deeps. It was she who entrusted me to the care of the nuns, leaving me outside the convent gates as an infant. Never had they seen such an ugly child. In those times, they believed that inner evil was betrayed in the flesh. I must have seemed like the very devil to them. Still, they were as kind to me as their courage allowed. I was fortunate they did not burn me for a witch's brat."

Jennet felt her eyes prick with tears; she felt so awful about calling the aufwaders "creatures" and "things." "I'm sorry," she cried. "I didn't realize."

"It matters very little now," Sister Bridget replied. "The years have taught me much; there were many bitter lessons to learn, and I survived them all. But the hatred of mankind was easier to bear than this yearning for the sea that binds my heart. Do you know what it is to ache for what you cannot have? All my life I have been mesmerized by its beauty.

It plagues my dreams and torments my soul—if indeed I possess one." She closed her eyes and said softly, "How well I know the sights and smells of the sea. How many times have I watched it, that slumbering beast that waits for me? Yes, it is waiting—it knows that the day will come when I can resist no more and must give myself to the waves. Perhaps that moment is coming. For many long, weary years I have tried to suppress my desire and have prayed for redemption. Alas, my attempts to keep away have failed. I fear that one day soon I may walk into the water and not return."

"That would be a tragic waste," said Miss Boston.

"No," murmured the sister, "it would merely mark the end of my life. No one would mourn my going, and the Deep Ones will rise to drag me to their dark realm."

Aunt Alice touched her hand sympathetically. But it was not pity that Sister Bridget wanted. "I have dared all tonight to bring you here," she said. "Now that I have surrendered my secret, the number of my days is short, but before I take the cold road, I must be certain that Rowena Cooper is thwarted."

"May we know now what she said to you that night?" asked Miss Boston. "What was she after?"

"She is a desperate woman," the novice replied. "Inside she is eaten away. The pain I feel for the sea is nothing compared with her lust for greater power—it is that which she seeks. That is why she attempted to enlist me in her service, first with promises she could not fulfill and then with threats. I would never have aided her—you did not have to fear that. What she wanted was too much for any mortal."

Aunt Alice held Jennet tightly. "And what did she ask?" she ventured.

The sister fanned out her fingers and spread her hands before her, motioning to the invisible horizon of the sea. "She seeks the moonkelp," she answered simply.

"But that's what Ben's looking for!" exclaimed Jennet. "He said it was to save the aufwader tribe. What can she want it for?"

"The moonkelp is a great treasure," returned Sister Bridget. "The Lords of the Deep would pay any reward that is in their power to get it back. Rowena undoubtedly has a deadlier prize in mind than the lifting of the Mothers' Curse."

Miss Boston peered at the novice with twinkling eyes. Quietly, she said, "You know when and where it will bloom, don't you?"

The sister nodded. "There are many memories one carries from childhood —who knows, perhaps a half-child can recall more than most. I remember when my father was alive, before the day he set sail to cast his nets and caught only death." She paused, and a strange light glimmered in her eyes as she cut through the centuries of adulthood. "I can still hear the rain battering against the walls and hammering on the roof," she began. "The noise of the thunder was frightening, and to allay my fears, Mother sang to me. Her face was lovely; I remember the softness of her cheeks and the scent of her hair as she held her face against mine to lull me to sleep. That memory of that precious afternoon when I was loved and cared for is the one thing that I have clung to down through the years. The following day, my father set out in his boat and was lost."

"What did Oona sing to you?" asked Miss Boston.

"Rhymes of lore, chants to raise the tide and stir the waves. Everything she knew she put into song to ease her child. You see, she must have loved me that day."

"And one of the songs was about the moonkelp," said Jennet.

"Yes, only she knew the time and place of its flowering." The novice looked at them both and lifted her head proudly. "It is time to share that secret with you," she said. "See how the moon rides full in the sky; soon it will be at its height, and then we must be ready. For the treasure of the Deep Ones blooms tonight!"

For a moment, Jennet and Miss Boston were speechless. "Tonight?" the old lady repeated eventually. "Gracious, what can we do?"

"We must claim the wish and lift the Mothers' Curse. That way Rowena Cooper will never achieve her goal." Sister Bridget glanced down at the shore and moved quickly back to the path. "Come, we dare not delay any longer, for the moon-kelp will not wait. If we miss its flowering tonight then never in our lifetimes shall we see it again!" With her robes billowing behind her, she hurried to the steps, followed by Jennet and Miss Boston.

Jennet tugged at the old lady's cloak. "She can't go into the town looking like that!" she said. "Why doesn't she put her veil back on? People will stare."

"Do you still not understand?" Aunt Alice asked. "None of that matters now. The moonkelp is the only thing that can stop Rowena from growing more powerful. If she gets her evil claws into it and her wish is granted, then I shudder to think what will happen. There are more important things at stake here than I think you realize, and Sister Bridget has sacrificed her secret to help us. I do not think she will ever wear that veil again."

As they reached the church steps Jennet muttered, "I wish I knew where Ben was."

The churchyard was still, but in the wells of darkness behind the arc lights, two narrow slits gleamed.

"There's a tidy bit o' news," croaked a sneering voice. "So daft old Hesper were reet all along. I'd better tell 'er sharpish."

A dark shape emerged from the shadows. The evil aufwader who had tried to murder Ben shot a poisoned glance at the sky. "Gonna be a deadly night," he cackled, before darting between the graves to run in the direction of The Hawes.

CHAPTER TWELVE

ONCE IN NINE HUNDRED YEARS

Ben's feet were soaked, so he sat down on the sand and emptied the water from his shoes. Ever since leaving Jennet fast asleep at Aunt Alice's house, he had spent hours searching for Nelda and Hesper. At first, he had gone directly to the agreed meeting place but found that deserted. There he had waited till long after the light failed. He assumed that they had abandoned all hope of seeing him again and no longer came to check whether he would turn up.

So Ben had decided to go looking for them, but so far he had been unsuccessful. He could not see the little aufwader boat on the water, and he had hunted far along the shore of the West Cliff. But all he found was a courting couple who chased him away. Now it was getting very late.

Ben had only wanted to tell Nelda that her father was alive and had intended to slip back to the cottage without Jennet realizing that he had been out at all.

"She's bound to have woken up by now, though," he mumbled sadly. "She'll be so mad. I bet she tells Aunt Alice on me. Prob'ly won't see Nelda ever again."

The boy kicked the sand wretchedly as he walked home. It was no use hurrying, as he was already in so much trouble that being late would not matter. His ears were filled by the soft sound of the waves as they washed over the shore and dragged away the sand in their retreat.

It was a beautiful night. When the moon appeared through the clouds, it shone with brilliant silver fire. Long, tapering shadows were cast along the beach, and the wet sand glittered about Ben's feet, mirroring the moon's rays in a magical way. It was like walking on a carpet of tiny stars, and he grinned broadly at the wonder of it.

He turned his head. A great silver road shimmered and sparkled over the sea. The gentle waves absorbed the light and, as they broke against the land, the moonbeams fractured and scattered a million pearls in the air.

Ben was enthralled and stared breathlessly at the moon; the enchanted light glimmered on his face. Then through the sighing rush of the sea, another sound began. It was the sweetest music he had ever heard, and he looked around to see where it was coming from. Abruptly the sound was snatched away, and the light was extinguished. Another cloud glided before the moon, and the shadows swallowed the glowing sands completely.

Ben was in the dark. It was a shock to his senses, and he stumbled forward blindly. The world seemed to have been plunged into black despair, and he longed to see that mysterious light once more. He shivered in his damp shoes and wondered if he had dreamed the whole thing.

The shore was grim. Now that it had been deprived of the moonlight, it was a dismal place and even the lapping of the waves sounded harsh and cruel.

Slowly, the boy began to realize what was happening. The light and the music had been a signal, like a herald's fanfare of trumpets. The time had come—the moonkelp was in bloom.

With a yell, Ben jumped up and down and danced on the sand. At last, somewhere out there the marvelous treasure was flowering. Once in nine hundred years Hesper had said, and that was tonight.

Ben was not certain exactly where the aufwader caves were, but he knew from what Hesper had said that beneath the East Cliff there was a maze of tunnels and grottos. He had to find the entrance: if he failed then the tribe was doomed to extinction.

Desperately, he stormed across the harbor and dashed onto Tate Hill Pier. He felt ready to burst as he scrambled down the old stone wall and dropped onto the flat, slippery rock below.

The sea had not yet flooded the shore beneath the cliff face, but already its creeping outriders were filling the rock pools. It was a treacherous place to be caught by the tide, and even the strongest of swimmers had met their end there. But Ben was too inflamed by the importance of his news to think about the danger, and he ran into the deep cliff shadow, calling at the top of his voice, "Nelda! Hesper! Can you hear me? It's Ben!"

Behind him the water gurgled up through the channeled rocks and flowed ever closer, while in front the sheer wall of shale reached into the night sky over the boy's head. It contained many clefts and crags that in the darkness resembled eyes and mouths. They seemed to stare down at him balefully, laughing at the little voice that went unheeded in that lonely spot. It was as if the whole cliff was mocking him, and he felt microscopic compared with its black vastness.

Ben tried to push these thoughts to the back of his mind and attempted to explore the large fissures and crannies that were within his reach. It did not take long for him to find out that they were only shallow gouges in the rock and not real caves at all.

"Nelda, where are you?" he shouted.

Only the incoming sea answered him. Ben whirled around and, to his horror, saw that the way back to the pier was totally cut off. The path was now flooded—he was trapped.

Orange firelight flickered over the rough cave walls. Bunches of drying weeds were suspended from the fishing nets that were draped from one side to the other, and they gave a sweet, salty tang to the damp air. These were Hesper's quarters, and they suited her admirably. Since the decline of the tribes there was plenty of room for everyone—too much room. The ancient galleries had not been visited for many years, and the long halls were bereft of song. Some passages had even been blocked up because they were no longer needed, and this saddened the kindly aufwader. Beyond those blockades were the wondrous ammonite caverns where, in days long gone, important festivals were celebrated. The revels had been high then; sometimes there was music and light for a whole three days.

Hesper brought herself back to the present and peered into the flames. Tarr sat cross-legged on the rush-matted floor beside her, his wiry white hair untied and tucked beneath him. He drew on his pipe and watched his daughter thoughtfully. The net that lay across her knee would not be mended tonight, he told himself.

"Tha'd better put it down if'n that's the best ya can do," he said. "Get thee to bed. Theer's nowt worth stayin' awake fer." He jabbed the air with his pipe and pointed at Nelda, who was idly pulling the loose rushes from the mat. "Tha too," he told her.

Nelda looked across at Hesper. This was the first night they had stayed in the caves. It seemed pointless to go on searching for the moonkelp without the human boy. She had no idea what had happened to Ben or why he had stopped meeting them in the evening. Perhaps she had been wrong about him. Were the elders right after all—could no humans be trusted?

"Ah'm to bed," said her grandfather grumpily. He reached for his staff and pulled himself up. With the briefest of nods, he bade them goodnight and hobbled out.

"It is over," Hesper said miserably. "Oona was wrong; there never was any moonkelp. I have fooled myself all this time. We are all to die, and our kind will disappear."

Nelda hung her head and said nothing.

In the passage beyond, Tarr slowly made his way to his own quarters. He could never understand what went on inside the heads of his children. Why, for instance, had they remained in the caves that night? They had been so despondent over the past few days, too. If he lived to be 600, which seemed likely, he would never work them out.

The ringing of heavy boots brought him to a halt. Some-one was coming down the tunnel.

"Prawny?" he called. "If'n tha's come t'pinch me purse, Prawny Nust, tha can—"

But it was not the aufwader Tarr had expected. Out of the gloom hurried a squat, busy-looking female. She was a scowling, bad-tempered creature who loved to put others in their place and wore a string of beaded shells on her brow to show her self-importance. Old Parry, the tribe called her—a nasty, small-minded widow with a sharp tongue and ears that flapped at any conversation she was not a party to.

"Oh," muttered Tarr, "it's thee, Parry." He quickened his limping pace and spluttered, "Ah canna stop; sithee tomorrer."

But old Parry was determined, and she caught hold of Tarr's sleeve. "Don't you scaddle off yet, Tarr!" she told him fiercely. "Come listen what I've heard—gives me great gladness it do, but I don't think you'll like it none."

Tarr sighed. "What be it?" he groaned, hoping this was not another petty scheme of hers.

She led him down the tunnel to a point where it opened out into a high, echoing chamber. This was the Hall of Whispers, the one place in the aufwader caves where you could hear the outside world. In here, the fisher folk would gather at times of storm and listen to the roaring tempest of the sea as it hurled its fury against the cliff. Old Parry, however, was fond of this spot because it was not just the sea you could hear from it. If she stayed very quiet and kept her ears glued to the rock, she could listen to humans walking along the shore. She hated those ugly land animals and blamed them for everything, but her enmity did not prevent her eavesdropping on them.

Tarr looked around huffily. He wanted to go to sleep. "Well," he said, "what be it?"

Old Parry drew him to the rock wall. "Do you not hear?" she asked with a giggle.

He regarded her disdainfully. There was nothing unusual out there, just the noise of the tide coming in. "'As tha gone doolally?" he barked. "Theer's nowt—"

Tarr's words failed as his large ears caught the sound. It was a human voice crying in panic; someone was trapped by the tide. He turned away, disgusted. Old Parry was a cruel piece of work.

"Ah dunna want t'hear such," he muttered. "Tha's got a heart o' stone."

"Puh!" she snorted. "'Tis only a human boy. Just one less of them—won't make no difference, there's so many."

"A life, all t'same," Tarr spat as he shambled out. "Thee's gone bitter 'n' twisted, Parry. Jus' cos thee canna'ave bairns, dunna gloat when others perish."

This struck a nerve, and she countered with all her petty spite. "You dare preach at me, Tarr Shrimp?" she squealed. "Look to yer own door afore you lord it!"

He glared at her and demanded, "What's thee on about?"

"Where's yer son?" she shouted accusingly. "Who killed Silas Gull, and where do Hesper and Nelda vanish to at night? Taking vittles to Abe, are they?"

He gnashed his teeth and raised his staff fiercely, but she laughed in his face and dodged to one side. "A curse on your line, Tarr!" she sneered. "Childless I may be, but it's folk like you that made me so." She lifted her hand and triumphantly declared, "There, hear now the voice that condemns your own children!"

From the outside world, the cries of the boy were growing fainter, but they could still make out the words. "Help!" came the pitiful shouts. "Nelda! Hesper! It's Ben—help me!"

Tarr charged back along the tunnel with Old Parry's taunts ringing in his ears. "Get you gone from this place," she called after him. "It's to the elders, I'm bound. Consortin' with the humans! Your folk are a disgrace to the tribe. It's exile for you till the end of your days—you and your family!"

Ben stood on a tiny island of rock, but it was rapidly shrinking. He had climbed as high as he could to escape the encroaching water and was now truly stuck. He had called for help until it hurt his throat and his voice was weak and croaky. All he could do was watch as the sea rose steadily and lapped ever closer. He screwed up his face and sobbed with despair. One big wave was all that it would take to sweep him off and drag him under. The boy's fingers gripped the shale tightly as he waited for the inevitable.

Suddenly, the cliff trembled. A loud cracking and grinding issued from the darkness above, and a shower of small pebbles rattled down.

The doorway to the aufwader caves was opening.

A familiar voice called, "Ben, take my hand." It was Nelda.

After leaving old Parry, Tarr had stormed back to Hesper's quarters and demanded to know why a human child was calling for them outside. They did not stop to tell him but jumped up and sped to the entrance.

Ben reached up and clasped the small aufwader's hand, then, helped by her aunt, she began to haul him up. He scrabbled over the sharp rock, scuffing his shoes and cutting his knees, but at last he was safe. As he lay gasping on the threshold of the aufwader caves, a large wave crashed onto the ledge he had just left. The spray hit their faces and they staggered back.

They were in a damp chamber, dominated by a primitive mechanism overhead that operated the two huge slabs of stone that were the main doors to the fisher folk dwellings. When closed, they fitted so precisely that it was impossible to see them from the outside, and they made a perfect seal against the sea. Stacked in rows in the near wall were the little wooden boats the aufwaders used and beside them the nets and weights needed for fishing. Ben took it all in and then remembered what had driven him here.

"Close the entrance," urged Hesper quickly. "The others will be here soon. They will throw the boy into the sea if they can."

Nelda ran to one of the two rusty chains that dangled from the lofty ceiling and tugged with all her strength. The massive doors began to swing back into position.

Ben staggered to his feet. "Stop!" he said. "We haven't got much time."

"We know that, boy," sniffed Hesper. "Oh, nine times bless me! They will be here all too soon—hurry, Nelda." She turned on Ben and said scoldingly, "Do you realize the trouble you've caused us, child? The penalty for merely talking with you is great enough, but now you have stepped inside our domain, where no human has ever been." She buried her face in her oilskin hat and paced about in a circle, nibbling the brim.

"No, you don't understand," said Ben. "It's the moonkelp! It's time!"

Nelda released the chain, and Hesper ceased her pacing. The cork lifebelt slid down to her ankles, but she took no notice. "Tonight—are you sure?"

"Positive!"

Hesper stared at her niece and let loose a terrific hoot of happiness. "It's true after all!" she cheered. "It's true! It's true—Oona was right!"

Nelda looked at Ben. "I knew you would be the one," she said. "I fear that when you stopped meeting us I thought—" She stopped, seeing the boy's troubled face. "Why do you turn away?" she asked.

"It's your father," he said quietly. "I've seen him."

"You have seen my father?" she cried joyously. "Where? Was he well?"

A vivid image of that night flashed into Ben's mind. He remembered the cruel lines that scored the aufwader's face and the glint of the knife that he had raised. He shivered, and for the umpteenth time wondered how such a wicked creature could possibly be Nelda's father.

When Ben looked back at Nelda, he realized that she was waiting for an answer. He nodded, but before he could tell her any more, the tramp of many feet filled the chamber. The tribe was approaching, running down the tunnels to the entrance.

Hesper yanked up her lifebelt, ran to the row of boats, and dragged one to the doorway. "We have not the time to explain our actions," she said. "For three hours only does the moonkelp bloom—we must not miss it. Nelda, the gap is not wide enough for me to get the boat out."

Nelda ran to the other chain and heaved hard. The doors opened a little more, and the craft was through.

The sea had risen a great deal. Now it was not far below the doorway, and Hesper studied the waves keenly. "A calm tide," she said. "We shall be safe. Fetch me the oars, Nelda."

Ben watched as the funny little aufwader stepped aboard, took the oars from her niece, and gave the signal.

"Push!" she shouted.

Ben and Nelda put all their weight behind the small boat. Lurching, it slid along the ledge and flew through the air, landing with a great "smack" on the water. Expertly, Hesper steadied the tiny craft and brought it as close to the threshold as the current permitted. "You next, boy," she called. "All you have to do is step down. Do not be alarmed, it's perfectly safe."

Ben was not sure—it didn't look safe at all. Taking a deep breath in case he fell into the water, he stepped out. With a bump, he found himself sprawled in the boat at Hesper's feet. He pulled himself up gingerly as the vessel tilted from side to side.

Hesper laughed. "There, that caused you no hurt, did it?" She looked up at Nelda. "Now you, child."

But her niece was not looking at them. She had turned away and was staring into the chamber. Hesper frowned. What was she up to? At that moment, the clamor of angry voices burst into the night, and Hesper realized that the rest of the tribe had arrived.

On the threshold, Nelda faltered as the fisher folk poured in. There were 35 of them, the sole survivors of the aufwader race. They made no attempt to rush forward but shouted and screamed their contempt. She was caught. Trapped by the aufwader snare, she could neither speak nor run. Nelda had never seen them stirred to such anger before; the light in their eyes was terrifying.

Abruptly, the noise died down, and the crowd parted, making a clear path down the center. "Esau approaches," they whispered reverently.

Through the assembled fisher folk moved a single figure: Esau, oldest of the ruling triad. His face was withered, and the burden of eight centuries lay heavily upon his gnarled brow. Thick white whiskers trailed from his chin, knotted and threaded with stones and shells. Seaweed twined amid his bristling hair and hanging about his neck was a single pearl. Of all the elders, he was the most respected. He seldom spoke—only in the direst emergencies, when judgments or important decisions were needed, had he been known to utter a word.

Grimly, and with his twisted back bowed by age, he crept closer. Nelda watched dumbly as he halted just three paces in front of her. The atmosphere was tense. Everyone held their breath and waited for him to proclaim the judgement.

Nelda knew that the elders had the power of life or death over wrongdoers. It was a power they rarely wielded, as such a severe punishment was reserved for only the most heinous crimes like murder or treason. An ice-cold dread stole over her—in the condemning eyes of Esau, she had betrayed the tribe.

In silence, the elder raised his wizened arm and pointed an accusing finger at her. "Treachery!" came his cracked old voice. "Thou art a traitor to thy kind." His words rang harshly around the chamber, and he waited for the echo to die down before turning his back on her. "All bear witness to my judgement," he cried. "Henceforth the line of Tarr is banished from this place—let no one give them aid."

Everybody hissed and began to stamp on the ground. At that moment, Nelda felt the snare release her, but instead of leaping into the boat below, she turned on Esau. "Be silent, you old fool!" she shouted defiantly.

Everyone gasped at this disgraceful behavior—had she no respect? "Insolence!" they roared.

But she had not finished with him yet. She stood her ground and cried, "For years, we have hidden away from the world and bemoaned our lot. Our numbers have dwindled, and why? All you elders can do is huddle together, despising any who tries to bring about change." She threw back her head and proclaimed triumphantly, "Tonight the moonkelp blooms, and when we find it, the curse of the Deep Ones will be lifted for ever."

Esau stared at her incredulously. "It cannot be so," he muttered. "It is but a legend. The moonkelp does not exist."

Nelda snapped her fingers at him. "Yes it does, Long Whiskers," she said.

"Impudent whelp" snapped the elder. For a moment, he glared at her, then he relaxed and said with a shrewd smile, "Very well, child. If thou do indeed bring back the treasure of the Deep Ones, I shall lift my judgement. But if thee return empty-handed, then expect the full measure of my wrath and abide by my decision."

Nelda agreed. "So be it," she said, and with that she leaped off the threshold.

Hesper chuckled and rowed away from the cliff. "Well done, Nelda," she said. "Imagine Old Parry's face when we succeed." The two aufwaders looked back to the cliff entrance where the tribe was watching them leave and laughed. Then

Hesper turned to Ben. "Tell me," she asked. "Just where may we find the moonkelp?"

Ben bit his lip; he had been dreading that question. "I don't know," he answered flatly. "Out here somewhere, I suppose."

Jennet, Miss Boston, and Sister Bridget ran down the alleys that led to the beach. Most of the summer visitors were snugly downing their final pints in the pubs, but those that were still wandering in the streets stared at the novice with goggling eyes. She was certainly a striking figure, with her dark-green hair streaming behind, stark against the dazzling whiteness of her habit.

Jennet saw how the people were staring. The last thing they wanted was a crowd of spectators following them, so she smiled at every passerby and said in a casual voice, "Costume party." That seemed to satisfy everybody, and they reached the sands of Tate Hill Pier with no one in tow.

It was quiet on the gloomy shore. Sheltered by the two piers, the waves that were driven on to the sand were small and gentle.

"Will we require a boat for this?" asked Miss Boston, eyeing the dark water uncertainly.

Sister Bridget said nothing but stared out beyond the harbor entrance toward the horizon. The old lady followed her gaze. Something was slowly moving over the water; it was a strange, hazy sight, and she wished she had brought her binoculars with her.

Jennet also looked, but although her vision was stronger than Aunt Alice's, it was not as sensitive. What she saw made her shake her head and look again. It appeared to be a small figure hovering over the surface of the sea. Jennet was taken aback, but when she turned her eyes upon it a second time, she saw that the figure was actually sitting in a little boat.

"It is an aufwader vessel," said Sister Bridget unexpectedly. Her sight was the keenest of the three, and quickly she identified those on board. "I see two of their folk," she murmured. "One wears an oilskin hat, the other is younger, and beside her there is a human child."

"Is it Ben?" asked Jennet.

The novice nodded. "Yes," she confirmed, "it is your brother. They are searching for the moonkelp—they will never find it without my guidance."

"Then we must attract their attention," said Miss Boston excitedly. "Soon they will pass out of sight. Come along." With her cloak flapping madly, she ran over the sand to the pier and clambered up the few stairs that led on to it. Along the flat stretch of stone she scurried, unwinding the scarf from her neck and waving it madly in the air. "Hello!" she called to the boat in the distance. "Hello, Benjamin!"

Jennet caught up with the old lady just as she had reached the end of the pier.

"Jump up and down, Jennet dear," cried Aunt Alice desperately. "They must see us."

"Do not worry," came the voice of Sister Bridget as she joined them. "Look—the boat has changed course."

Gradually the small aufwader vessel came closer. It was Hesper who had seen them, and she gazed curiously at the tall figure dressed in white.

Miss Boston let out a great breath of relief and wrapped the scarf about her neck once more. Eagerly, she waited as the boat drew near. "How splendid," she cooed when she discerned the two strange figures beside Ben. She had never before had the chance to examine an aufwader closely, and it was a thrilling prospect. The craft bumped against the side of the pier far below, and Aunt Alice stooped and glanced over the side. "Oh, what a pity," she tutted in disappointment. To her, the fisher folk were still blurred and fuzzy. "Botheration," she tutted.

Jennet had watched the boat approach with mounting concern. The poor girl could not see the aufwaders at all; the only things real to her were Ben and the boat. She had no idea how the vessel was being steered or how the oars moved through the water. Her brother looked up at her and waved cheerfully. "Just you wait," she muttered under her breath. "I'll teach you to run off like that."

Miss Boston pattered along the pier to where iron rungs were set into the stone. "Come up here, you little marvels," she shouted at the fisher folk.

Hesper and Nelda stared up at the old lady and the girl on the pier. Nelda was not sure if this was such a good idea. She leaned over to her aunt and said, "We waste precious time here. I still do not see why you were so set on this—the moonkelp must be our main concern."

"So it is," Hesper replied, "so it is." She gave her niece the oars and stood up in the boat to see if she could get a peek at the figure who had so fired her interest. Above her, Sister Bridget appeared and gazed down. "As I thought," nodded Hesper. "Look, Nelda. Now do you see?"

Nelda looked at the novice and immediately saw the faint shimmering aura that surrounded her. Confused, she turned to her aunt for an answer to this riddle.

"Behold the daughter of Oona," Hesper announced, "after all this time. Hurry, Nelda, take us to the ladder."

The oars dipped into the sea, and swiftly Nelda brought the boat alongside the lowest rung. Hesper checked that her lifebelt was secure and then clambered up. Ben was not sure if he should follow. He was certain that if he tried to stand up in the boat, it would probably capsize.

"Delighted to meet you," chatted Miss Boston as Hesper climbed up beside her. "And whom do I have the honor of addressing, may I ask?"

"There is no time for that," interrupted Sister Bridget suddenly. "Only an hour remains. I must take your place in the boat." She brushed past Hesper and began to climb down the ladder.

The aufwader fell to her knees and called after her, "Eska, Eska—you must not venture on the open sea!"

Sister Bridget paused in the descent and threw her head back. The face she turned to her was pale but grim. "I no longer recognize that name," she said, trembling. "For many years, I have been Bridget, and that I will remain—whatever happens." She looked away and concentrated on the rungs of the ladder once more.

When she reached the bottom, the novice glanced at the deep water all around and shuddered. Nelda and Ben stared at her from the boat in surprise. "Are you really the daughter of Oona?" asked Nelda.

"For my sins," she returned solemnly. "Now hold the craft steady and make room for me."

Nelda and Ben squashed themselves against the sides of the boat. "You coming with us, then?" asked the boy.

Clinging to the ladder with one hand, Sister Bridget crossed herself and replied, "If my courage allows." With her heart pounding in her breast, she reached out her foot and stepped into the aufwader vessel.

Ben gripped the sides in alarm as the boat rocked uncontrollably. Sister Bridget cast her eyes despairingly upon the surrounding water. For the first time in her long life, she was putting herself at the mercy of the waves. It was a chilling sensation. She knew full well the consequences if she were to fall in—the Lords of the Deep would claim her.

"Hurry, child," she called to Nelda. "I shall be your guide now."

Nelda put the oars into the water and struggled to pull away from the pier. High over their heads Jennet called to her brother, "Be careful, Ben!" He gave an answering shout, and the boat sailed out onto the dark wide sea.

Miss Boston put her arm around the girl's neck. "Don't worry, dear," she said. "He is in excellent hands."

Hesper stamped her foot with irritation. "All this time I have wandered the shores to find it!" she snorted. "Now I shall never see the moonkelp."

They watched the little craft move away, so engrossed that they failed to hear the footsteps that approached from behind.

Miss Boston smiled at the blurred shape next to her. "You have played your part," she told the aufwader. "Now it is up to them."

"All the same," added Hesper quietly, "I would wish that Eska had remained here—the sea is no place for her."

Miss Boston disagreed. "Oh no," she replied mildly, "she had to go. Not just because she knew where to find the moonkelp, you understand. No, Sister Bridget has endured her entire life for this one night—it's what she was born for. I pray she survives."

Hesper bowed her head. "Poor Oona. I wish she had brought her daughter to me—I would have gladly left the tribe to look after her."

"Things are as they should be," muttered Aunt Alice darkly.

Jennet had taken her eyes from the boat that was now in the distance and had been listening to this exchange with growing annoyance. To her it was a one-sided conversation. Not only could she not see Hesper, but all that she said escaped her hearing.

"What a charming little scene," a sneering voice broke in.

The three of them whirled around. Silhouetted against the lights of Whitby was Rowena Cooper.

CHAPTER THIRTEEN

STRUGGLE AT SEA

The woman was dressed in black robes that were tied around the middle by a thick purple cord. On a chain about her neck she wore a five-pointed star that gleamed against the midnight material. She played with the amethyst ring on her finger and mocked the group before her, laughing at the dismay on their faces.

"A child, a shore vagrant, and a senile old woman," she spat contemptuously. "What a ridiculous combination."

Hesper moved forward, bewildered. "Yet another human with the sight," she said. "Is the gift not as rare as once it was?"

Miss Boston put her hand on the aufwader's shoulder. "Beware," she whispered, then cleared her throat and said aloud, "I do believe Mrs. Cooper is showing her true colors at last. What do you think, Jennet? A little too crude for my taste, perhaps, but then what can one expect from a black witch?"

"A witch?" repeated Jennet, and she gaped at Rowena. The woman seemed to have grown. In her black robes, she was like a great dark cloud. Even Aunt Alice seemed to have shrunk in comparison.

Miss Boston folded her arms. "Oh yes," she said. "Mrs. Cooper—though I doubt if that is her real name—has been using her treacherous arts from the moment she arrived."

Hesper removed her oilskin hat. "Is there such a breed left in the world of man?" she asked in astonishment.

Rowena sneered at her and moved a little closer. She was now effectively blocking the way back, and they were caught between her and the end of the pier. She glared at the horizon, the boat now only a small speck upon it, and tossed her head with anger.

"They are out of your reach now," smiled Miss Boston blithely. "I'm so sorry, but we couldn't wait, you see."

Rowena hissed venomously at her, "Old crone, I am not defeated yet!" She took a step nearer, forcing them dangerously close to the pier edge—one quick shove and they would all topple backward. The woman seemed to consider this for a moment, flexing her fingers with anticipation, but for some reason she decided against it and, instead, cupped her hands around her mouth. "Gull!" she shrieked. "Come here, Gull!"

Hesper clutched her hat anxiously. With wide eyes, she watched as a short figure hurried along the pier toward them. The leering aufwader, knife in hand, ran to Rowena's side and licked his brown teeth. He shot a despising glance at Hesper and wiped his nose on his sleeve. She could only stare at him, utterly horrified, as the truth dawned.

"Cat bit yer tongue, Hesper?" he asked. "Not like you, that—always 'ad a word or three t'say, you did. Ain'tcha glad t'see me, then?"

Hesper's heart grew cold. "Hello, Silas," she said eventually. "I thought you were dead."

"Hoped I was, ya mean!" he laughed. "But that's what I wanted yer to think."

She looked at his gansey—it belonged to Nelda's father. "Never was there a more loathsome worm," she said. "I curse the day I wed you, Silas Gull."

He spat on the ground. "Dunna fret yerself, me darlin.' Abe weren't worth any tears. Poked 'is nose a bit too far into my affairs—'e 'ad to be kept quiet."

"So you took his life and robbed his clothes," she said with disgust. "The black boat that we burned contained my brother, yet his name has become reviled by the tribe."

Silas chuckled maliciously. "Hah, I 'oped it would. Serve 'im right I says, fer all them times 'e shamed me." He grinned and added in a whisper, "Listen to this, Hesper my love. If I 'ad the chance I would gladly throttle your 'oly brother nine times over."

Hesper flew at him. Whipping out one of her little fishing poles, she beat Silas on the side of his head.

Her husband fell back but immediately sprang to his feet and flourished the knife before him. "No one does that t'me no more!" he yelled.

"Enough!" snapped Rowena suddenly. She seized Silas's knife and threw it into the water below. He turned on her, but the look in the witch's eyes daunted him. "There will be time for this later," she barked. "But first things first." Rowena pointed out to sea. "Out there that half-breed could already be claiming the wish. You must stop her!"

"What d'yer expect me t'do?" he asked. "We ain't got no boat, 'ave we?"

"You can swim, can't you?" Rowena snarled back at him.

Silas stared at the black, uninviting water and shivered. "I'm not goin' in theer!" he said firmly.

"You will do precisely what I command!" shouted Rowena, grabbing him by the scruff of his neck. "I haven't put myself through all this for nothing. If we don't find it tonight, then neither of our lives shall be worth living. But know this. When my husband discovers that I have been plotting behind his back, rest assured that before he arrives to tighten the leash about my neck I shall dine off your putrid flesh." With a fierce push, she thrust him over the edge, and he tumbled into the sea.

Silas floundered in the waves. His whiskers were plastered over his spluttering face, and he looked like a drowned weasel. Coughing up the brine, he glowered at Rowena, hating her yet fearing her more.

"Bring the moonkelp back to me," she called down to him.

Swearing and grumbling under his breath, Silas kicked his legs in the water and began to swim after the little boat.

"Your lackey will never reach them in time," said Miss Boston confidently. "You have lost."

Rowena did not reply, directing all her powers of concentration elsewhere. She bent her thoughts toward the little aufwader boat, and in the black maze of her mind, the scene was revealed to her.

Hesper looked questioningly at Aunt Alice. "But why should this human desire the moonkelp?" she asked. "It will not aid her."

Aunt Alice thought she knew the reason. "I think Mrs. Cooper would disagree with you there," she replied. "No doubt it possesses certain qualities vital to particular rituals."

Suddenly, Rowena sighed, and the vision that she had conjured up melted before her eyes. "Excellent," she cried. "They have not found it yet." She turned to the group beside her and caught the gist of what they were saying.

"The moonkelp!" she roared, throwing back her blonde head. "Is that what you think, you old hag? Pathetic! How amusing the feeble-minded can be!"

This cruel derision made Jennet furious. She moved forward, but Aunt Alice's arms held her tightly. "Peace, dear," said the old lady softly. "Ignore her, and she may ignore you."

Rowena's thin, twisted lips pulled wide apart and revealed all her teeth. "The moonkelp is not my goal," she told them. "What use to me is such a weed?"

"Then what do you want?" asked Hesper.

Rowena touched the star pendant at her throat. "I seek my freedom," she answered in a hushed voice. "Once I return the wretched moonkelp to the Lords of the Deep, I shall have it— the power to control and destroy will be mine alone to wield."

"The Deep Ones will not aid you in that, witch woman!" protested Hesper. "If you think to obtain some of their might, then you shall perish. For their craft is too great for any mortal—it would consume you."

"I want none of their baseness!" Rowena snorted. "But they alone know the precise location of what I seek. Somewhere in this squalid, dingy little town a most wondrous thing was hidden and forgotten many ages past—an artifact charged with the magic of the ancients."

"Balderdash!" retorted Miss Boston. "Whitby is full of legends, but I've never heard anything to suggest *that* before. Absolute rubbish!"

Rowena prowled before her, and the old lady teetered on the brink of the pier. "Have you not?" she growled with menace. "What of Hilda?"

"St. Hilda?" said Aunt Alice, in a voice that had lost its confidence. Somewhere in the back of her mind, there was an idea . . . if only she was less flustered. But the sound of the sea slapping the wall below scattered her thoughts, and she glanced down warily. The heels of her shoes were only just on the pier; if Rowena compelled her to move back any more, she would certainly fall. The old lady shuffled her feet forward and desperately groped among her memories. "St. Hilda," she repeated. "What has this absurd fantasy got to do with her?"

"*Saint* Hilda!" scoffed Rowena. "Before she came here, Hilda was a sorceress! If she had not found your God, she could have ruled absolutely with the power that she possessed."

Miss Boston uttered a cry as finally it came to her. "And she cut off the heads of the serpents," she said, fearfully repeating the old legend, "with a whip or . . . staff." The old lady glanced at Rowena and trembled, momentarily losing her balance. "Can it be true?" she stammered.

Rowena Cooper swept the short, bleached curls off her forehead. Forming her bloodless white lips into a horrible smile she laughed softly and murmured, "Yes! Tonight the staff of Hilda will be mine."

Ben's eyes smarted. They ached from staring at the endless stretch of water, and he had rubbed them until they were bloodshot. "Is it much further?" he groaned. His initial excitement had worn off, and the chill wind of the open sea numbed his cheeks and had turned his fingers purple.

Sister Bridget was absorbed in studying the night sky. There were too many clouds for her to be certain—if only she could get a clear view of the stars. "I feel it is near," she said.

Nelda ceased rowing, for her arms were tired. She gazed about them, but all was dark—not a sign of the moonkelp anywhere.

The novice caught her doubtful glance. "Patience," she told her. "The moonkelp will not show itself until I speak the charm of the cold realm."

She put her hands together and rested her chin upon them. Then, quietly at first, she began to recite the words her mother had sung to her. Her voice grew in strength as she repeated the strange-sounding charm. Cutting through the blackness of the night like a blade, it rose to a shout. Words of power challenged the spells of darkness that Irl had wrapped about the moonkelp long ages past and that blinded their eyes to it still.

Ben looked all around him. The air was charged with expectation, and he held his breath—something was definitely beginning to happen.

A faint glimmer appeared about the boat. High above, the clouds moved quickly, fleeing to the far rim of the world, and in the clear expanse blazed the moon. It was swollen and full, bright as the sun but cold and ringed with a halo of frosty light. The icy rays poured down and the sea became molten silver.

Ben and Nelda looked at each other in wonder as sparks danced over the timbers of the boat. They pulled their tingling hands away from its sides hastily. The shining water crackled, and a flash of green lightning streaked through the waves, encircling them in a mesh of magical fire that radiated outward, weaving a dazzling net upon the calm sea.

Abruptly, Sister Bridget stopped chanting. She collapsed into Nelda's arms, gasping for breath. Her work was done.

Nelda felt her pulse. "She will recover quickly," she told Ben. "You keep a watch for the moonkelp."

The boy leaned out of the boat and scanned the shimmering sea. The quality of the light was changing—it became softer, and when he looked at the waves, he noticed that they were now edged with gold.

From the deep, empty reaches of the seabed, the moonkelp rose. Beneath the silver sea, a rich yellow glow welled up. Bubbles of flame erupted on the surface and burst against the keel of the aufwader vessel. With a hiss of steam, the treasure of the Deep Ones surged upward and met the air.

Ben fell back at the incredible sight. The many strands of the moonkelp shone gold and green. The light that pulsed from them was like midday at high summer, and it laced the surrounding sea.

"Hurry," Nelda instructed Ben. "Gather it before it sinks again."

He reached over the side and put his hand into the water. It was deliciously warm, and when his fingers brushed the waving weed, all weariness left him. Quickly, the boy began to haul the moonkelp out of the sea. Fiery jewels dripped from it. The marvelous light flooded his face when he held the treasure in his hands, and the boat brimmed over with its glory.

Sister Bridget stirred in Nelda's arms. She raised her head, and the sight of the moonkelp invigorated her. With its brilliance mirrored in her eyes, she turned to the aufwader. "Send it back to them," she said urgently. "Claim the reward and release your people."

Nelda could not quite believe what was happening. She felt as though she was inside one of the old legends that Hesper had told her. Hastily, she foraged in the canvas bag by her side and brought out a large scalloped shell. "Place it on this," she told Ben. "I must call to the Deep Ones and dispatch their treasure."

Ben did as he was told, leaning forward to put the glowing moonkelp into the shell. Nelda took a deep breath, hesitating until Sister Bridget gave a nod of encouragement.

The aufwader faced north and held the shell aloft. "Hear me," she shouted into the wind. "Listen to my words, ye Lords of the Deep and Dark. Let my voice journey to your cold realm and may you—"

The boat tipped suddenly. Ben was thrown to one side, and the novice screamed. Terrified in case they fell into the water, she gripped the sides and sobbed with fear.

Above her frantic cries a harsh voice said, "May the deeps swallow the lot o' yers!"

Nelda lowered the shell and forgot everything; the shock of what she saw overwhelmed her. For, clinging to the boat, drenched and malevolent, was the uncle she had presumed dead.

"Silas!" she exclaimed.

Just as Ben had gathered the moonkelp, Silas had caught up with them. Silently he had swum closer, gloating in the sure knowledge that they were unaware of his approach. This was going to be too easy, he had told himself.

Ben stared at Silas fearfully. "I thought this was your father," he told Nelda.

"No," she muttered tearfully. "He is my uncle and a murderer."

"Shut yer whinin'!" Silas roared, and his rough hand snaked out and struck the side of her face. It was a vicious slap, and Nelda yelped with the force of it. The shell and its golden treasure dropped from her grasp and crashed to the floor of the boat.

Ben sprang forward but was too slow. With a sideways dig of his elbow, Silas shoved him down, winded and spluttering. The little craft lurched, threatening to capsize. Sister Bridget, petrified with terror, could do nothing to prevent Silas from reaching in to snatch the moonkelp away.

He laughed as his grubby fingers clawed up the shining prize, and he spat at each of them in turn. "A curse on all," he growled. "Man, kin, and half-blood—yer fishbait now." With a cackle, he rocked the boat deliberately. Sister Bridget sobbed, and Ben held on tightly.

Anger to the point of madness furied up inside Nelda. Still stinging from his last blow, she lashed out at her evil uncle. "You killed my father!" she screamed.

Silas pushed her down once more, enjoying watching them suffer. A few more rocks, and the boat would tip over completely. Then, to his surprise, Nelda staggered forward again. Lunging at the hand that held the moonkelp, she seized it in her own, bared her teeth and bit deeply into his skin.

"Aaaaaaggghhhh!" he screeched, tearing his hand from her mouth. "You've drawn blood," he yelled, gazing at the torn flesh. "Well, you'll not do that again!" With his other hand, he punched his niece for all he was worth.

Nelda reeled backward and, as she fell, her head struck the side of the boat with a dull crack. She slumped senseless to the bottom.

"You've killed her!" cried Ben. He stared at Silas, appalled, then turned to Sister Bridget. "Can't you do anything!" he asked.

"Don't waste yer breath askin' 'er," sniggered Silas. "Afraid t'step in a puddle, that one is." He scooped up a handful of seawater and threw it at the novice. She shrieked when it hit her. "That's what comes of mixi' the two," Silas snarled mockingly. "I'll wager there's weaker stuff in her veins."

Sister Bridget raised her head and glared at Silas reproachfully. He did not notice the perilous look that had crept into her eyes. Very softly, she began to hum.

"Barmy, she is," Silas grunted. "Hark at her—cracked as an old bog pot."

Ben did not listen. He was cradling Nelda's head in his arms and did not care what happened to them any more.

Silas sucked the back of his hand and eased himself back into the water; it was time to return to Rowena. Let them sail where they wanted—they were not important now. Besides, if they thought they could escape they were mistaken. After tonight, nowhere would be safe. Keeping the glowing moon-kelp over his head, Silas pushed himself away from the boat and began swimming to the far shore.

Sister Bridget stroked Ben's hair. For a moment, the tune died on her lips. "Do not worry," she told him. "Nelda is not dead—she will awaken."

The boy looked up at her. "Why didn't you do anything to help?" he asked. "Why didn't you stop him?"

"I was afraid," she replied. "All my life I have been afraid. Yet it is strange, is it not, that the moment he threw the water at me, and I tasted the bitterness of its salt, all my fears vanished."

Ben stared after the determined figure of Silas as he swam away. "It's too late now," he said.

"I think not," she answered secretively. "He will never reach the shore. For Oona was my mother, and I am proud of that, for she taught me much that day when she sang to me. Now I know it was not I, her child, whom she could not bear, but the thought of returning to the life of an aufwader. That is why she left me in human care. Finally, I understand." With a deadly smile, the humming resumed.

Ben watched Sister Bridget doubtfully. Perhaps Silas was right—maybe she had gone mad. Why else would she behave like this?

Almost imperceptibly, words began to creep into the tune. It grew stronger until Sister Bridget was singing loud and defiantly. Ben felt a chill pass over him. The song was unsettling and made him want to get away. But how could he?

Suddenly, the melody changed: the tone became harsh and prickled the hairs on his neck. A shadow fell over the novice's face, but her voice continued. The discord mounted, seeming to jar every bone in Ben's body until he covered his ears in an attempt to block it out.

The silver moonlight faded, and all around them the sea darkened threateningly, as if responding to the sister's song. The gentle wind now blew in strong gusts that whipped up the waves and crowned them with foam. The boat spun around as the breakers smashed into its sides. Ben stared at Sister Bridget—somehow she was responsible for this.

"Weathercharming!" he cried. "You're singing up the storm."

The waves swelled all the more. Huge volumes of water reared up and raged toward Silas. The aufwader cried out, but his voice was lost amid the tumult as hammering waves swept him up, then hurled him down again. Silas fought to keep afloat, with the moonkelp held over his head. He gulped down deep breaths, and the sea battered into him. The full fury of the mounting tempest was focused on him, and he floundered in its wrath.

Ben thought the piercing notes were going to burst his eardrums. Though the storm was at its height, he could still hear the shrill song, and it pounded in his head.

With one final shriek that seemed to madden the wild blasting gale, Sister Bridget stopped. "Take the oars," she shouted to Ben. "You have to row to him."

"Into that?" spluttered the boy. "You must be mad. We'll be dashed to pieces!"

"Do it!" she commanded. "It is our last chance to retrieve the moonkelp."

Ben seized the oars and plunged them into the churning water. The current snatched at them, and the rough wood rubbed the skin from his palms. With his teeth clenched, the boy clung on determinedly and began pulling the boat through the frothing waves.

They rode the boiling sea, skimming bravely between the steep water valleys, gaining with every dreadful moment upon the toiling figure of Silas.

"Closer," demanded the novice. "Hurry, boy!"

Ben heaved on the oars, but they bucked and tugged at his arms. It was like riding a mad horse. "I can't," he yelled. "I'm not strong enough." But even as he said these words, the wind drove the craft into the center of the tempest.

The light of the moonkelp was dimmed by the black brine that rained down as the waves broke over Silas, but it was still firmly in his hands.

"Hold her steady," Sister Bridget called to Ben as they rammed through the water.

Silas was almost within reach now. He turned his stricken face to them and battled against the waves. Never had he been so afraid, but although his heart rejoiced to see the boat, he cursed the novice with all his strength. "Damn her!" he cried. "Damn her to her Deep!"

But neither she nor Ben heard him. Sister Bridget stretched out her hand. "I have it!" she shouted as her fingers closed about the moonkelp in Silas's clutches.

But the aufwader would not let go, and with the waves crashing over his head, he grimly held on. Suddenly, the boat lurched, carried by the foaming tide. Sister Bridget cried out as she was yanked back. For an instant, her fingers slipped from the moonkelp, but she leaned over even further and caught it again.

Silas tried to pull the treasure free of her grasp, but most of his energies had been spent laboring in the waves. With dismay, he saw the novice wrench the moonkelp from his fist.

Sister Bridget sat back in the boat and waved the shining treasure over her head. "At last," she cried triumphantly.

Ben cheered with relief, but he turned guiltily to the aufwader, still struggling in the water.

"Help," spluttered Silas. "Don't leave me here. I can't make it—" His head disappeared beneath the waves, and when he bobbed up again his eyes were wide with despair. "I'm drowning!" he screamed.

Ben glanced at the novice. "We can't leave him," he said.

Sister Bridget looked at the boat uncertainly—it wasn't big enough for the four of them. Silas would just have to hang on to the side. "Here," she said to the boy, "take the moonkelp. I shall pull him from the water."

"Be careful," warned Ben as she leaned over the side once more.

Silas waved his arms in panic as he went under for the third time. "Save me," he gargled. "I'm done fer!"

"Take my hand," called the novice, stretching out as far as she dared.

Silas reached up and grabbed the offered hand. "Got you now, half-breed!" he snarled, dropping the pretense.

Too late, Sister Bridget realized she had been tricked. "No!" she pleaded. "I beg you!" But it was no good. Using his last reserve of strength, the aufwader dragged her out of the boat. "Time to come home," he yelled, as she fell into the sea.

A great spout of water flew up when she hit the seething waves. "You'll not be welcome where you're going," Silas bawled.

Sister Bridget was gasping and choking when she reappeared. Terror was graven on her face, and she splashed hopelessly, gagging on the saltwater she had swallowed.

"Are you all right?" shouted Ben, too worried about her to notice Silas swimming toward him.

A change came over the blackened sea. Far below, a sickly greenish light began to pulse, as if her presence in the water had triggered some strange alarm. From the fathomless depths, a great bell began to toll. Sister Bridget wailed when she heard it, and her tears mingled with the sea.

"Don't just sit there, boy!" spat Silas, grabbing hold of the side of the boat. "Don't yer know what that is? It's the Lords o' the Deep—they're comin' fer'er."

Ben put down the oars and stared at the horizon. In the dim distance, there rose an immense wall of water in a thunderous rush. It reached into the night sky and savage lightning flickered around its towering height. It was like a mountain of glass that fed on the surrounding darkness sucking up the sea and ever increasing in size.

With a rumble that shook all the oceans of the world, the nightmarish spectacle roared toward them.

"They know I am here," the novice cried. Ben held out an oar to her but she pushed it away. "Flee!" she shouted. "All is lost. Save yourself—it is too late for me."

"You 'eard 'er," bellowed Silas, fearfully looking over his shoulder. The vast wave was sweeping nearer, and he trembled when he caught sight of those contained within.

Sister Bridget knew she faced death. All those years of cringing from the world were finally over. The wrathful Lords of the Deep had found her, just as they had found her father, and they had come to claim her. It was the end of everything. She sobbed hopelessly—had it all been for nothing?

"Row, damn you!" Silas screamed at Ben. "I'll not be 'ere when they come—I'll not be dragged to the cold regions."

But Ben was petrified and could not move; the awful vision of the Deep Ones in all their fury paralyzed him. Silas swung one leg over the side. "I'll do it myself," he growled.

But the other leg refused to follow—in fact it pulled him down again.

"What the . . .?" He stared down at his foot and what he saw made him squirm maniacally. "Leave go!" he screeched.

Below him, Sister Bridget laughed. It was a terrible sound, filled with doom and despair. Her hands were fastened about his ankle, and she held on tenaciously. "Come, stunted one!" she cried. "Let me embrace you."

Just as he had pulled her, she dragged Silas out of the boat. He fell into the water with a great howl of fear. "Keep away from me!" he begged.

But she merely laughed all the more. "Come to me," she taunted. "I only wish to hold you."

Silas kicked out at her, truly panicking now. Flailing his arms in the water, he tried to escape, but she was too quick. Her strong fingers grabbed the gansey he had taken from the body of Nelda's father and hauled him back down. He was caught like a fish on a hook.

The huge wave was almost upon them, its deadly pinnacles rearing over their heads. With a fierce light in her eyes, Sister Bridget turned to Ben. "Row, fool!" she shrieked. "Row!"

The boy snapped out of his terror and strained at the oars. The novice watched the boat pull away and dragged Silas in the opposite direction.

"Curse you!" he whined, but his protests died in his throat as he looked up.

The sheer wall of water towered over them and within its ominous bulk he saw three shadowy figures. The Lords of the Deep wore crowns of glowing green stars. Their eyes were huge, lidless discs that glared down at Sister Bridget accusingly, and the hair that cascaded from their bloated, coral-crusted heads was like the branches of great trees. A deafening thunderclap issued from their mouths, and they revealed row upon row of sharp, jagged teeth.

"Wait," screamed Silas. "I am not to blame—let me go free."

The novice laughed at his futile efforts. "They do not hear you," she cried.

"Nooo!" he begged. "For pity's sake."

But she took no notice and grimly wrapped her arms about him. "Take the cold road with me, Silas Gull," she hissed in his ear. "Let them drag us down together!"

With terrible violence, the Deep Ones smashed down on them. The sea convulsed at the impact, and shock waves sped inland and smote the cliffs of Whitby.

The aufwader boat was tossed like a matchstick on the water. On board, Ben clung to Nelda for dear life—in its ruin he had seen monstrous tentacles writhing and thrashing in the wake of the wave. For several minutes, he lay shaking on the bottom of the boat, then it was all over.

The sea became calm, and when Ben peered over the side, it was as though nothing had happened. Only the empty sea met his gaze—there was no sign of Sister Bridget or Silas anywhere. He stared at the dark water—they had been taken below. It was a horrible thought.

A painful groan came from the still form by his side. Ben patted Nelda's face, and she opened her eyes, but the pupils were unseeing, and she sank into unconsciousness again.

What am I to do? He thought. He was cold and exhausted, and the night seemed to press around him. At his feet, the moonkelp was dying, for the time allotted to its flowering was nearly over. Carefully, Ben picked it up. The treasure that had been so hard to win and had cost so many lives was disintegrating before his very eyes. The golden light that pulsed through its stems waned and grew weak.

"Oh, no!" he said and, searching in the cold water that sloshed in the bottom of the boat, he brought out the large shell. It was chipped but still whole. Maybe it isn't too late, he told himself. If only I knew what to do.

Quickly, he put the shriveling moonkelp on the shell and held them both aloft. "Listen to me, Lords of the Deep," he shouted to the bleak expanse of the sea. "Take back this treasure and let me have my wish."

The moonkelp suddenly burst into flames, and a tongue of yellow fire soared into the sky. The Lords of the Deep had heard him.

On the pier, Aunt Alice squeezed Jennet's hand. They had all seen the terrible wave rise up but had no idea what was happening. Then the sea flung itself upon the cliff, and fierce waves battered against the pier. Miss Boston took hold of Hesper and, with Jennet, pushed past Rowena. They ran to the old lighthouse and clung to its rails as the waves crashed over the edge.

While the spray foamed up over the stone, Rowena pressed her fingers to her temples. "I must see," she whispered. "I must know." Locking her muscles until they were rigid, she sent her thoughts flying over the water toward the aufwader boat once more.

There, Ben was standing in the craft, the brilliant thread of flame scorching upward from the shell in his hands. The wish was his now. Rowena's thought returned to her body, and she staggered back.

"You idiot, Gull!" she cried. It was hopeless. The reward would go straight to the boy, he would save the tribe, and she would never know where the staff of Hilda was concealed.

Then an awful smile flashed over her lips. "There is a way," she murmured.

She threw her arms wide and screwed her face up, summoning every ounce of power. "Channel through me, ye demons that feed off my soul," she cried. "Put my voice in his mouth, let my words be his—for evil's sake!"

Unholy laughter boomed across the sky and, with her black robes flapping madly in the gale, Rowena's face turned white as she strove to control the forces she had unleashed.

Nelda grunted; she touched the tender lump on her skull and winced. Very slowly, her eyes fluttered open. The world was swirling, and strange voices echoed inside her head. She did not know where she was, but something bright was shining above her, and she blinked to bring everything in focus.

The last sparks from the moonkelp drifted up from the shell in Ben's hands, and then she remembered. She realized that she had awoken just in time, for the boy was about to lift the curse. This was the vision Nelda had seen on the cliff top, and she held her breath with anticipation. At last, the tribe would be able to grow, and children would be born again.

But the smile froze on her mouth—something was wrong. The boy looked ill. His face was drawn, and he swayed like one in a trance. "Hear me, ye Lords of the Deep and Dark," he shouted, in a voice that sounded forced and unfamiliar. "Grant to me the reward you promised ages past for returning to you your treasure."

A cloud of soft gray ash blew out of the shell and hovered in the air. "Hear now my wish!" he cried. The sea became smooth—not a ripple marred its perfect surface. Everything was silent, waiting for his demand.

"Reveal unto Rowena Cooper," he uttered hollowly, "the precise location of Hilda's staff!"

The shell fell from his hands. It shattered on the side of the boat, and the cloud of ash was snatched away by the breeze.

"What . . . what have you done?" stammered Nelda.

Ben fell to his knees, and the spell that had bound him melted. He stared at Nelda in disbelief. "What did I say?" he cried. "What did I say?"

On the pier, Rowena Cooper shuddered. In the far northern sky, a point of light appeared. A slender shaft of green slanted down over the sea and shone on the witch's forehead. It burned into her mind the knowledge she so desperately sought and Rowena crowed with delight—at last she knew.

Spinning on her heels, she threw Miss Boston and the others a triumphant glance, then hurried back to the town with her robes billowing behind her.

CHAPTER FOURTEEN

THE EMPRESS OF THE DARK

The gables of the late Mrs. Banbury-Scott's house cast odd, angled shadows on the lawn. With no lights behind its mullioned windows, the building was a sorry sight. There was no one at home, for both Grice and Mrs. Rigpath had fled from Rowena that afternoon as she had rampaged through every room. Panels had been splintered, hangings torn, and the attic spaces poked and peered into, but without success. She had not found what she sought, and now the house settled uneasily on its foundations, its ancient timbers creaking and complaining.

The serene peace did not last long—Rowena had returned. Eagerly, she let herself into the house and stormed through the hall, leaving the front door wide open. Charging through the debris that littered the floor, she kicked open the French windows and hurried into the garden.

Grice's shed was lost in shadow, nestling against the garden wall. Rowena ran up to it and pushed open the heavy door. She fumbled for a switch and clicked on the electric light. The walls were covered in tools, and on one side there were three shelves stacked with tins containing nails and tacks, nuts and bolts, and old bits of wire.

Rowena sneered at all the patient hours the man had spent in this place, and with one sweep of her arm, knocked every tin to the floor. "There!" she whispered. "The mark of Hilda." On the bare wall between two of the shelves was a curious sign gouged into the plaster. Circling it were three others, but they were meaningless to her and she ignored them. "All these years," she said admiringly, "and no one knew. All this time locked away here—a perfect hiding place. Grand houses are easy targets, yet who would notice a hut like this? Even I overlooked it."

She ran her fingers lovingly over the mark. "And now you're mine," she snorted. "I have beaten you, Hilda!"

The witch threw wrenches and screwdrivers to the ground as she looked for something to break through the plaster. The axe she had borrowed was still in the house, and she was too impatient to fetch it, so she seized a pair of garden shears and drove them into the wall.

The plaster was dry and crumbled easily, as she hacked and stabbed with the blades.

"Oh, Hilda," Rowena said, "you should have destroyed your staff instead of sealing it in a wall for me to find. Were you so unsure of your newfound God? How its very existence must have tormented you—how you must have longed to wield it once more."

A ragged gash now grinned in the whitewash. With the next strike of the garden shears, the plaster gave way. A sound like a rifle firing blistered through the hut, and all along the wall hairline cracks appeared.

Rowena stood back as the cracks widened, and in an avalanche of dust and dirt, the whole lot slid down.

When the choking cloud settled, she wiped her eyes and laughed. At her feet, half hidden in the rubble of long buried centuries, was the staff of Hilda.

It was a long piece of polished black wood, carved round the handle with Celtic snakes that twined into knots and swallowed their tails. A beautiful thing, it had been untouched by age since the day Hilda herself had walled it up. Rowena could feel the power beating from it. She licked her dry, dusty lips and held out a quaking hand.

"Mine," she said softly as she felt the magic of the ancients surge through her. "It really is mine." The witch threw back her head and laughed madly.

Miss Boston watched the little boat drift closer. At her side, Hesper was fretting. "I see only Nelda and the boy. Where then are Eska and Silas?"

Jennet waved to her brother as the craft sailed into hearing distance. "Ben! Ben!" she called out.

He looked up but did not return the wave.

Aunt Alice clasped her hands behind her back and her chins shook querulously. "I fear all is not well," she said.

"But Rowena's gone," Jennet told her. "That must mean she's failed."

The old lady said no more, but the last look of triumph on the witch's face had been troubling her. The only thing they could do was wait for the boat to return and learn the truth.

The aufwader vessel bumped against the side of the pier, and Nelda slowly rowed to the iron rungs. Ben scrambled up the ladder. When he was safely on the pier, he ran to his sister and flung his arms around her. "It's all my fault," he cried. "It's all my fault."

Jennet stared at Aunt Alice. What did he mean?

Hesper pattered over to the edge of the pier and helped her niece up next. "My heart rejoices to see that you are safe," she said, "but what happened to Eska? Why is she not with you?"

Nelda raised her head, and Hesper saw that tears were streaming down her cheeks. "So the Deep Ones took her," she murmured. "Well, perhaps she is happy at last."

Miss Boston removed her hat and gazed at the ground. "Then Sister Bridget is no more," she clucked sorrowfully.

Nelda wiped her eyes. "They took Silas too," she put in, "and . . . and that is not all." She glanced quickly at Ben and hung her head.

"Weep not for Silas," Hesper said, trying to comfort her. "I was a fool to think he would ever change. A rogue he was when I wed him, and a rogue he remained. The shore is a cleaner place without him."

Aunt Alice looked from Ben to Nelda, trying to understand their despair. She moved forward and tapped Hesper on the arm. "I think there is more to this than we know," she told her.

"But what else might there be?" Hesper returned. She gasped suddenly as a suspicion crept into her mind. "No!" she exclaimed. "Nelda, tell me I am wrong. Tell me you found the moonkelp and returned it to the Lords of the Deep."

Nelda did not reply—she avoided her aunt's eyes and stared at the ground.

It was Ben who answered for her. He let go of Jennet and said in a wavering voice, "It's my fault. I had it in my hands but instead of . . . instead of asking for the curse to be lifted . . ." He was too ashamed to complete the sentence.

"Then what did you ask for?" Hesper cried angrily.

Ben felt rotten. "I'm not really sure," he mumbled feebly.

"Not sure!" shouted Hesper. "How can you not be sure? Are you a total simpleton, boy? The moonkelp was our only chance—have you doomed us to extinction, human?"

Miss Boston covered her face. "Of course," she groaned. "Rowena—I thought she looked too happy."

"What has that witch woman got to do with this?" snapped Hesper. "Do you not understand that this child has betrayed our trust in him?"

"Nonsense," Aunt Alice retorted. "Don't you see? He was a victim of her devilish arts." She laid her hands on the boy's shoulders and looked him squarely in the face. "Tell me, Benjamin," she began, "what was it you asked for? Was it for the whereabouts of Hilda's staff to be revealed to Mrs. Cooper?"

"How did you know?" he asked.

Miss Boston groaned again and stuffed her hat back on. "Then we have all failed," she said. "If that staff is as powerful as Rowena believes it to be, nothing can stand in her way."

They fell silent, for the situation seemed hopeless. Miss Boston was deep in thought. If there was a solution to all this, then it eluded her.

Nelda chanced to look into the sky, where heavy clouds were now gathering. "The weather is changing," she said. "I think a storm is coming."

"A storm *is* coming," Aunt Alice affirmed, "but not the kind you were thinking of."

Nelda continued to look at the dark heavens. She had never seen clouds quite like these; they seemed to ooze overhead like thick molasses. Her gaze followed their slow, deliberate progress over the harbor toward the East Cliff.

Suddenly Nelda cried out. "Look!" she shouted, pointing to the church.

Miss Boston, Hesper, and Ben turned and fixed their eyes upon the floodlit building.

"Gracious," breathed the old lady.

Curious as to what her brother and Aunt Alice were staring at, Jennet peered up at the church.

Standing before the arc lights, as Sister Bridget had done hours earlier, was Rowena Cooper—and the staff of Hilda was in her hands.

Even from that distance, they heard her harsh, gloating laughter. Rowena was insane with joy, and she revelled in the newfound strength that flowed through her veins.

"Now we'll see," she yelled. "The time has come for you to serve a new mistress." With both hands clasped firmly about the staff, she raised it over her head. "Obey me!" she screeched.

A jagged streak of black lightning erupted from the staff. It crackled upward and split the night sky apart. With a mighty roar, the clouds exploded, and ripples of destruction radiated out to the far reaches of the world.

Rowena hugged herself. She was amazed—the power of the staff was greater than she had ever dreamed. The thrill of it was delicious. She looked down on the little town of Whitby, which would have the honor of being the first place to suffer. "I am Empress of the Dark," she exulted. "Armies shall fall before me, and nations tremble at the mention of my name."

Down on the sands, Miss Boston was appalled. "She's testing the staff's powers!" she exclaimed.

Whitby flickered beneath the flashes of darkness that issued from Hilda's staff. The very fabric of the night seemed to swirl over the rooftops, and the heavens were alive with black thunderbolts. Rowena laughed all the more, her shrieks of mirth carried on the gale that tore around the graveyard. Her voice ricocheted off every headstone, and it seemed as though the dead themselves were rejoicing with her.

"Now for a true demonstration of your power!" she cried.

The staff blazed with evil energy, and she flourished it in the air. A large whirlpool of shadow began to form above her. It spiraled out, growing larger with every swing and changing everything it touched.

The tombstones blistered, and moss fell from them as the ancient magic passed over. The weathered inscriptions glowed with purple fire until they were as clear and sharp as the day they had been carved. Still the staff poured out its might. The solid, immovable shape of St. Mary's quivered as the coils of blackness pounded its walls and the years fell away from it.

Rowena looked around at what she had done, impressed and delighted. Even as she admired her handiwork, the expanding web of darkness engulfed the abbey. The majestic ruin shimmered, and its ragged walls switched in and out of past ages. For an instant, it was the grand structure it had once been, whole and with light shining through its high stained-glass windows, and the next it was partially built. Then it disappeared entirely, replaced by a collection of smaller buildings. Rowena was unraveling time.

Lowering her arm, the witch pointed the staff at the huddled houses below her and screeched with glee. The twisting helix of magic spun toward the town. It blasted through the narrow lanes, and confusion rampaged in its wake. Street lamps dimmed as they became gaslights, and then they too were whisked away. Paved roads buckled, and the tarmac split apart as cobbles forced their way to the surface. Modern buildings vanished, and the surrounding houses grew shabby, while in the harbor the fishing boats were replaced by high-masted whaling ships.

On the sands of Tate Hill Pier, five figures gazed at the town, bewildered.

"What's happening?" asked Jennet in disbelief. "The houses are changing."

"Rowena is dragging Whitby back through its own history," said Aunt Alice. "But this is only the beginning. If she is not stopped, then everywhere will be plunged into chaos." The old lady held on to her hat and darted over the beach. "We must take that staff from her," she told them, "whatever the cost."

"How?" Jennet began, but Miss Boston was already scampering up the path toward the 199 steps. Hesper ran after her, closely followed by Ben and Nelda.

Jennet was scared; anything might happen to them. "Stop!" she shouted. "Wait! You won't be able to take it from her. Stop!" But they were caught up in the urgency of the moment and did not hear her.

The girl glanced wildly at the town. Whitby continued to judder through the past, but the rate at which the centuries devoured it was not constant. Some areas were still untouched by the crackling power of the staff, while others were totally devastated. Primitive stone huts stood beside Victorian houses, and next to them an arcade sparkled.

Jennet looked at the church steps. As yet, they were unchanged, and she saw Aunt Alice striding up them with Ben close behind. There was nothing she could do to make them turn back, so, with her heart pounding, she rushed after them as fast as she could.

Upon the bleak, empty cliff, where the churchyard had once been, Rowena Cooper flung her arms open and embraced the glorious spectacle below. As the town hurtled down through the ages, she contemplated, with relish, the new life that stretched before her. "No more will you rule me, Nathaniel!" she hooted ecstatically. "No more will I be bound to you. I am free at last—free to do whatever I choose—and you shall cringe before me." She breathed a great sigh of contentment and drank in the devastation all around. Her glittering eyes swiveled from barren marshland to the rapidly shrinking piers and along the wide expanse of cliff. There her gaze was arrested as it fixed upon the five figures that toiled up the steps.

Miss Boston had almost made it to the top. Hesper was at her side, and below them came Ben and Nelda, while Jennet was right at the bottom of the steps. And even if she ran for all she was worth, she would never catch up.

Rowena regarded them as she might a collection of insects.
"Futile creatures," the witch spat. "How they plague me.
Will they never learn that I have beaten them?" She pounded
the staff on the ground in irritation and then smiled cruelly.
"Perhaps I could have some sport with them." Filled with evil
purpose, she raised the staff and pointed it at Ben and Nelda.

The boy and the young aufwader were running side by
side. The clamor of the tormented night was rising behind
them, but neither dared to look on the horror that Whitby
had become. Ben's ribs ached, and the blood thumped in
his head. He felt responsible for everything—if only he had
not succumbed to the enchantment Rowena had put on his
tongue. If he had been stronger, then none of this would have
happened. Tears of guilt trickled down his cheeks, and he
blamed himself with each step.

The anguish Nelda had felt before was nothing compared
to this. If the alternative was living in a world of Rowena's
making, the curse of the Deep Ones was a thing to be welcomed. In all the legends of the tribe, there was never a more
deadly threat than that vile witch woman. Nelda glanced
quickly at Ben, feeling the torture of his guilt. Suddenly, her
face fell, and she stumbled.

"Ben!" she screamed. "Look out!"

Too late. A twisting jet of power streamed down from the
staff and cannoned into them with staggering force.

Ben and Nelda were plucked off the steps and swept into
the air. Torrents of unstable time thrashed about them as the
full fury of Rowena's might was unleashed. The staff blazed,
and a yawning fissure opened in the sky above their heads.

"Jennet!" the boy shrieked as the swirling chasm widened
over him. Hideous forms rushed through the cyclone of

darkness that bore him into the heavens, and the coils of the past seized him utterly. Nelda yelled and kicked, but the gaping mouth bore down on them both. With a flash of purple fire, they were sucked into its spinning center, and their cries were swallowed by the night.

On the steps beneath, Jennet staggered to a halt. She howled her brother's name, but he had vanished into the whirling void. "Ben, Ben," she sobbed, falling to her knees.

The maelstrom crackled and spun toward her prostrate form. Jennet stared up at the awful vision that threatened her with oblivion. Springing to her feet, she ran down the steps but the wind tore at her hair and dragged her backward. Jennet clung to the railing as the gale lifted her off the ground, and the spiraling maw of night closed on her. She felt her fingers slip from the rail then, and, with one final cry, she was lost.

Rowena crowed with amusement. "Back you go," she laughed, "out of reach forever!"

Miss Boston's breath rattled and wheezed in her throat. She glared at the empty steps below and threw her hat down in dismay. "Cooper!" she cried. "May God forgive you!"

Hesper was distraught. "Nelda!" she wept bitterly. "What has happened to her?"

"I don't know," murmured the old lady. "I just don't know."

Whitby was almost completely destroyed—gone were the houses, and only the River Esk glinted between the rippling shadows on either of its muddy banks. The menacing waves of power crept over the bottommost steps, and they melted beneath it, dissolving into clay and shale.

The sound of Rowena's laughter broke into the night. "Fools," she cried. "See how easily I vanquish you."

From out of a shimmering rent in the fragmented heavens, there suddenly came a fierce burst of gunfire. Above the valley, two aircraft appeared, locked in combat, their engines roaring in the shredded clouds.

Miss Boston looked up incredulously. "Good Lord," she muttered.

The planes swooped low over the cliffs. Hugging the ground, they zoomed perilously close to Aunt Alice and Hesper, and a blizzard of lead hailed from their spluttering guns. Sparks rang off the steps, and the bullets plunged into the soft soil beyond. That was too close for comfort, and Miss Boston staggered back. One of the planes bore a swastika: they were witnessing the dogfight that had taken place over the rooftops of Whitby during World War II. Rowena had snatched the planes out of time to fight again.

"She's toying with us," declared the old lady, "using history itself to do her dirty work!"

The aircraft soared upward, gaining height and preparing for another strike.

"Run," Aunt Alice shouted to Hesper.

The aufwader turned, but even as the Nazi fighter bore down on them and lethal rain blasted the steps, the air trembled, and both planes faded from the sky. Miss Boston looked uncertainly across to Rowena. She knew what the witch was up to: taking them to the brink of disaster and dragging them away again. Dangling the inevitable before their eyes, watching them squirm and beg for mercy. "Well, I'll not gratify her ego," declared Aunt Alice firmly. "I won't play her games—if I die, then so be it, but I shan't abase myself before that one!"

"You may not have to," cried Hesper at her side. "Look!"

The creeping darkness that had swiftly consumed Whitby finally reached them. Boiling mud bubbled up through the cracks in the stonework, and the steps sank into a mire of soft clay. Before they had a chance to escape, the ravenous time floe devoured them.

Everything was dark—an eternity of blackness seemed to have passed since Ben and Nelda had been swept into the twisting gulf. He felt an icy wind rush up to meet him, then his feet struck something solid, and his legs gave way.

It was bitterly cold. Sleet hammered into Ben's face, driven by a savage northeasterly gale, and the freezing air hurt his lungs. His mind was reeling—where was he? Stinging ice pelted his cheeks and chapped his skin. He shivered, and the veil before his eyes began to lift.

The lifeboat crashed through the sea, and huge gray waves smashed over its bow. Twelve bush-bearded men wearing lifejackets of cork pulled on the oars while another grappled with the rudder.

"Put yer backs into it, lads," he boomed. "We've done aright so far this evil day."

"Ben," a voice called, "what's happening?"

He shifted uneasily and turned. Through the drizzle that the breakers threw at them, he recognized the aufwader at his side. "I . . . I'm not sure, Nelda," he replied with a shout.

"You there!" bawled the coxswain. Ben jumped and looked around, but the man seemed to look straight through them. "Henry Freeman, pull yer weight! Want them folk to die on that schooner, does yer?"

The man he was addressing glowered, and his clenched teeth showed white within the frost-dripping beard. "I'll clout thee over t'side, John Storr," he growled. "I've done as well this day as all t'others 'ere." His great hands tightened around the oar, and he bellowed like a bear as he heaved it through the squalling water, his face turning purple with the strain and the cold.

"Aye, five crews we've saved a'ready," the coxswain shouted to the rest of his valiant men, "so we're not gonna let thissun confound us. Heave on it, we'll get through!"

Nelda held on to Ben and stared ahead as the boat smashed into the towering, ice capped waves. They were making for a ship that had been driven ashore, but the surf was treacherous and pummeled their boat ferociously. Nelda squinted over her shoulder at the East Cliff. It was shrouded in mist, but the sight of an aufwader is sharp, and hers was no exception. Very briefly, the fog parted, and there was Rowena Cooper.

The witch invaded all times now. She was the one fixed point around which all this confusion spun: a beacon of despair that shone only misery and death.

Nelda turned away and studied the faces of all the doughty, stern men at the oars—they were from an earlier time. She nudged Ben. "They can't see you," she told him hoarsely. "We are phantoms here."

Ben didn't feel like a ghost, but he was in no mood to argue. It took all his strength to hold on to the side of the boat, and he felt violently sick. At that moment, he didn't care whether anyone could see him or not. The storm was filthy—a veritable devil's tempest.

He choked back a cry as that phrase surfaced in his mind. Where had he heard it before?

"Nelda," he yelled, "what's the name of that ship?"

"Does it matter?" she cried.

"Just tell me! Can you make it out?"

She stared at him for a second, then shielded her eyes from the constant battering spray. "It is called *Merchant,*" she told him. "What does that signify?"

"Oh no!" Ben wailed. "Nelda, we're done for!"

He knew exactly what was going to happen, for he had been told the whole story before. All but one of these men were going to die.

Ben was too terrified to look at them. With the seawater flattening the oilskin hats against their skulls and their faces drenched and pinched with cold, the lifeboatmen seemed drowned already.

"Watch out theer," warned the coxswain as a giant wave rolled toward them. "Hold hard, theer's another girt beggar this side."

This was it! Ben clutched Nelda's frozen hand and waited, with his round eyes defying the smarting spray. The storm-mad sea charged at them. With a terrible crash, the two waves smashed into one another, and the lifeboat was hurled into the air upon a massive spout of water. Fifteen souls were cast into the freezing brine, their cries smothered by the tumult.

Nelda struggled in the water. The tide was too strong to swim against, and, although her race was suited to a harsh life, the dreadful cold numbed and pained her.

Overwhelmed by the mountainous waves, Ben could not remain afloat. The sleet-covered sea filled his mouth and poured into his ears, cutting off all sound from the world above. Swiftly, he sank beneath the surface, and his frantic thrashings grew weaker until he moved no more.

"Ben!" called Nelda. "Ben!" But soon her voice too was drowned.

Jennet fell onto the cool turf, and the last traces of the shadowy void curled away from her, swirling into the night. She rubbed her head, dazed, her thoughts a disordered jumble. Then she remembered her brother.

Scrambling to her feet, the girl looked around desperately. The abbey reared up behind her, but without its floodlights, it seemed unfriendly and larger than before. She was standing near the edge of the cliff, but there was no sign of Ben. Everything seemed back to normal, and she wondered how this could have happened. There was Whitby sleeping peacefully below. It was a calm December night, and columns of smoke rose from the many chimneys. Jennet frowned: something was not quite right. Where was the hospital, and what had happened to the amusement arcades? Gradually she realized that she was looking on some bygone time, before she was even born.

A black figure stepped from the shadows under the church. Rowena Cooper was tall and monstrous, transformed into something beyond humanity. A nightmare to harry the waking world.

The witch turned slowly and faced Jennet, her eyes glinting sinisterly. "I do not believe you have met *Derflinger* and *Von der Tan,*" she cried. "Allow me to introduce them to you."

Jennet wondered what she was talking about until Rowena stretched out her hand and gestured to the sea. Two dark shapes were on the water. The girl peered at them—they almost looked like battleships.

A small explosion burst from one of the vessels. Overhead something whistled through the darkness, and suddenly the cliff top was ablaze with flame. Jennet dropped down as the ground shook from the force of the blast. Another missile screamed through the sky, this time hitting the cliff face, and large chunks of rock fell into the sea. The ships were firing on Whitby.

The air seemed alive as shells exploded. Flowers of death flashed and flared, as dazzling blooms of yellow and orange fire raged above the cliff. Jennet crawled along the ground, trying to get under cover quickly. With her head down, she wriggled toward the abbey; if she could only reach the west wall, she would be safe. Flying shrapnel sliced through the grass around her, and streams of liquid flame showered down.

Seconds felt like hours as she labored along the ground toward the high walls of the ruin. She breathed a thankful sigh when she passed under the tall arches and cowered against the pillars of stone within.

The abbey flashed beneath the volleys of fire that erupted around it, a well-lit target for the German cruisers to bombard. In a deafening blast, one of the mortars struck the west wall, and the stones flew apart. The place Jennet had chosen to shelter behind was blown out of existence.

* * *

Shrieks of death stabbed into the gloom, and the dragon boat rammed onto the beach. Brandishing fiery torches, the raiders jumped ashore, spears and swords flashing in their hands.

From the small collection of wooden and stone huts built near the marshy estuary there came a shout. "Northmen! The Northmen are come!"

Panic and fear filled the air. Out of the small buildings, women and children poured. "To the abbey!" they called to one another.

With their eyes blazing and their faces hungry for war, the raiders charged through the village. Torches were thrown into the thatches, and soon the huts were aflame. The men-folk had few weapons to defend themselves with, and the thirsty swords of the invaders eagerly drank their blood.

On the slope of the cliff, Miss Boston and Hesper slithered in the soft clay. Harsh war cries resounded in their ears, and they looked fearfully on the burning settlement below.

Miss Boston clapped her hands with wonder at the unfolding scene. "Extraordinary!" she exclaimed. "Positively marvelous—a real Viking raid."

Hesper was not so enthusiastic. "We must not linger here," she said urgently. "Listen to those screams; they are the sounds of death."

Aunt Alice blinked. "Heavens," she muttered, "how dreadful. I don't know what came over me. You're right; people are dying down there."

"Not all," Hesper put in. "See, some have crept out unseen."

The old lady stared down and there, fleeing barefoot through the undergrowth, came the women and children. Crouching low, they ran to the cliffside and scrambled up.

"Are they aware of us?" murmured Hesper curiously.

Miss Boston shook her head. "I doubt if they can see you," she said, "or me either, for that matter. No, it is sanctuary they are seeking. Look!"

Upon the cliff top, Hesper saw the Anglo-Saxon abbey with the smaller monastery buildings clustered around it. This abbey was not as tall as the later one, but a proud and noble structure nonetheless. Hidden in the deep shadows, a solitary figure watched and waited.

"Will these folk be safe in there?" Hesper asked Miss Boston.

"No, the Norsemen had no respect for the church. They will chase those poor people up here and kill them, and then the abbey will be robbed of its treasures and razed to the ground. I'm afraid we are an extremely barbaric species."

Hesper looked at the villagers clambering toward them, very close now. The hair of the women was braided, and they wore coarse, woollen garments pinned at the shoulder by large brooches.

From the ruin of the settlement, the raiders emerged. Blood smeared their faces, and the swords they held aloft were scarlet. This was too easy: there was little honor in slaughtering peasants. They lifted their heads and gazed at the true prize—abbeys were always full of gold plate and silver chalices. As one, they rushed up the cliffside howling for glory.

"Come!" cried Hesper. "We must run. A spear does not have to see its target to slay it."

But at that moment, the villagers were upon them. Blind to the two strangers, they surged on regardless. Many stumbled into the old lady or tripped over Hesper, cursing the unseen obstacles in their fright. But so wildly were they driven by their fear that the frenzied rush of their bodies swept the aufwader and Miss Boston with them up the cliff.

"Hesper!" called Aunt Alice as she tried to drag herself out of the panicking crowd. "Hurry, we must go the other way. Don't let them carry you to the abbey! It's too dangerous there." A fat Saxon woman with matted hair unwittingly barred the old lady's way so Miss Boston gave her a hard shove. "Sorry, my dear," she apologized, even though the woman could not hear her.

The spears of the Vikings were launched into the night. From the back of the thronging group, a voice gasped, and a body tumbled, lifeless, down the slope.

Finally Aunt Alice broke free of the crazed villagers. She scurried and skidded to the right, out of the pursuing invaders' path. Sliding through the mire she ran for cover. Only when she had dived behind a thick hedge of brambles did she realize that she was alone.

"Hesper!" she shouted in dismay.

Above the heads of the shrieking Saxons, the old lady saw the nets of the aufwader's fishing poles bob up and down— she was still trapped among them.

More victims fell, with spears embedded in their backs. Hesper staggered over the ground, too small to barge her way through the humans. She was hemmed in on all sides and could not stop running, for if she did, they would trample her to death. They herded her further up the cliff, and her piteous cries went unanswered.

The bells of the abbey began to ring, warning the surrounding country of invasion. Startled out of sleep, monks hurried from their cells and pushed open the great doors to let the villagers in. Spurred on by hope, they made for the blessed sanctuary and streamed inside.

Hesper whirled upon the threshold, battling against the human tide, suffering the knocks from careless elbows and knees. When the last of the villagers had fled into the abbey, the oaken doors slammed shut violently, and she was left out in the grim dark.

"Quickly!" Miss Boston shouted, "over here. The Vikings are coming."

In terror, Hesper saw the Norsemen raging nearer, storming with their axes and swords raised toward the abbey entrance. She was caught in the middle.

"Run!" cried Aunt Alice.

Hesper hitched up the lifebelt that had fallen around her ankles and dodged out of the way just as the fury of the Danes crashed into the doors. The oak splintered before them, and they lunged inside.

Down the slope to Miss Boston, Hesper scampered. She was nearly there when a faint noise brought her to a halt: a child's voice was whimpering. She spun around and saw a figure lying facedown in the mud. It was a boy, about four years old. Evidently, in the panic to find safety within the abbey walls, he had tripped and been left behind.

Terrible sounds issued from the abbey entrance, and Hesper shuddered at the thought of the butchery taking place within. Soon all the innocents would be dead, and the Vikings would swagger back down the cliff, taking their spoils with them.

She dithered on the slope, not sure what to do. It was sheer luck that this boy had been overlooked in the first place. If those murderers came out now, he would not escape with his life.

Hesper rushed hastily to the child and turned him over. He groaned and opened a bleary eye. "I know that you cannot hear me," the aufwader said, "but you must not remain here. Go hide until the danger passes." Stooping low, she slid her hands under his shoulders and hauled him to his feet.

The boy stared about him too awestruck to utter a single word. It was as if the angels themselves were lifting him.

One of the Vikings dragged a sack laden with clinking treasure through the doorway of the abbey. The massacre was still raging within, but he had slaked his thirst for blood, and the axe in his belt dripped a gory trail on the hallowed threshold. He was swigging back the abbot's finest wine but choked when he saw a Saxon boy rise unaided from the ground. The Norseman started and shook his ugly head. A foul curse rang from his lips, and he reached for his spear.

Hesper set the boy down. "Now you skedaddle," she whispered into his unhearing ears. The child refused to budge, for the fear of God was on him, and he nearly fell to his knees. Hesper scowled. "Men children," she grumbled, "always the worst," and she gave the boy a kick on the backside to start him on his way. With a yelp, he scampered along the cliff.

An infuriated roar came from the abbey behind, and Hesper whirled around to see the tall red-haired man draw back his spear, his sight fixed on the escaping child.

"No!" she screamed, and ran forward. Not caring for her own safety, she darted between the Viking and the boy. Removing the fishing pole from her pack, she charged toward the pagan brute, thrashing the stick before her as though it were a rapier. "You leave him be!" she yelled gallantly.

The spear hurtled from the Viking's grasp and plunged into the aufwader's chest, throwing her down.

The Dane spat on the floor with disgust. That was a bad spear; it did not fly straight and true, so let it rot in the ground where it had fallen.

Miss Boston stumbled over to the wounded aufwader. The weapon had gone right through her and was embedded in the soil beneath. Hesper felt the darkness tighten all around, and her large eyes looked imploringly up at Aunt Alice.

The old lady knelt beside her in the reddening mud and gently lifted her head.

"Did the child get away?" Hesper asked.

Miss Boston nodded, the tears trickling down her wrinkled face.

"Good. It is fitting that I give my life for one so young," Hesper whispered. "Weep not for me; my troubles are ended. Save your sorrow for your own kind." Her voice grew weaker, and her features twisted in agony. "I go now on that loneliest of voyages," she murmured, "but no black boat shall sail into the night with Hesper Gull on board."

The aufwader closed her eyes and died in Miss Boston's arms.

Flames crackled up through the roof of the abbey, and their flickering light banished the shadows from its walls. The one who had been watching all this time stepped forward at last. Rowena Cooper's bleached hair glowed in the dancing firelight. She raised the staff in her hand, and the flames vanished. The abbey shifted through the ages once more while below the town of Whitby jolted into view.

Upon the 199 steps, Miss Boston, stained with mud of long ago, laid Hesper down. The havoc of the present assailed her ears once again.

"Don't waste your grief on that!" sneered Rowena contemptuously.

Aunt Alice glared up at her. Never had she been moved to such anger and outrage. "How dare you!" she yelled. "How dare you!"

She sprang up and rushed at the witch, lashing out in spite of her fears. So fierce and unexpected was the attack, that it took Rowena utterly by surprise. Miss Boston's hands seized her robe and yanked her sideways. With a startled shriek, she fell, and the staff flew from her clutches.

The old lady made a grab for it, but the witch recovered swiftly. She bristled with wrath, and a vicious growl rumbled in her throat. Savagely, she leaped up and, thrusting Miss Boston aside, snatched the staff once more.

Aunt Alice rolled backward, clasping her stomach, for Rowena's shove had winded her. She was too old for physical combat, and she scolded herself crossly. "What do you think you're doing wrestling at your age, Alice?" she wheezed. "Your body's clapped out, so use your brains."

"Hag!" screeched Rowena. "I should kill you now!" Trembling with anger, she raised the staff and brought it smashing down. Miss Boston scuttled backward as it drove into the soil, which burst into flames.

"Temper, temper," puffed the old lady. "What's the matter, my dear? Everything getting out of hand, is it?"

Rowena hissed through gritted teeth, "Have a care! One command from me, and you will suffer untold torments."

"Oh, I do beg your pardon," Miss Boston rallied. "I thought you'd already tried that."

Sable lightning flashed from the staff, and Rowena shrieked with fury. "You haven't seen a thousandth of my power!" she snapped.

"Your power!" scoffed Aunt Alice. "Don't flatter yourself, madam. The staff obeys no one now. It was made for Hilda alone to wield, but even she became afraid to use it. That is why she had to hide the thing: it started to take over. It has a will of its own; can't you see that?"

Rowena's confidence was not shaken. "Don't be absurd," she laughed. "I am in full control. Hilda was weak; she listened too long to the whinings of the bishops and abandoned the way of the night. That is all."

The old lady struggled to her feet. "Use your head, woman," she said. "If that were true, then Hilda would have had the staff destroyed. The fact that it still exists must tell you something. The staff is invulnerable—it cannot be broken. Over the centuries, it has increased in strength, waiting for another to discover it. If you pursue this folly, then you shall be bound to it forever. It is using you—it needs a human vessel to work through, and you shall be utterly enslaved."

The witch looked uncertainly at the staff in her hands. Could the old fool be right? Is that why she desired this so much; was it really the staff tricking her into subservience? Then an unpleasant smile crossed her lips, and she tossed her head. "Be silent," she told Miss Boston. "I am the Empress of the Dark. The staff of Hilda obeys me!"

"Does it?" shouted Aunt Alice desperately. "Look around you, you poor deluded woman. Is that what you call control?" And she pointed at the town to convince her.

Whitby was still lurching in and out of time, with confusion everywhere. In the sky, the sun and the moon traversed the heavens, wheeling great arcs of light and darkness about the world. Winter and summer mingled in the chaos, trees shrank into the ground, and buildings glimmered through the spinning ages. The Norman abbey rose about them. For the briefest of instants, they were enclosed within its covered walls, then these fragmented, and they stood amid ruins once more.

"It's a mess!" Miss Boston declared. "The staff is out of control."

Rowena studied the town with suspicion. At first, she had enjoyed watching it gallop into the past, but now it irritated her. "I will have order," she barked. "I have the mastery."

"Never," goaded Aunt Alice. "The staff won't listen to you any more—you have become its servant."

The witch turned on her. "Name a time," she demanded. "Name a year, a day if you wish, and you shall see who rules here."

The old lady seemed taken aback. "A time?" she asked in a fluster.

The witch ground her teeth impatiently; she was being pushed too far by this senile idiot, and she advanced on her menacingly. "Come on, hag—choose!" she barked.

Miss Boston stammered and shuffled backwards. "Er . . . let me see, any time did you say?" She counted on her fingers and scratched her woolly head idiotically. "Nineteen, no, . . . six, dear me, no—of course, June 25, 1830," she said at last, "my grandpapa's birthday, don't you know."

Rowena threw back her head and held the staff high in the air. "Hear me!" she announced. "Show your devotion; acknowledge my sovereignty."

At once, the wind died down, and the sun slowed and came to rest in the bright blue sky of a hot June afternoon.

The hazy images of Whitby stabilized and fused into a solid collection of houses. The harbor was filled with whaling ships. Seagulls flew over the church of St. Mary and flapped lazily around the cliff, riding the air currents and crying with contented voices. From the streets below, the bustling sound of a busy town drifted up, and the majestic abbey ruins shone rich and gold in the sunshine.

Miss Boston was overawed at the speed of the transformation—Rowena really was in control. The witch smirked, greatly pleased with herself. She could see that the old lady was impressed, for that know-it-all look had been completely wiped from her face. The smile broadened as she thought of an even more conclusive way to prove the extent of her powers.

With the end of the staff, she tapped the ground three times and closed her eyes. "From the very jaws of death, I snatch thee," she muttered.

A blaze of purple fire burst over the grass and out of Whitby's history crashed three figures. Ben and Nelda gasped for breath; they were soaked to the skin and icy seawater dripped from them onto the summer grass. They flopped onto their backs and gulped down the sweet air. Jennet crouched nearby, still with her fingers in her ears and her eyes squeezed shut.

Miss Boston was overjoyed. She longed to run to them, but her difficult task was not yet finished. For the moment at least, they were safe. Her eyes rolled cautiously upward as she turned back to Rowena. "A good twelve or fifteen feet to go yet," she told herself quietly.

The witch was glowing with satisfaction as she smugly gazed at the tranquil scene around them. "See how wrong you were?" she breathed. "I have total control over absolutely everything."

"Yes," Aunt Alice mumbled, "I rather think you have." She stole another glance at the children and the aufwader. Ben and Nelda were recovering already, and Jennet was tending to them. Good—so long as they stayed there, all would be fine. The old lady wrung her hands and, in a small, frightened voice, asked Rowena, "What will you do with me now? Have mercy, I beg you." Very slowly, she started to shuffle away through the high archway below the central tower.

Rowena stalked after her. "The time has come for me to end my business in Whitby," she said with a sneer. "I have other matters to attend to, but as for you—you have been a thorn in my side for too long, old crone. Before I leave I shall deal with you in my own way."

Miss Boston cowered further back. "Please," she cried, "have pity. I'll do anything you ask—just spare me!"

The witch laughed. Her teeth were long and sharp, and when Aunt Alice saw her eyes, they were red as blood. "Only now do you understand," howled Rowena. "Look at me and die!" Her face was pulled into a dreadful snarl, and hackles prickled from her neck. The fingers that held the staff twisted into claws, and in a deep, rumbling voice she roared, "Your life is over."

The old lady recoiled. "No!" she blubbered pathetically.

Jennet and the others watched in disbelief as Miss Boston groveled and pleaded for her life.

Rowena's hellish laughter rang through the abbey ruins as she summoned all her black powers, and the ancient stones shook around her. "I'm going to rip you apart!" she screamed.

With her jaws slavering, the witch sprang at Miss Boston. But the old lady was not as cowed as she had pretended to be. She stepped nimbly aside and, as the terrible creature lunged, she gave it a mighty stab with her hat-pin. Rowena howled and yammered, but then she turned again on her prey. Miss Boston looked hurriedly at the vaulted ceiling above. Why was it taking so long?

Rowena prowled toward her, half woman–half hound. She had Aunt Alice pressed into a corner and advanced with her teeth snapping. A stone rattled down and bounced over the ground by her feet, but the witch ignored it. The muscles in her shoulders tensed, and she prepared to pounce.

As the fiery eyes blazed malevolently at her, Miss Boston bellowed, "I've waited a long time to do this!" and punched the witch for all she was worth.

The blow had little effect, but that little was enough. Rowena stared at her, not believing the audacity of it. Seizing her one chance, the old lady bolted for the archway.

"You can't escape me now," screeched the witch. "I am the hunter of souls!"

From the structure above, there came an ominous crack— the great arches were splitting. Rowena looked up warily; her burning eyes widened with shock as she realized that she had been tricked. In a thundering crash, the central tower collapsed. A shrill howl pierced the deafening tumult as Rowena Cooper was crushed beneath the tons of falling masonry that

toppled and smashed down. A cloud of dust billowed out and, when it cleared, all that remained of the tower was a mound of rubble.

Beyond the vast pile of broken stones, the children and Nelda were standing with fearful looks on their faces. Where was Aunt Alice? Jennet and Ben rushed forward, calling her name.

"What do you think you are doing?" came a voice. Miss Boston's head popped up from behind a wall, and she peered at the devastation.

"We thought you were under there," cried Jennet.

The old lady stepped carefully through the wreckage. "Don't be silly, dear," she said. "Give me a hand here, would you?"

Ben and Jennet dashed over and threw their arms around Aunt Alice's neck.

"Oh, Benjamin," she said with a grimace, "you're all wet."

"I thought you were dead," the boy cried.

Miss Boston pulled the children from her and became serious. "Quickly," she told them "We must search through this rubble and find the staff of Hilda—it is our only link with the future. If we don't find it, then we may be stuck in this time for good."

She and Jennet began pulling the stones from the great mound, but Ben did not join in. He was looking for Nelda. "Where is she?" he asked. "Did you see where she went?"

The old lady straightened her back and glanced past the church—Nelda was there, and she knew what she had found. "I believe she is on the steps," she said, a little croakily. "She is with Hesper—leave her alone for a while, Benjamin."

Aunt Alice clasped her hands together and stared at the ground. A forlorn, soul-wrenching cry floated on the warm breeze, and the old lady covered her face so that the children would not see her weeping.

Jennet dragged a huge square stone from the pile and sent it rolling onto the dusty grass. "Aunt Alice," she shouted excitedly, "I think I've found it—look!"

She had uncovered a corner section of the ruined tower. It was balanced precariously on one of the fallen pillars but, in the shade beneath, the carved end of the staff was plain to see.

"Wait," said Miss Boston, drying her eyes and scrabbling anxiously over the debris. "No, Jennet, don't you touch it."

The girl reached in and her fingers closed around the black wood. "It's alright," she told her. "I've got it." Jennet tugged at the staff, but it was held fast. "It must be wedged under all this. Just one more . . ."

She staggered down the side of the heap and stared, horrified, into the hole—the staff was in the grip of a large black paw.

"Hush, dear," Miss Boston whispered in the girl's ear, "don't let Benjamin know."

"But that's the hound," Jennet stammered, "the Barguest. Where is Rowena—what happened to her?"

"You're looking at her, dear," Aunt Alice answered mildly. "That was Rowena's true nature." She patted Jennet's arm and stooped down to retrieve the staff herself. It came free in her hands and, reverently, she held it up.

"Oh, what a divine creation," she breathed, examining the intricate carving. "Simply marvelous."

"Do you really know how to use it?" Jennet ventured. "I mean, it's not as if you're a witch like Rowena."

Aunt Alice smiled. "I seem to remember somebody saying otherwise not too long ago. I think I told you then that I preferred the term *wise woman*."

She held the staff before her, but a call from Ben interrupted her concentration. "Look up there!" he cried.

In the east windows of the abbey, a white light shone. At first, they thought it was only an illusion, but then the blurred shape took form, and the old lady gasped in wonder. So intense was the radiance that it cast long shadows over the abbey lawns, and the summer sun seemed pale by comparison.

"My word," murmured Miss Boston and humbly bowed her head.

Jennet shielded her eyes but found that she could look into the light quite easily without it hurting. The girl blinked; for a second she thought she had seen the figure of a woman.

Miss Boston lifted the staff and offered it to the dazzling vision. "Take it," she said respectfully. "It is too dangerous a thing for this world."

Briefly the light welled up and then was extinguished. Jennet gawked stupidly; everywhere seemed dull and chill. Aunt Alice lowered her hands, which were empty. The staff had gone back to its rightful owner. "All is as it should be," she sighed, "thank the Lord."

"But how will we get home without it?" asked Ben.

The old lady chuckled. "Look about you, dear," she said.

It was a gray September dawn, and the town was waking. Cars lumbered down Church Street, and the fish market was